ALSO B

M000285588

The Language of Spells

The Secrets of Ghosts

The Garden of Magic

In The Light of What We See

Beneath The Water

The Lost Girls

The Crow Investigations Series

The Night Raven

The Silver Mark

The Fox's Curse

The Pearl King

The Copper Heart

The Shadow Wing

The Broken Cage

The Magpie Key

The Unholy Island Series

The Ward Witch

For the bookshops I have loved and the ones I have yet to discover.

THE BOOK KEEPER

UNHOLY ISLAND BOOK TWO

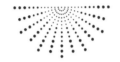

SARAH PAINTER

Siskin Press

Published by Siskin Press Limited

Cover Design by Stuart Bache

WELCOME TO UNHOLY ISLAND

Lindisfarne, or Holy Island, is a tidal island in the county of Northumberland in northern England. Visitors can gawp at the impressive remains of its ancient priory, established in 635AD - a beacon of religious learning and salvation in a cruel world, enduring as a place of pilgrimage and piety throughout the years. When the priory was abandoned as part of the dissolution of the monasteries in the sixteenth century, religion gave way to military concerns. Henry VIII demanded fortifications against the Scots, and a castle was built on the highest point on the island.

Unholy Island sits a few miles northward, in an area that has been Scotland and then Northumberland and then Scotland again throughout recent history, but in ancient times was just the Old North. Unlike Holy Island, it escaped royal and monastic notice, and has endured without much external interference.

Unholy Island is a mile further out in the cold sea than Lindisfarne, but it has a similar causeway. Stable enough for vehicles twice a day, if you stick to the window of opportunity provided by the tide. Holy Island is also accessible on foot, the final destination for the famous pilgrimage of St Cuthbert's Way. The more distant position of Unholy Island means that only the strongest or most foolish would attempt to reach it on foot. Or the desperate.

On an average day, you can see Holy Island from the mainland, with the distinctive shape of the castle rising on its rocky hill.

Unholy Island is only glimpsed when the air is clear and the sun is high in the sky. It seems to have its own weather system, staying almost permanently shrouded in mist. Even for those who live close to the causeway on the mainland, it is easy to forget it is there at all.

The island community is very small and the visitor numbers are not large. Few people know about the island and those that do, those who bring delivery vans or visit to fix utility poles or water pipes or fibre broadband, don't really think about the place after they leave. It's not that they forget about it completely, it just passes from the front of their mind. In the case of the delivery drivers and the post office, this is a regular recurrence. A weekly knowing and then unknowing that becomes a familiar part of their mindscape and doesn't unduly trouble anybody.

There are tourists. Throughout the summer, a handful make the crossing. They walk the quiet beaches, watch the ringed plovers, skylarks and oystercatchers, birds which can still successfully nest as there aren't enough humans to trample their homes, and eat lunch in The Rising Moon. If the bookshop is open, they squeeze between the packed shelves and browse the used stock and usually come out with a small stack of books. They might buy some home-made tablet from the general store or a painting of the waves from the owner of Strand House, and as the sun crosses the sky and the tide begins to turn, lapping at the edges of the causeway, they get back into their cars and drive back to the mainland. The sea reclaims the island and the visitors eat their tablet, read their books, hang their new artwork, but never really think about Unholy Island again.

CHAPTER ONE

L uke stood on the main street of the village on Unholy Island and stared at his phone screen. The moon was close to full and its light fell around him as his world fell apart. He wanted to step back in time. To rewind a few seconds to the pure contentment and joy he had been feeling. He had been contemplating whether to walk on the beach and look at the star-filled sky and the dark waves rolling onto the shore, or to head home to his bookshop where warmth and his current read were waiting.

Instead, he felt like the universe had reached out and smacked his face. He had given up on his twin brother, stopped looking or even thinking about looking. He had been planning to stay here on the island, to embrace his new role as the island Book Keeper. And maybe, in time, his friendship with Esme, the island's Ward Witch, might have the time and breathing space to develop into something more. Maybe.

Now, he was thrown back into the sick feeling of terror for his brother. And guilt that part of him wanted to have not seen the message. For it to have got lost in transit. He knew that wasn't really accurate. What he truly wanted was for Lewis to be living happily and healthily and not causing Luke a single night of lost sleep, but he couldn't separate his guilt at his initial reaction.

The rush of adrenaline was scrambling his thoughts and he felt as if he had been standing, struck with a maelstrom of feelings, for a long time. It had probably been seconds, but the thought that he was wasting time, time that might turn out to be crucial, pushed him into action.

His first instinct was to run. Hard exercise would clear his mind, and his muscles itched to get moving. Instead, without giving himself a chance to stop and think about it, he walked past the turning to Esme's and on to the mayor's house. Ringing the bell, he hoped Tobias was home from The Rising Moon, but that he hadn't gone to bed yet.

Much to Luke's relief, Tobias opened the door fully dressed in his customary tweed. When he saw Luke's face, he invited him straight into the house.

Inside, Luke declined refreshments or a seat. He was too strung out to sit down, had to keep moving. A well-tended fire was leaping in the grate and Winter was lying in his customary position in front of it. Tobias looked well, colour in his pale cheeks and the hollows of his face less deep and shadowed than before. Luke commented on it, and Tobias smiled faintly. 'I sleep better at this time of year. Makes all the difference.'

Luke had only been on the island for ten weeks, but he had come to trust Tobias's opinion. There was something steady and wise about the older man. He showed him his phone. 'I'm sorry to visit this late,' he said, not for the first time.

Tobias waved away the apology. 'You are troubled.'

Luke opened the WhatsApp message and passed his phone to Tobias. 'I got this.'

Tobias read the message and then met his gaze. 'You don't think this is good news.'

Not a question, but Luke shook his head. 'Someone else could have Lewis's phone. They're warning me off.'

'Or Lewis is alive and well,' Tobias offered. 'And he is telling you that he doesn't want to be found.'

'Why? Why would he just say that? After all this time.'

Tobias stayed quiet as Luke ranted, his words tumbling out in a stream. His frustration, his confusion, and the fear. Always the fear. Gradually, he wound down and managed to sit on the edge of the armchair opposite Tobias.

The older man was stroking Winter's head and Luke sensed he was waiting for him to get a hold of himself. He took a breath and forced himself to stop speaking, to give Tobias space to answer. He clasped his hands and squeezed hard, feeling the bones of his knuckles.

'It might not be as bad as you fear,' Tobias said.

'I can't believe he's alive.' Luke squeezed his hands harder, willing the discomfort to anchor him.

'Why not?'

'Because that means he has been deliberately avoiding me. Deliberately not being in touch, putting me through this. He's no saint, but I can't believe he would do that. Not after everything we've been through. We're the only family left.'

'There's another possibility.' Tobias leaned forward, his hands loosely clasped.

Luke frowned. His head had begun to pound and he felt a wave of exhaustion as the adrenaline began to ebb from his system. 'What?'

'Your brother could be alive, but not in a position to be in touch with you before now.'

'I don't get...'

'If he hasn't been at liberty.'

'Like kidnapped?' The word didn't seem right, not for Lewis. Lewis would not be easy to capture, to hold against his will. And given neither of them were rich, why would anybody bother?

Tobias smiled gently, sadly. 'Or he's been staying at His Majesty's Pleasure.'

It took Luke a second to catch on. 'Jail? Wouldn't I know?'

'Perhaps not,' Tobias said, leaning back. 'I'm not entirely sure how these things work, but if Lewis didn't give your contact details, then I see no reason for the prison service to track you down.'

Luke passed a hand over his face. He was tired. And now he had to leave his home and go looking for his twin. Again.

'That scenario does suggest that the message is from your brother and that he is alive and well. That is cause for celebration.'

'Yay.' Luke said flatly. Then he shook himself. 'Sorry. Yes. You're right. I'm just gutted... I was starting to feel...' He realised that he had thought of leaving Unholy Island as 'leaving home'.

Across the village, Esme woke up with a start. The moon was bright, sending a shaft of light across her bed from between a gap in the curtains. Her cat, Jet, had been curled up with her when she fell asleep, but he wasn't there now. Probably out hunting.

Esme didn't know what had disturbed her. She tried to recall what she had been dreaming about, knowing it couldn't have been frightening or her heart would be racing and she would most definitely not need to wrack her brain to remember. Her nightmares were hyper-detailed, and

4

always continued for a few seconds, even after she became conscious.

Something was wrong, though.

After waiting, listening intently for any sound that would indicate what had awoken her, Esme decided to brave getting out of bed. When her thoughts veered toward the possibility that she had been woken up by a sound in the house, such as somebody breaking in, she shut it down. A lid slamming shut on a box that she could not afford to open. Esme knew that, while she was a great deal less anxious now that she was settled in the community of the island, she was never far from a panic spiral. To distract herself, and ensure she didn't peek inside that box of fear, Esme forced herself upright. She was wearing flannel pyjama bottoms and a t-shirt, but the air outside of her duvet was cool. She pulled on her winter dressing gown and pushed her feet into her boot-shaped slippers before creeping out of the bedroom.

There is nobody here, she told herself. Everything is fine.

Esme didn't ever feel lonely or that the guest house was too big when it was just her and Jet. She relished the peace and quiet and the extra empty space. Having grown up in the system and then endured a short and traumatic marriage in a poky one-bedroom flat, having a bedroom that was all her own, let alone an entire home, was nothing short of magical.

Downstairs, Esme padded cautiously through the rooms. She wouldn't let herself think, not really, that anything would be wrong, but that she was just going to check anyway. Nothing was amiss, and the moonlight was glowing through the kitchen window. Esme put the kettle on to make a tea, knowing that she was fully awake and unlikely to get back to sleep anytime soon.

She chose a chamomile and valerian tea and stared out at the garden as it brewed. The moonlight silvered the edges of leaves and the deep shadows of the bushes and trees seemed to grow as she watched, as if the garden was responding to her attention.

With her hands wrapped around the mug for warmth, Esme unlocked the kitchen door and stepped onto the back step. The island's winter festival had passed, and the season was just getting into its stride. The air was cold, but not unbearably so, as it was beautifully still. She breathed in deeply, savouring the island bouquet. Esme hadn't travelled extensively and, truthfully, couldn't base her claim on hard evidence, but she believed the sea air of Unholy Island to be the freshest and most delicious in the world. In the summer she would be enjoying the night jasmine as an unlikely addition to the salt-and-ozone island base note, but right now she could detect the earthy mulch of a garden bedding down for its winter sleep. But the air of the island wasn't just fragrant and clean, it meant freedom and safety.

The branches of the rowan tree that stood between the vegetable patch and the wall that ran along the back of the garden began to sway a little, as if animated by a stiff breeze. Nothing else was moving, including the air. The hairs on Esme's arm lifted and she felt a pricking sensation across her scalp.

Bee had been working with her for months, trying to get Esme to relax the parts of her that remained hypervigilant and screaming for control. She said that once her mind was truly calmed, her intuition would open like curtains being drawn back.

She ignored the electric panic that was fizzing through her body, counting a long, slow breath in and then out. The tree was moving more violently now, whipping in the still air until Esme feared it would lose a branch. Then it stopped. She forced herself to step across the grass to the tree. This was her garden. Her home. She was the Ward Witch and she refused to be afraid. Not here.

The bark of the tree under her fingertips was an answer to a question. She felt instantly calmer and she put her other hand onto it, instinctively anchoring herself. 'What's wrong?' Whispering to a tree in the dark of night was not the action of a sane and rational woman, but luckily Esme had left that notion back on the mainland.

The tree didn't answer.

At the other end of the village, in the last cottage before the wild land of the island took over, Bee awoke with the moon shining through her window. Lucy was standing at the end of the large bed they shared when Bee was home. Diana had her own space and, besides, rarely slept. 'What's wrong, Sister mine?'

With a flash of white teeth and light feet on the wooden floorboards, the youngest of the Three Sisters was gone. Bee lay still for a moment, warm underneath the covers, and contemplated staying put. Then, slowly and with some dissension from her joints, which had a tendency to seize up a little at night these days, despite her daily stretches, she got out of bed and drew on a thick flannel gown and slippers.

Downstairs, the door to the back garden was wide open and the cold night air was streaming through. She passed the mirrors they used for scrying, safely shrouded with swathes of thick fabric. In the half-light, they looked like three figures standing in the middle of the room. Waiting.

Lucy was standing on the patch of shells and stones that served as the back garden to the cottage. It was a yard, really, and was filled with colourful pots of foliage and flowers. At this time of year, they were dormant or dead. Diana could keep things blooming all year round, if she chose, but she respected the wheel of the year. *Every living thing deserves to rest.*

'Can you feel it?' Lucy asked, not turning around.

Bee stopped thinking about Diana's plant pots and her ageing bones and instead opened her mind. It was as easy as breathing for her. Too easy, in fact, and something she had spent her young years learning to close. There was a ripple of something unsettling. A dark vein of *wrong* that was obvious when you knew what *right* felt like. She opened her mouth to say the words, but Lucy beat her to it. Her sister turned, her pale face glowing luminous in the moonlight. 'Something's coming.'

CHAPTER TWO

The next day, Esme called into the pub for lunch. Seren came out of the kitchen, tucking a pencil behind one ear. Her dark hair was twisted off her face in a chic knot, and she was wearing a red checked shirt that matched her lipstick. It made Esme think that she ought to start making an effort with her own appearance. At least occasionally.

Bee arrived shortly after and they chatted about this and that, avoiding the big subjects, and focusing on their lunch orders.

When Seren brought over their food, she lingered. 'Will there be someone new?'

'What?' Esme had a forkful of quiche ready to go, and she put it back down.

'We're a man down,' Seren said, referring to the sudden departure of Fiona's husband, Oliver. 'Does that mean someone else can stay? I've got a cousin looking for a place to live and I just wondered...'

Only residents could stay on the island for longer than two nights. It was a rule enforced by the protective wards that cloaked the island from the mainland, keeping it forgettable to the wider community of Britain and the world.

'I don't know if it works like that,' Bee began.

Seren waved a hand. 'Oh, that's all right. I told her I would ask and now I have.'

'You don't want her to move here?' Esme guessed.

'It's not that. I don't think she would enjoy island life. It's too quiet for her.' Seren flashed a smile. 'And, yeah, she would drive me bloody mad.'

AFTER SEREN HAD LEFT, Esme asked Bee how it did work. 'Does the island have a quota of residents? Now that Oliver has gone, does that mean the next person who visits will be able to stay if they want?' She felt a shiver of anxiety at the prospect. Change was not her favourite thing and new people were even worse.

'I don't know if there is an exact quota,' Bee said. 'And it may be that family members of residents get a pass.' She was vigorously grinding black pepper over her food and paused to sneeze.

'Bless you,' Esme said automatically.

Bee shot her a piercing look. 'I thank you, Witch.'

Esme felt herself blush. 'I didn't...'

'Get a hold of yourself,' Bee said, but not unkindly. As one of the mysterious Three Sisters, Bee was inherently terrifying. But she was also the kindest and most approachable of the three. Having known her for seven years, Esme was mostly comfortable in her presence, but it didn't take much to throw her out of that relaxed state. One big step forward was that Esme could now confidently admit that Bee was not of this world. Not human. Or not just human.

'But it's a possibility? That we'll have a new resident?'

They hadn't long acquired a newcomer, Luke, and that hadn't been all bad...

'When Alvis died, we needed a Book Keeper. There are roles that must be filled. Oliver wasn't important.'

Well, that was blunt. But also, Esme had to admit, entirely true. The man had done something to do with investing and given financial advice, but he had only been on the island because of his wife, Fiona. 'I don't want somebody new.' The words were out before Esme realised she had been going to say them.

'New can be good.'

'New can be dangerous.'

Bee smiled widely. 'That, too.'

Luke was settled in his reading chair with a fresh mug of tea and the closed sign flipped on the door of the shop. After his late-night conversation with Tobias, he had come back to his bedroom above the shop and slept like the dead. The day had been spent in a stupefied state between sleeping and waking. He could feel the concern over his brother and the confusion over what he should do, but his mind seemed determined to keep it turned down low. It all felt muffled and somehow distant in the light of a new day. It wasn't something he could defer forever, he knew, but he was grateful for the reprieve.

He reached blindly for the paperback spy novel, which he had left on top of the pile of books next to the chair, but felt an unexpected texture. Instead of the soft cardboard of a vintage Penguin, worn smooth with time, his fingers brushed the rougher surface of a clothbound book.

The tiny jolt of confusion made him sit straighter. He looked down and discovered that the pile of business books, thrillers and Penguin classics was no longer crowned with

John le Carré's The Spy Who Came in from the Cold, but with a small clothbound book. It had probably been red once, but was now a faded pink. He looked around at the bookshelves. The air in the shop was tingling, almost like a small current of electricity was running through the atmosphere. It was the same feeling you got when there was somebody else hidden in the room and they were holding their breath, trying not to be discovered. He knew that phenomenon. Had played a lot of hide and seek when he was a kid. Mostly with his twin brother, but also sometimes as a teen, with his drunk father.

'Where is my book?' He kept his voice even. The bookshop was his friend. At least, he hoped that was true.

There was no answer. Which was probably the less alarming outcome, really. After another ten seconds of waiting and listening, Luke allowed a small sigh. He picked up the clothbound book and turned it over. The cover was blank. No stamped letters on the cover or spine. Flipping it open, he was halted by Alvis's name, written in perfect cursive on the inside of the front cover. Alvis Knott 1939. The writing was in soft pencil and blurred with age, but it was perfectly legible. And it made no sense. Alvis hadn't been a young woman when she had died, murdered by Fiona's husband Oliver in a fit of rage when she had refused to give him a lump of sea glass that now sat on Esme's kitchen windowsill. But this date was eighty-four years ago and, assuming she hadn't popped out of the womb writing in cursive, had to have been written when she was at least ten. He pictured Alvis. Was ninety-four possible? He would have guessed early seventies, but he supposed it wasn't the strangest thing he had encountered on the island.

He was just about to flip to the title page when the landline rang. As the mobile signal on the island was patchy, residents still used their landlines as a matter of habit. The bookshop's telephone was chunky and red and had an actual dial. It lived on the counter and Luke pulled himself out of his reading chair to answer it, betting it would be Tobias checking in after his late-night visit.

Instead of Tobias's voice, there was a kind of confused gasp and then a pause.

'Hello?' Luke tried.

'Is Alvis there?'

Luke leaned against the counter and looked out of the front window. The sun was low and reflecting golden light onto the glass. 'No. I'm very sorry, but I have some bad news.' He explained that Alvis had died.

The voice on the other end of the line was male and slightly quavery, as if it belonged to somebody quite elderly. 'Alvis knew what to look out for. She knew my area of specialism. I don't think I can... Oh dear.'

'I run the shop now. If you tell me what Alvis did, I can try to do the same.'

'Oh dear,' the man said again. 'This is very bad. There was another place... A local shop. It wasn't all that good, truth be told, but that's gone, now, too.' His voice had an aggrieved tone. 'This really is most inconvenient.'

'I'm sorry for your loss.'

Silence. And a bit more breathing.

'Can I help you with anything?' Even before Luke had finished his sentence, there was a click, and he was left speaking to dead air.

TOBIAS WALKED from the spit of rock known as Seal Point along the eastern edge of the island to the ruins of the castle. Winter trotted beside him, content to go at the same pace as Tobias, at least for now. As a younger dog, Winter had roamed widely throughout their walks. Running ahead to investigate and repeatedly dashing back to check in with Tobias, looping circuits around him so that he had to have covered ten times the distance by the time they returned home. It was natural for a dog to calm as he aged, Tobias reasoned, and it surely meant nothing more than maturity of spirit.

The day had started overcast, but now the clouds had cleared, and a pale sky stretched from the horizon. The sun was still low and wouldn't climb very high at this time of the year. Tobias felt his lungs expand with deepening breaths and his muscles stretch pleasantly as he strode out along the path. He was more vital in the cold season, could feel his thoughts snapping to attention and his body responding more readily to his commands. Strength ran through his limbs, and he flexed his fingers against the wooden handle of his walking stick with satisfaction. The drowsiness of the summer had been cleared out by the north wind and he was fully awake.

The ruins of the castle came into view and Tobias could see the original building, the ground as it had been before those stones had been laid, and the vast rock sill that had formed before the island millions of years before that. This palimpsest was everywhere for Tobias, but most clear on the island that was his home. He was adept at filtering the multiple views, focusing on the latest layer and letting the others fade to the background, but they were always present.

Winter broke away from his side, letting out a sharp bark of warning. His hackles were up and he stared toward the castle.

'What is it?'

Winter barked again, low and quiet. A secret warning that was more alarming than a loud one. It meant he wasn't sure whether he could frighten the threat, and his uncertainty pierced Tobias's heart. Was Winter feeling his age? He joined the dog where he stood a few paces along the path.

He heard the singing first. Then the group appeared around the corner from the castle. Five people dressed in warm puffy coats and sensible walking boots, the leader of the pack with walking poles and all of them with brightly coloured daysacks, no doubt filled with sandwiches and Kendal Mint Cake. They were singing and didn't falter even after they must have seen Tobias. He didn't recognise the song, although the melody reminded him of one of the old border ballads.

Tobias patted Winter. 'It's all right,' he said. 'They're harmless.'

Winter looked up at him with an expression that begged to differ, but his hackles were no longer raised and his ears lay normally.

Tobias moved to the side of the path to give the group room to pass. He leaned on his stick and Winter sat obediently next to him, forming the perfect image of the country gent with his faithful hound. Winter slightly spoiled this by letting out a pungent fart just as the group came level.

Tobias nodded to the walkers and they waved cheerily, not breaking their song to say 'hello'.

After their voices had faded and Tobias had started on his way, he said, mildly. 'That wasn't very polite.'

Winter ignored him, springing away to some undergrowth to chase something more interesting.

CHAPTER THREE

The bookshop had been surprisingly busy during the afternoon. Luke knew the island was quiet over the winter months and he hadn't been expecting the group of cheerful ramblers. They bumped around the narrow passages of the shop, threatening to knock books from the shelves, until he asked them to pile their rucksacks onto the floor while they walked around. When the doorbell jangled as the last of them left, he heaved a sigh of relief and could have sworn he felt the bookshop do the same.

The sun had set at four and it was full dark by five. It made it feel much later. Flipping the sign to 'closed', Luke was ready for a pint and some food. The shop clearly had other ideas. When he walked back through to the register to cash up for the night, he found the red clothbound book sitting on the counter.

'Later,' he said out loud. 'I'm going to sort the money, go for a bite and then I'll read it. I promise.' He wasn't entirely sure why he was putting it off. Perhaps a stubborn part of him didn't want to be bossed around by the shop.

The lights flickered and he held his breath, waiting to see if they would go out entirely, but they stayed on. He patted the counter in a conciliatory manner and opened the register.

IT WAS quiet at The Rising Moon. Tobias and Matteo were sitting at the main table in the middle of the room and Luke joined them. If they had wanted to dine alone, they would have taken one of the smaller tables. 'No Bee tonight?'

Tobias shook his head. 'The Sisters go through times when they are less sociable. Like us all, I suppose.'

The words weren't serious, but his tone gave them an ominous note. Giving Tobias a second look, Luke thought he looked concerned. Weirdly, he also looked healthier and, somehow, younger than he had a few weeks ago. 'Is everything all right?'

'All is well, thank you. I miss Fiona and the boy, that is all.'

'When will they be back?' Fiona, Oliver's wife, and her son Euan, had taken a trip after Oliver had been... dealt with. Island-style.

'Alas, they did not share that information with me. I would have thought they will be a few more days, at least.'

Luke studiously didn't look at Matteo.

'I believe it's called 'needing space' and I gather that means more than the sea and the sky.' Tobias smiled a little after this, as if he was making a small joke.

Luke nodded.

The door to the pub opened and Esme walked in, closely followed by Hammer. Winter, drowsing by the fire, lifted his head, saw that he knew the incomers, and put it back down.

Luke wondered if they had walked together. He wasn't jealous, he told himself. Just interested. He wasn't one of those possessive men who wouldn't want his partner to have friends and a life of their own. He was just interested in whether Esme was as fond of Hammer as he was of her. And whether it was purely friendly. It was a matter of information.

Of course, Esme wasn't his... anything. She was a friend. He thought there might be something there. A possibility. But there was also a wall of reserve around the woman, and he didn't know if that was caution or a deep disinterest in acting on the attraction that he thought was mutual. Or the attraction wasn't mutual at all and he was reading signals that simply weren't there. He drained half of his pint while he ruminated on this depressing possibility.

Esme stopped at the bar, perching on a stool to chat with Seren, while Hammer came and sat next to Matteo, opposite Luke. He nodded a greeting, which Luke returned by lifting his glass slightly. Two could play at the strong, silent type.

'Good evening,' Tobias said, polite as ever.

Matteo was writing on his notepad and he angled it for the group to read.

Did the walking group leave?

'They did,' Tobias said. 'I checked the car park.'

'Good thing,' Luke said. 'It would have been a squeeze for all of them at Esme's.'

Esme ran the island guest house and it had two bedrooms, three if she gave up her own room and slept in her painting studio.

Strange time of year for rambling.

The words on Matteo's notepad were innocuous enough, but Luke could see the concern on the older man's face.

Tobias, the oldest of them all, was the most relaxed. 'It's

fine,' he said. 'Some people like to get into baths of ice. Going for a winter stroll is nothing.'

'Are you talking about Wim Hof?' Luke asked, amused. 'I didn't peg you for a health bro.'

'I beg your pardon?'

Luke caught Matteo's eye and he let out a single wheeze of laughter, the most audible sound he had ever heard from Matteo in the months he had been on the island. Even Hammer cracked a smile.

HAVING FINISHED her evening meal and a detailed conversation with Seren about the best way to make scones, Esme decided to head home. Other than a casual 'goodbye' to the whole table, she hadn't spoken to the Viking, and he had barely looked in her direction. Which she didn't care about. Not one bit.

Outside the pub, Esme was bundled up in her coat and scarf but could still feel the biting edge of the wind. The door opened behind her and Luke appeared, as if she had summoned him with her oh-so-casual thoughts. She felt herself flush even though he couldn't possibly know that she had just been thinking about him.

Luke had his hands stuffed in his jacket pockets. 'Well,' he said at the same time as she had started to say 'have a good night.'

'Sorry. What?'

'Nothing,' Esme said, feeling her cheeks flush even more.

'I have some reading to do.'

'Okay. Right. Enjoy that.' She cursed herself for sounding so stilted. Why couldn't she speak like a normal human woman? She had thought that she had got more comfortable around Luke, that they had become friends.

Just because she found him easy on the eye was no reason to lose her mind.

'Actually,' Luke glanced away and then back to her. His eyes bright in the light spilling from the pub windows. 'It's a bit of a weird one. It belonged to Alvis.'

Well, that sharpened her up. 'What's it about?'

'I don't know, I haven't looked yet.'

'You haven't looked?' Esme tamped down on the feeling of irritation. Luke hadn't really known Alvis. Naturally, he wouldn't feel the same pull to look at her belongings.

'I've been a bit distracted,' he said, his gaze sliding away as he stuffed his hands into his pockets. 'I don't know... Do you mind if I walk with you?'

They started in the direction of Strand House. Esme remembered when Luke had first arrived on the island. He had offered to walk her home from the pub because it was dark and she had laughed at his big city ways. Now, she was grateful for the sign that he wanted to spend time with her. Pathetically so.

It was too cold to dawdle, and they kept a good pace as they chatted. Esme waited for Luke to say what was on his mind, but he seemed content to chat about the bookshop and his meal and when Fiona and Euan might return to the island.

Once they arrived at Strand House, Esme had relaxed enough to casually invite Luke in for a coffee.

'I would love a tea,' he said, dipping his head. 'If that's all right?'

It didn't take long to boil the water and make a pot and soon they were sitting at Esme's kitchen table. She could see them as they had been a few weeks earlier, back when Luke had first arrived. He had stayed in one of her guest rooms for a couple of nights, and she had made him breakfast. It seemed strange that it was a relatively short time ago. She felt she knew him so much better now, and couldn't really imagine island life without him at the bookshop. The thought made her start, and her hand jerked as she poured the tea, slopping a little over the side of the mug. She shouldn't be that attached to him. That invested. He was a newcomer. Just because he had inherited Alvis's bookshop and the role of Book Keeper, didn't mean he would stay. Island life was quiet. He might decide he wanted more excitement in his life.

Luke added a splash of milk and then picked up his mug, cradling it between his hands. 'You were saying you were distracted this evening. With Seren. Everything all right?'

Esme tried not to notice how big his hands looked and how nice they might feel spread across her skin. She felt a blush ignite and dipped her head to hide her face. 'I had a broken night.'

'Bad dreams?'

'Something like that.' Esme lifted her mug and blew across the surface of the tea. 'Is everything all right with you?'

'Fine,' he said, looking away from her.

Esme felt the rebuff like a slap. Jet chose that moment to wake up from his nap underneath the table. He stretched against Esme's legs and then she felt him move away. A second later, Luke jumped and reached a hand down to rub his leg.

'Jet?'

He nodded. 'Claws.'

'That's unusual,' she said. She ducked under the table and saw two green eyes staring insolently. 'Luke's not a scratching post,' she said, while giving his head a gentle fist bump.

CHAPTER FOUR

Luke didn't know if it was the cup of tea and easy chat or the pain from Esme's cat sinking his claws into his ankle, but he found himself speaking again.

'I couldn't sleep, either. Last night. I got a message from Lewis.' He hadn't intended to mention it, having become accustomed to dealing with his problems on his own, but now that Esme was sitting in front of him he found he wanted to talk about it. First Tobias and now Esme, what on earth had happened to him?

Esme was frowning. 'Your brother? The one you've been looking for?'

'My twin, yeah.'

'Is he all right? Did he tell you where he is?'

Luke grabbed his phone and thumbed to the message, then showed Esme. There wasn't a chain of messages above it, as it was the first time Lewis had ever used WhatsApp. It had to be using his old mobile number for the account, though, as the display name was 'Lewis' and not an unknown phone number.

'What kind of message is that?' Esme's eyes were

23

flashing in anger. 'I'm sorry, I know he's your family, but what the...'

He was gratified by her reaction, realising that a small part of him had been simmering in frustration. All of this time. All of the worry. And then Lewis sends him this curt dismissal. Problem was, it only sparked more concern. 'Yeah. It's not great. But I don't believe he's just being a dick. He can be one, don't get me wrong, and he loves to wind me up, but this is...'

'Messed up.'

He nodded. 'Extremely. And it doesn't feel like him. Like his brand of fuckery, if you know what I mean?'

'Are you going to reply?'

'I've tried ringing his number a few times since. He doesn't have voicemail so it just says 'the person you've called is unavailable'. Same as it has all the other times I've tried. Could be switched off, could be dead.' He winced as the last word seemed to hang in the air.

To her credit, Esme didn't flinch. She didn't bail on the conversation now that it was heavy. 'You think somebody else sent the message? Using Lewis's phone?'

Luke picked up his mug of tea and then put it back down. His throat had closed up.

'Even if that's the case, it doesn't mean Lewis is... incapacitated.' Esme's expression was gentle and Luke felt dangerously close to crying. He managed a grimace and a nod that he hoped conveyed 'maybe' and appreciation of her words without him having to speak.

'Or,' Esme continued, her voice brighter, 'someone could have stolen his phone. He might have a shiny new phone and be living his best life and have just not been in touch to give you his new details. For some petty reason. Families can be weird. So I've been told, anyway.'

'Yours is normal?' Luke was glad to change the subject a bit. Maybe get some light relief.

'No siblings, parents died, foster care from six.'

'Holy shit. I'm sorry.'

Esme shrugged. Her expression had closed back down to the blank, guarded one he remembered from when he first arrived on the island. His chest tightened in misery. And then she flashed him a reassuring smile and looked like herself again. 'I don't talk about it. Not because it's a big secret or too terrible or anything. I just... honestly, I don't know what to say. It was shit. But it's over. And I'm not going to go through the rest of my life being defined by my crappy childhood.'

'That's a very mature attitude.'

She stuck her tongue out at him.

IT WASN'T until Luke went home that something very obvious occurred to her. She rang his mobile, feeling like it wasn't the sort of thing she ought to put in a text. He answered quickly. 'What's wrong?'

'Nothing,' Esme smiled at his concern. 'I just thought of something. Don't know why I didn't think before...'

'What?'

'Are you going to speak to the police about Lewis? I mean, the message from him is a lead.'

There was a short silence. 'Probably not.'

'Because he's an adult? Or do you think they'll stop looking because he's asked you to?'

'I haven't been to the police at all. He's not registered missing.'

'But...'

'My brother hasn't been living a good life. He would never forgive me if I called the law on him.'

At that, Esme realised why it hadn't been her first thought, either. The police weren't bad in her mind, not her conscious mind anyway. But underneath that, there was a fear of authority and of bureaucratic systems. She had been swallowed up by the care system and it had been filled with many good people who meant well, but the overall experience was of being churned through a machine. No control. No exit. She felt a burning in the back of her throat as if she was going to cry. Or throw up. 'I get it,' she said.

'It's a good thing, anyway,' Luke said. 'I don't think the other islanders would thank me for bringing police attention here. Lewis isn't here, I know that now, but I came here looking for him. An investigation might have them asking questions, looking into us all.'

'We do like our privacy here.' They all had pasts they were running from or secrets they wanted to stay hidden.

'And it would be causing trouble for no good reason. Lewis didn't come here, whatever rumours I heard. Nobody here saw him, I'm sure of it. They would have told me by now.'

Esme was touched by his trust in the community. And it seemed like a good sign for him sticking around.

People came to Unholy Island for sanctuary and sometimes the safest thing of all was to disappear.

HAMMER HAD THOUGHT he was working on a new carving. He had his favourite whittling knife in one hand and a beautiful chunk of elm in the other, but he had been staring into the flames of his log burner utterly motionless for what, he now realised, was the best part of an hour.

He wasn't upset about Oliver. Not about the man's death, anyway. And he didn't think he was particularly upset about Alvis, either. Hammer had seen a lot of death and, while Alvis might have been helped along by Oliver, she had reached an extremely good age and didn't have too much to complain about.

All of that made good sense, so he didn't understand why he had been watching the orange flames and thinking about his gran. The only family of his worth a damn. And long dead, now. No reason for her image to be haunting him.

He put down the wood and closed the knife. He would go to the pub, have some food and maybe a pint. Hammer wasn't a big drinker, but he would have one or two tonight, he could feel it. With any luck, Esme would be in and he could speak to her for a while. Or not. Just being in the same place as her would make him feel better. He didn't think it was because she was the island's witch, didn't know how much of the island lore he believed, but he knew she was a good person. And that being near her made the thing inside him that was snarling and snapping quieten down.

THE NEXT DAY, Esme's house phone rang. Seren sounded excited and worried in equal measure. 'A woman's interested in renovating the cottages down near your place. She's called Kate.'

'What?'

'She just came into the pub and I gave her a bacon roll. For breakfast. She wanted granola and fresh berries but I told her it was winter so she could have jam or compote from the freezer if she wanted raspberry. But she seemed to enjoy the bacon.'

Esme broke in as soon as Seren paused to draw breath.

'What do you mean she's interested in the cottages? What for?'

'The ones down by your place. One of them, at least. I'm not quite clear. And she might have been talking nonsense anyway. Do you think it's possible? What do the wards say?'

'They don't speak to me,' Esme said, more sharply than she intended. Her heart was pounding. Another new person. She thought about the strange wind the other night. The sense of foreboding.

'She said she was going to speak to Tobias, so you might be able to catch her there if you leave now.'

'Right.' Esme realised she was being given an order.

WALKING across to the mayor's house didn't take long and, as Seren had predicted, the visitor was still there.

'Good,' Tobias said when he opened the door to Esme. 'You're here.'

'Seren called,' Esme said, stepping over the threshold. The house smelled of beeswax polish and wood smoke.

'We have a visitor.'

'So I hear.' Esme wanted to ask more, but Tobias was already leading the way into the sitting room. The fire was crackling in the grate, but Winter wasn't in his usual position in front of it. She looked around, expecting the dog to come and greet her, but he was nowhere to be seen.

A young woman was standing in the middle of the room. She was wearing slim jeans, leather ankle boots, and an over-sized grey jumper that looked like cashmere. She had expertly applied make-up and her honey blonde hair fell in perfect, swishy loose curls.

'Hello,' Esme said, and introduced herself.

'I'm Kate Foster,' the woman said.

Her smile was warm and seemed genuine. Esme felt her shoulders ease down a notch. This woman looked like money. When she realised there wasn't a development opportunity on the island, or a shop selling ruinously expensive candles, she would no doubt head back across the causeway.

'I was just telling Kate about our little community,' Tobias said. 'Do sit, everyone.'

Esme wondered which version of the island Tobias had gone with. She waited for Kate to take a seat before sitting cross-legged on the hearth rug. Winter's usual spot. She wanted to ask where the dog was, but it felt too private a question in front of a stranger. Tobias must have guessed what she was thinking, though, as he answered her anyway. 'Winter's out in the garden. He wouldn't come in, so I've left him to it for now.' He shook his head fondly. 'He's getting stubborn in his old age.'

Tobias sat in his usual chair, his hand dangling as if expecting to find Winter. Esme wondered if he would absent-mindedly pat her on the head instead.

'My friend visited,' Kate was saying. 'She said it was really pretty. And quiet. I like quiet, there are so few properly wild places left now, don't you think? Where you can get back to nature? And the old ways of life. We're always in such a hurry these days. It's good to slow down. Anyway, I just had to come and see for myself. And then I saw those darling cottages and it felt like fate.'

Esme glanced at Tobias. Word sometimes spread about the island, of course, people didn't always forget about the place instantly. It took varying amounts of time for thoughts of the island to fade and sometimes people talked. And, for the most part, Unholy Island welcomed day trippers and one-night visitors. They brought money and life to the place. But wanting to complete a renovation project was different. That was medium-term at least, even if Kate didn't plan on staying on the island overnight for more than two nights at a time. It still violated the spirit of the two-night rule, even if it would technically be allowed.

'And what do you think?' Tobias asked Kate, surprising Esme.

'I think they're beautiful, but they need some love.'

The woman was exuding sincerity. It put Esme on her guard. 'They're not for sale, I'm afraid.'

Kate shook her head. 'Forgive me, but I don't think that's quite true.'

Esme realised that she didn't actually know who owned the buildings on the island. She had been given the bed-and-breakfast when she arrived and Luke had been given the bookshop as well as the job of Book Keeper. But it wasn't a name on a piece of paper, not the kind of ownership that meant selling the building. It was more of a role. A tenancy or stewardship. Esme understood that when she died there would be a new Ward Witch and whoever took on that responsibility would also live in Strand House.

'I'm sorry?' Tobias was saying, his expression mild. 'I don't think we quite follow you.'

Kate Foster shrugged an elegant shoulder. 'You know how things are these days. Everything is for sale.'

CHAPTER FIVE

W alking back to Strand House, a cold wind whipping at her cheeks and making her eyes tear up, Esme's mind was filled with thoughts of Kate Foster and her confident manner. Could they really be getting a new resident? Just like that?

Her only comfort was Tobias's utter calm about the whole thing. After Kate Foster had left, saying that she was going to speak to her financial advisor, Tobias had assured Esme that nothing else would come of it. 'The young lady will go home and forget all about this notion. This sort of thing happens every so often. How many times have visitors told you that they would love to stay longer?'

Having just got into the house and begun to unlace her boots, Esme's phone buzzed. She picked it up to find a message from Luke.

Are you free for a chat?

Esme tapped out a reply. *Yes! Shall I come to shop?*

Thanks. I don't have any milk though.

· · ·

Having stopped at Matteo's to buy milk, Esme headed to the bookshop. The window display hadn't changed in all the time that Luke had been in residence, and she realised that he had never seen Alvis at her best. She had slowed down over the last couple of years and had been quite distracted in her last months, but before that she had put real effort into the front window of the shop. Not just changing the books on display, but adding seasonal decorations like autumnal leaves or summer flowers, wintergreens in the cold months and a bottle of whisky at Hogmanay. It wasn't exactly Harrods, but it was cheery and inviting.

The bell on the door of the shop jingled softly and Esme inhaled the scent of old paper and warm wood. She found Luke in the front room of the shop and knew he would have seen her walking past the window, maybe even pausing to look at it. She hefted her shopping bag. 'I brought milk.'

'Kettle's just boiled,' he said, heading to the tiny room that served as his kitchenette and office. It had a kettle, a microwave and a fridge, and it occurred to Esme that she didn't know how Alvis had coped with such bare facilities for so many years. She had the pub for her main meals, of course, but even so... She thought about her own cosy, well-appointed kitchen and felt a surge of gratitude for all she had.

Once they had mugs of tea, Luke led the way back to the front room. He offered Esme his reading chair and perched on the stool behind the counter. He looked uncharacteristically nervous. 'I've got a favour to ask.'

'Okay.'

'It might not be possible. It's probably not possible...'

'Just say it.'

He took a breath. 'Could you put a ward on Lewis? To protect him?'

'Oh,' Esme felt a wave of disappointment. She wanted, very much, to say 'yes' to anything Luke asked of her. 'I don't think that is possible.'

Luke nodded, as if that was what he had been expecting, and Esme's stomach dropped in sympathy. 'I'm sorry. The wards are physically here. On the island. I don't know how I would add one remotely. Even if I knew where he was and could picture it...' She trailed off, remembering her vision of Lewis in a bed. It was unlikely he was still in that room.

'I'm sorry,' she said again, feeling useless. Worse than useless. 'I wasn't really given instructions for this stuff. Just how to keep the wards going on the island.'

'It's okay.' Luke's shoulders were hunched and he looked miserable.

'Do you know what you are going to do? About Lewis?' Esme didn't want Luke to say he was leaving to look for his brother, but it seemed inevitable. It was a quest that had brought him to the island in the first place. Now that Lewis had been in touch...

He shook his head. 'I feel like I should start looking again, but I wouldn't know where to start.' He looked at Esme. 'One message telling me to butt out of his life doesn't really help.'

'No.'

There was a short silence. Luke wasn't drinking his tea, but he wasn't looking at Esme anymore, either. She could see he was thinking and she waited quietly, lost in her own swirling fears. She had been happy on Unholy Island before Luke arrived. She would be happy again. There was no need to be afraid.

'Would you hate me if I didn't go?' His face twisted and he laughed self-consciously. 'That came out a bit

33

weird. Sorry. I mean, would I be a really bad person if I didn't start looking again?'

'If you did what Lewis is asking?'

'It might not be him,' Luke's face was now utterly bereft. A mix of misery and hope.

'I don't think you would be a bad person,' Esme said. 'Not at all.' She just didn't think he was a man of inaction and her gut told her that Luke Taylor would not be able to leave the mystery alone.

Tobias was standing in the front room of the bookshop, waiting. Luke had heard the door while he was in the cubby making himself a tea in his favourite mug. It was a misshapen pottery thing that had been clearly made by an enthusiastic amateur. Or a genius. It had wobbly sides but was a dream to drink from, with the most comfortable lip. God help him, he was thinking far too much about mugs.

'You look settled,' Tobias said, approval in his voice.

It was a phrase that Luke would have expected to send him running for the hills. But it made him feel warm. 'I like it here.'

Tobias wasn't looking at him. Instead, he was gazing at the bookshelves and Luke expected him to ask about 'that mystery with the yellow window on the cover' or an obscure first edition. Normal bookshop questions.

'These shelves are made from French oak,' he said instead. 'They were grown in the ancient Forest of Rouvray, between Paris and Normandy, and cut down for a monastery library. When the order made their way to Melrose to found an abbey, they brought their library with them, shelves and all. Imagine how difficult that journey would have been back then. How highly they valued their library to transport it by cart and boat. Books are important.

34

They keep the knowledge so that it can be passed down. They stop things from being forgotten.'

Luke wondered if Tobias knew about the internet.

Tobias reached out and ran a finger along one of the shelves.

Luke felt a tingle on the back of his hand, as if someone had touched his skin.

'They may have been misguided in a few of their beliefs,' Tobias continued, 'but those monks had one thing right. It's a sacred duty to care for books.'

'Right.' Luke lifted his mug and took a sip of his tea. It was too early for this.

'You are our Book Keeper.'

Bee had said the same. The same emphasis on the phrase as two words. 'I'll look after the shop,' he said, trying to reassure Tobias.

The older man seemed to relax. At once he was the usual Tobias. A kindly old gent. 'If the shop shows you Pliny the Elder's second book of natural history, I would very much like to see it.'

'I can look for it now,' Luke said, putting his mug down.

'Oh no, don't trouble yourself. I've looked many times.'

'Right... I don't know if it's something I can order.' There were a few contact numbers for book suppliers and Luke assumed that on occasion he would need to order books in. Or by request. He really needed to read up on how to run a bookshop.

'The bookshop will provide,' Tobias said. 'But there are volumes it is reluctant to reveal.'

'I don't think I understand.'

'I don't know what the problem is with it either.' He looked around, as if addressing the shop. 'But I would dearly like to read it. I will bring it back in mint condition. I solemnly promise that there won't be a repeat of Cassell's Volume Four.'

'Why do I feel as if you aren't talking to me?'

Tobias smiled at him gently and raised a hand. 'Chee-rio, Book Keeper. See you at dinner.'

The witch was more distracted than usual. Bee opened her eyes during their meditation and contemplated the woman sitting cross-legged on the floor, obediently breathing slowly. There was a feeling around people when they relaxed and entered an open state. Esme had been here for almost an hour and Bee hadn't sensed it once.

Bee rose to her feet and went to make tea. She wasn't a quitter by nature, but she knew the edges of her sphere of control. If Esme wasn't focused for today's session, then there was little Bee could do about it.

As soon as the kettle began to boil, Esme opened her eyes. 'Is it twelve already?'

'Eleven. I thought we'd stop early today.'

'Okay.'

Bee turned away. If Esme had thought she had hidden her relief, she was mistaken.

Bee put her blend of tea into the warmed pot and added the water. The sound of the china lid against the rim of the pot reverberated strangely, and she knew there was an answering memory or premonition somewhere in her consciousness, the sound playing at the same time to make that unmistakable layered tone. A chorus.

She ignored it and carried the tea tray to the seats near the front window of the open plan living room.

After they had taken their first sips and Bee had noticed Esme studiously avoiding her gaze, Bee was ready to interrogate the witch. It wasn't just a matter of neighbourly concern. In fact, it wasn't neighbourly concern at all. Bee was Esme's tutor. Her guide. She had a responsibility to make sure the island's Ward Witch was performing at full capacity. And currently, she really wasn't.

'I am not your friend.'

Esme put her cup down.

Bee felt, rather than saw, Esme draw herself together. A surface knitting tightly to form an impenetrable shield. It wasn't physical or something Bee could actually see with her eyes, but she knew it had happened all the same. 'I am your guide. Your teacher.' She tried to make her next words gentle, but it was difficult. They were true and Bee didn't know to soften the fact. 'And you are honoured.'

Esme sat a little straighter. 'I know. I am very grateful.'

'I don't want you to be grateful. I want you to concentrate. To work.'

'I am trying,' Esme said, a little sharpness in her tone.

Bee took a sip of her tea before changing tack. 'How much do you know about the island's history? Do you know, for instance, why we have a Ward Witch?'

'To protect the island from the mainland. The wider world. Keep us hidden.'

'Yes, that. But why?'

'It's a place of sanctuary?'

'And we are lucky to have it. All of us incomers have been granted sanctuary here, but the island was here before the first residents.' Apart from Tobias, of course, but Bee wasn't going to tell another's story. Especially not his. 'Have you wondered why?'

Esme frowned. 'I don't know what you mean... It's a place. Places... form. Tectonic plates. Geology and all that.'

Bee watched the other woman. She had been waiting for Esme to complete her training before revealing the full extent of her responsibilities. But it had been seven years, and she was starting to worry that Esme's progress wasn't ever going to speed up. It could put more than the island in danger if she didn't know what she was protecting. But if she freaked the witch out and she panicked, maybe ran away, they would be even more vulnerable. Not to mention that she was fond of Esme. 'This place formed for a reason. A spirit, not sentient at first, but becoming increasingly so over time.'

Esme nodded. Her eyes were wide and fixed on Bee's face as she listened.

'You know about thin places?'

'Like on Hallow's Eve?'

'This place is like Hallow's Eve all year round. The spirit formed. Or, more likely, came through thousands of years ago and stayed. It acts as a guardian. Stops more things coming through.'

'Unholy Island is a gateway and we're, what? The gate-keepers? The bouncers?'

You are the bouncer, Bee thought, but didn't say. The small woman in front of her with her messy bun and large eyes and spiral of terror wound tightly around her own power was the last line of defence between the other worlds and this version of Britain. Probably best not to tell her that. Just yet.

CHAPTER SIX

Luke didn't know if it was the guilt he felt over taking his eye off the ball, getting distracted by the bookshop and Esme and island life, or whether it was some buried seam of self-destruction that he had inherited from his old man, but he closed the bookshop early and walked down to the car park without telling anybody on the island where he was going. The sunset had been bleeding red across the sky, but the dark was rolling in fast now. He got into his ancient Ford Fiesta and took his phone out of his pocket, trying not to think about how big a mistake he was probably making.

Tobias had told him he looked settled and he knew it was true. He felt settled. But that was all wrong. His brother had reached out to him. And, ignoring the actual text of Lewis's message, it meant one thing only: that there was a chance Lewis was alive. To stay playing shop on Unholy Island, ignoring that reality, wasn't right.

Luke had kept in touch with some of Lewis's more reasonable friends, asking them to let him know if they heard anything from his brother, and one of these had a contact who could put him in touch with Dean Fisher, the supremely dodgy guy that his brother had been working for before he disappeared, in return for a Bitcoin payment. His thumbs hovered over the screen for a moment before he began typing.

A loud knock on the car window made him jump, dropping his phone. 'Fuck!'

Hammer was looming outside the vehicle in the twilight, looking terrifying and furious. So, pretty much the same as he always did. Luke wound down the window. 'You want something?'

'Going somewhere?'

'Maybe,' Luke said.

'Mind if I tag along?'

'Why?'

'I just have a feeling you're about to do something stupid.'

Just because Luke had made the same assessment, didn't mean he liked Hammer pointing it out. 'If I am, it's none of your business.'

'Tobias told me about your brother. He made contact.' Hammer wrenched open the door. 'Get out. Or I'm getting in.'

Luke weighed up the possibility that Hammer would be able to haul him bodily from the car and made a gesture that was halfway between 'be my guest' and 'fuck you'.

Hammer didn't crack a smile or move around to the passenger side, probably because he assumed that Luke would take advantage of the delay to drive away. Instead, he opened the door behind Luke's seat and folded his gigantic frame into the backseat.

'So, where are we going?'

Luke gave up. 'Nowhere.'

'Excellent choice, pal.'

. . .

WINTER WAS a time of rest and recuperation. All living things lying quiet under the frozen earth and waiting for the turning of the year and the return of the light. Bee, more than her sisters, felt these cyclical changes deep in her bones.

Sitting in the plant-filled front room of her island home, she closed her eyes and immediately felt the gentle sway of travel. Her summer was spent moving from town to town with the fair, some large and sprawling, some tiny, not much larger than a village. It was both strange and wonderful to wake up each morning in the same place she had gone to sleep, but she knew that if she lived on the island all year round, as Lucy and Diana did, that she would go slowly mad.

'Are you still up, sister mine?'

Bee opened her eyes to find Diana with her watering can and an absent expression. 'I can hear a thirsty plant and I knew I wouldn't sleep until I found it.'

'Just reading,' Bee said. She did have a book open on her lap and she turned her attention back to it. A sudden certainty flowed through her. She would finish the last chapter tonight and visit the bookshop in the morning to swap it for something new.

THE NEXT MORNING, Luke awoke to snow on the skylight of his bedroom. He got dressed in warm clothes and headed downstairs to make tea before opening the shop. As he walked through the rooms, he felt as if the bookshelves were leaning in a little, greeting him. The lights had gone on, too, bathing the shop in a welcoming glow.

He made a large mug of tea and took it to his reading chair. Alvis's book was waiting for him, back on top of his reading pile. 'Fine,' he said out loud. 'You win.'

Flicking through Alvis's book, Luke quickly realised why the shop had been so keen for him to read it. There were several things that he ought to have been doing, some to do with keeping drains running freely and home maintenance, and some to do with running the shop. And, most importantly, there was a stockroom. Well, he assumed Alvis meant stockroom. What she had actually written interchanged between 'repository', 'repository/public', and 'vault'.

'Where is the vault?' Luke asked out loud.

He looked around the empty shop and waited for a new doorway to appear. Then, feeling faintly foolish, he walked through the corridors and small rooms, asking 'hotter?' and 'colder?' like he was playing a game. The shop lights stayed unhelpfully steady, and the atmosphere was one of a breath being held. The shop was holding out on him.

He stopped moving and looked around at the bookshelves in an accusatory manner. 'I thought you wanted me to look?' The shop didn't answer.

Frustrated, and feeling slightly foolish, he headed back to the front room. Sitting in his reading chair, he flipped the red book shut and picked up his John le Carré.

He tried to lose himself with Alec Leamas, but his skin was prickling and his ears seemed to hum with the silence in the shop. Luke had felt atmospheres in buildings before, the sense that it was a place or calm or sadness or joy, but he had never known the feeling that the building was actively thinking. It shouldn't be possible to pick up on an atmosphere of petulance from a structure of bricks and wood and plaster, but that was exactly what was happening.

He wasn't going to give into the shop. He read the same paragraph for the third time, determined to ignore the silent battle and the rapidly cooling air. He had the feeling the shop wanted him to apologise, but he was damned if he would. For starters, he had no idea what he had done wrong so it would be insincere. He sighed and started the paragraph for the fourth time, hunching his shoulders against the chill.

Luke was a stubborn man and would probably have stayed locked in that cycle for a good while longer, but the bell on the front door jangled and gave him an excuse to put his paperback down and stand behind the till.

'Gies a hand, pal?'

The Scottish voice belonged to a small wiry delivery guy wearing a grey polo shirt with a stitched logo. He had a metal trolley stacked with boxes and was trying to manoeuvre it in the narrow entrance.

'I didn't order anything,' Luke said, confused.

The man shrugged. He had a clipboard resting on top of the uppermost box and he handed it to Luke.

The docket was from the delivery company and the bookshop was listed with the correct address. There wasn't a name under 'contact' and Luke wondered if that was because whoever had sent the boxes knew that Alvis had passed away or whether it was because this whole thing was a mistake.

Once he had signed and the delivery guy had wheeled his trolley grumpily back up the wynd, Luke carried the heavy box into the front room and hefted it onto the counter. He used his penknife to carefully slit the packing tape.

He wasn't entirely surprised that it was filled with books. They were, however, not books he had ever seen in real life before. Wrapped in layers of acid-free tissue paper, these books were old. The kind you saw behind glass in museums.

Luke was so intrigued that it took him a couple of minutes to realise that the atmosphere in the shop had changed, too. He felt as if the shelves were curving inward, as if the shop wanted to get a better look. 'This is beautiful,' he said out loud as he unwrapped a thick leather volume with detailed tooling on the cover and brass fixtures. The air in the shop warmed in response.

Soon, the counter was filled from the edge to the cash register with a stack of leather-bound books of varying sizes. The last book in the box was smaller and lighter than the others. He plucked the tissue-wrapped parcel and placed it on top of the sturdiest books on the counter to unwrap. The book inside was clearly modern, at least compared to the others. It had a thin, flexible leather or faux-leather cover and it was the size of a trade paperback. It looked a little like a high-end journal and he half-expected it to have blank pages inside.

He didn't get to find out, though, as the moment he flipped it open he felt a wave of fiery heat burning his fingers and racing pain ran through his entire body. It was pain so intense that his thoughts shorted out. All was pain, and he didn't know if he was going to be sick or pass out. Then his vision went black.

CHAPTER SEVEN

Bee liked the quiet of the winter. After a summer of travelling the mainland with the fair, she needed the seclusion of the island to recuperate. Not her powers, but her ability to deal with people. She liked humanity, for the most part, and valued her connections to them, but that didn't stop them from being irritating when taken in large doses.

The air was remarkably still and when Bee stepped outside her cottage, she found the land coated in white. Snow visited most winters, but this was the first proper dusting of the season and Bee returned indoors to add steel tracks to the soles of her thick walking boots. It was a thin-looking blanket and she suspected there would be patches of ice lurking beneath.

She took the path down to Shell Bay, enjoying the changed view. The frost clinging to the spiky grasses, and the lines of snow piled on fence posts and walls, blanketing the ground in clean white. It varied in thickness underfoot and she listened to the different sounds her steps made, and enjoyed the variegations of white and speckled white and grey, eventually giving way to sand and crushed shells, silvered by the low sun, in a wide band that met the sea.

She walked along the beach in the direction of the church ward, the old gravestones and ruined walls looking like something from a painting in their snowy clothing. She paused a moment, taking in lungfuls of iron-cold air and thanking the island for the lack of wind. It felt as if the whole place was honouring her need for peace, and every quiet breath was restorative.

A few minutes later, a figure broke her solitude. It was Tobias, bent double, and he straightened as she approached. He had a mallet in one hand and was wearing thick gloves. As usual, he was dressed in corduroy trousers and a tweed jacket with a knitted Fair Isle pullover underneath. He raised a hand in greeting. 'Beautiful day.'

'Yes,' Bee agreed. 'What on earth are you doing?'

Now that she was closer, she could see that there were a couple of fresh posts in the ground, another lying waiting on the frozen ground. Winter was sitting to attention, watching her approach. He was a friendly dog, but kept his distance from Bee. She wasn't offended. Animals showed remarkably good sense when it came to potential danger and she didn't begrudge the animal his instincts.

'This part of the wall needs supporting. I meant to do it in the summer, but I never quite... well. I'm here now.'

'Isn't the ground too cold for hammering into?'

'It would have been better in the warm.' Tobias looked at the half-completed job. 'But I just have more zest in the winter. And it's not too bad. The cold hasn't really set in, yet. This is just a dusting.'

'If you say so,' Bee said. Now that she wasn't moving, she could feel the chill of the day. The cool air was tinged with damp, and it was seeking every gap in her clothing.

Bee rubbed her hands together theatrically. 'I'm going

to keep moving. We can't all thrive in the snow. Not like you.'

Walking away, Tobias once again swinging his mallet and the dull thwacking sound echoing behind her, Bee tried not to think about how Tobias was going to cope when Winter got too old to accompany his master on tasks around the island. She knew that Tobias must have had many partings in his long life, but she also knew that wouldn't make them any easier. She could look in her glass when she got home, see what the future held for Winter, but there was no point. His end would be that of all animals. A return to the earth.

At the end of the beach, where the coast became too rocky to walk, she crossed the scrubby ground, coated in thrift and sea campion, and cut up Widdershins Wynd, heading for the bookshop.

Bee was stepping carefully, as the cobbled street hadn't yet enjoyed much sun and was a patchwork of ice, and had just reached the bookshop door when it flew open, almost knocking her over. She stopped, expecting Luke to come rushing out. She was going to fix him with one of her best stares and was pleasantly anticipating the fear she would see flaring in his eyes. No more than he deserved for startling her.

There was nobody in sight. And no sudden wind to have burst open the door. Bee was already walking into the shop, her body knowing before her mind that something was wrong, when the lights inside the shop started flicking on and off. She ran.

ESME WAS the second person that Bee called and she made it across the village to the bookshop in record time, her feet skidding more than once on the compacted snow and ice, as she hurried along the main street and down the wynd.

The bell above the door jangled and the woody smell and warm air of the bookshop welcomed her, but Esme didn't notice. She was running up the steep stairs and into Luke's studio where a new odour, sharp and wrong, was waiting.

Tobias and Bee were next to the bed and Luke was lying on top of the mattress, fully clothed. The duvet had been neatly folded at the bottom. Luke's foot jerked, kicking at it. He was very white. His lips bloodless. Esme was taking in impressions in staccato images. Her mind seemed to be protecting her from taking too much at once. Or it was malfunctioning. She could have sworn that she could smell burning, the acrid tang of smoke.

'He is very lucky,' Tobias said gravely. 'If Bee hadn't found him when she did...'

Esme stared down at Luke's prone form and swallowed hard. She was not going to cry. She was not going to disintegrate or freeze up. She was going to *work*. She could fix this. Fix him.

Luke was mumbling in his semi-conscious state and his limbs twitched. His skin was waxy pale, but when Esme placed a hand on his forehead, it was scorching hot. She leaned close and tried to make out his words. They were indistinct and, most likely, feverish gibberish. 'You found him?' She didn't glance away from Luke as she asked the question.

Bee's voice seemed to be coming from far away. 'He was on the floor downstairs.'

Esme wondered how they had got him upstairs, but instantly dismissed the question for another time. More importantly, she had to assess his vitals. She took out her phone and laid it on the bedside table so that she could see the clock, then wrapped her finger and thumb around his wrist and began to take his pulse. It was too fast. Racing as if trying to outrun a foe. His legs spasmed again and he moaned. She didn't need a thermometer to know that he was running a fever. But she ought to monitor it. Her thoughts were clicking into place. 'I need a thermometer. Small towels. Tea towels, anything. And ice. A glass of water and a spoon. Plastic, if possible. Liquid paracetamol. The stuff for kids is fine.'

Bee came back remarkably quickly with the supplies and the three of them got to work. Esme clicked into nurse mode, seeing Luke's body as a patient to be cared for, not a male threat. She and Bee wrestled his jumper over his head, and Tobias removed his jeans before replacing the folded duvet with a thin sheet. Luke's body convulsed with violent shivers, but his skin was still hot to touch and his temperature far too high.

Bee and Tobias soaked towels in ice water and wrung them out before laying them over Luke's body. His mumbling became low moaning and he whipped his head from side to side in clear discomfort. Esme lay a cold wet flannel on his forehead and another on the back of his neck. Within seconds, they were warm, so she dunked them into the waiting basin of ice and water to cool them down and replaced them. 'We need a stream of cool air.'

'What about a fan? I can see if Seren has some at the pub.'

Esme wasn't surprised they weren't common to every-one's homes. Unholy Island wasn't exactly prone to heat-waves. 'We can open the window.' The skylight was large and could be tilted and locked into position. The freezing air swirled through the room, but Esme barely noticed her own discomfort. She was running calculations in her head. She had to bring down his core temperature, but it wouldn't do to have the room too cold for too long. He needed to stabilise.

'Why isn't he sweating?' Bee asked.

Esme had started training as a nurse and she acted as the island's unofficial medic for minor injuries and illnesses. 'It's a really high fever. When it's this bad, the body doesn't function the way it should. We need to bring down his core temperature. Or we should phone for an ambulance.' She bit her lip, thinking fast. The snow overnight was still lying on the ground and she didn't know how quickly it would arrive. 'No. We'll try this first. Give it ten minutes.'

'St Anthony's Fire,' Tobias said abruptly. 'Comes from contaminated grain, I think. Or grain that had gone mouldy.'

'I don't think so,' Bee said gently, laying a hand on Tobias's arm.

'Or maybe we should call right away. They'll take time to get here and by then...'

'They might not know how to help,' Bee said.

This wasn't normal. That's what she meant. And Esme agreed.

'I'll get the fan,' Bee said. 'And some more towels.'

Esme didn't know how long Bee was gone or when Tobias had quietly placed two glasses of water, one with a bendy straw, on the chest of drawers near to Luke's bed. She just kept methodically soaking and replacing the flannels and repeating a silent plea to whatever deities might be listening. *Please let him cool down. Please let him be all right.*

Esme knew she had said 'ten minutes', but she took Luke's temperature before she checked the time. If it hadn't gone down, she was going to dial 999 regardless. Visions of what could happen to a body that stayed too hot for too long were flashing through her mind in a flickering reel. If his temperature hadn't come down, it might already be too late to avoid brain damage and organ failure.

Sticking the ear thermometer in place and hearing the beep made her grateful that she wasn't relying on an old mercury thermometer. Apart from anything else, Luke's teeth were clenched and the knots of his muscles standing out on his neck. She didn't know how she would have got a glass stick into his mouth without it breaking.

Her breath rushed out in a relieved sigh when she read the digital readout. Thirty-nine. Still too high, but lower than before. The cooling protocol was working. She dunked the flannels and wrung them out, smoothing the cold damp material back into place. Was it her imagination, or was he mumbling slower? She thought his breathing was getting deeper, as if he was slipping into a proper sleep rather than a feverish limbo state.

Bee arrived with a white stand fan. She set it up so that the cool air was blowing directly onto Luke's body. He moaned in his sleep and shivered, hands grasping as if to pull a duvet over himself. Esme caught his hands and held them gently, making sure he didn't dislodge his latest flannels and towels. The air would cool the damp fabric and keep him even cooler. It wasn't pleasant for the patient, who felt freezing already, but it was essential.

'His temperature has come down a bit,' Esme said. 'It's working.'

Bee nodded and took another seat. They worked

together for the next couple of hours, laying cold flannels onto Luke's forehead, cradling his head to feed him sips of water, spooning children's paracetamol between his lips. 'I thought he would be with it enough to swallow tablets by this point. His temperature is down. He ought to be awake.' Esme wasn't going to voice her worst thought: that they hadn't brought his temperature down in time and that brain damage had occurred. It wasn't likely, she knew that, but it was possible. And that was bad enough.

Bee was watching Luke, a furrow between her eyes. 'I don't like it.'

Esme had been hoping for reassurance, for Bee to say 'he's just exhausted from the fever and needs a long nap'. Instead, her insides turned liquid with fear and her skin prickled. 'What do you mean?'

'He's not just asleep, is he? It feels...' Bee stopped. Shook her head. She picked up Luke's hand and he jerked as if her touch burned, then subsided to unnatural stillness. A wax figure. She muttered something under her breath.

'What?' Esme demanded, properly panicking now. She had never seen Bee rattled before and she didn't like it.

'I need to talk to my sisters.'

BEE PUSHED the vision from her senses as she hurried down the stairs and out of the bookshop. Seeing the future was all well and good but it could give one a sense of hopelessness. Bee knew, though, that fate was malleable. Just because there was a most likely course of events, just because the universe was arranged a certain way, didn't mean that you were powerless to change that outcome. Fate wasn't a set pattern that would happen regardless, just that the mass of probability was sitting on one end of the scales and you needed a gigantic bloody load on the other end if you had any hopes of shifting the balance.

Luckily, Bee knew two such weights.

At the house, Diana was in the back room with her plants. She was snipping stray tendrils from an overgrown Senecio Herianus with gentle concentration. The room felt calm and normal, a strange contrast to the tension of Luke's home above the bookshop. 'I need your help.'

Diana put down her secateurs and rose to her feet in a fluid movement and stretched her spine, both hands on the small of her back. Bee knew that if Diana hadn't been her sister, the sight would have turned her into a molten puddle of lust. The sexuality and fecundity that exuded from Diana was so potent that men and women lost their wits. It was one of the many reasons that Bee was the sister that went into the human world and earned the family money. It wasn't so much the cash, of course, Diana could command any amount of riches with a single crook of her smallest finger, but the sisters had vowed a very long ago to step lightly and to keep their influence to a minimum.

This was an exception, however. For the greater good.

Diana was looking at her questioningly, but she followed and let Bee explain on the way. The Three Sisters did not always see eye to eye, but they trusted each other implicitly and Diana knew that Bee would not be asking her to leave her home and her plants if it wasn't for an extremely good reason.

The witch was keeping vigil over the Book Keeper. He was worse. Bee could see a grey haze hanging above his prone form. Diana shuddered as soon as she entered the cold room. The window was open and the fan was blowing, but as soon as Bee stepped closer, she could feel the heat rolling from the body in the bed.

Her sister was standing at the top of the stairs, a

regretful expression painted across her beautiful face. She shook her head slowly. When she spoke, her voice made Esme jerk and look around.

'I am sorry,' Diana said.

'Can't you try?' Bee asked, knowing the words were pointless. If Diana could help, she would do so. She closed her eyes, knowing what her sister was going to say. Knowing that this outcome was always what was going to happen. The moment she had seen Luke Taylor's future she had known it. Fate or not, Bee knew that some things were inevitable. And when a human had been cursed this badly, there was only one of them strong enough to deal with it.

Diana looked sympathetically at Bee. 'You need to get Lucy.'

CHAPTER EIGHT

E sme watched in terror as the youngest of The Three
Sisters leaned over Luke. Lucy had drifted into the
room, bringing a strange atmosphere. The cold room felt
suddenly charged with electricity and Esme had pressed
herself instinctively against the wall to let her walk past.
Now, Esme moved closer to Bee, who was watching her
sibling with focused intensity. Lucy climbed onto the bed
and sat astride Luke's prone body, her knees on either side
of his waist. The flowing fabric of her long white nightgown blended with the colour of her skin, in stark contrast
with her long black hair and red lips. It took everything in
Esme's power not to throw herself between them, as if he
were somehow in danger. Not that Esme would prove
much of a barrier. If any of the Sisters wanted to harm
Luke, he was as good as dead.

Still. Knowing wasn't the same as feeling and her body
wasn't listening to reason. Her palms itched and her
muscles twitched with the urge to move closer, to pull at
Lucy until she was further from Luke's still and vulnerable
body. She knew Bee was trying to help, but it was much

harder to believe that the unearthly-looking figure straddling Luke felt the same.

'Diana couldn't help,' Bee said quietly. She was almost whispering, leaning in close to Esme as if she didn't want to disturb her sibling. 'I tried, too. I'm sorry. This is the only way.'

Lucy put a hand onto Luke's bare chest, her fingers splayed and curving inward slightly, nails digging into his skin. Her lips were curved in a joyful smile as she gazed at his anguished face. She dug deeper. His expression twisted in agony, and he let out a low moan of pain.

Esme felt Bee's hand on her arm, her grip tight, and realised that she had been moving toward the bed. 'He's in pain,' she whispered urgently.

Lucy's head whipped around and the full force of her gaze rocked Esme back on her heels. She stumbled and would have fallen if Bee hadn't still been holding onto her arm.

After a long moment, Lucy turned her attention back to Luke. Esme felt the sweet relief of personal danger passing, but it was quickly swallowed by her fears for him.

The young woman, who was most definitely not a young woman, moved her hand away to tuck a strand of her long black hair away from her face. The movement revealed five small wounds on his chest. Blood was seeping from the deepest of these as she reached back down and calmly fitted her fingernails to the wounds, digging them back in. He moaned in pain and Esme bit the inside of her cheek to stop herself from objecting.

Lucy's nightgown was rucked up, revealing pale knees on either side of his waist. She leaned forward and bent her head to lick his neck. It was part sexual and part pure animal. Tasting food or marking a mate. Or playing. Lucy glanced across at Esme and smiled. Her teeth were very white and, suddenly, sharp. Her eyes sparkled with a hedonistic joy that Esme couldn't imagine ever feeling.

For a long moment Lucy stared at Esme, her attention shifted from the body in the bed. Esme felt the danger of the moment. If Lucy decided she wanted to play with Esme instead, she would be distracted from Luke. And, strange as that felt, that would seal his fate rather than save him.

She felt Bee utterly still beside her, and the atmosphere in the room swell and thicken. She couldn't look away from Lucy's face and could feel a pull to move closer. Esme didn't move. She didn't breathe. She couldn't trust herself to do anything in case she tipped the delicate moment into disaster.

After what seemed like an age, Lucy's head turned back to Luke. Her tongue darted out as her head dipped and she licked his cheek.

Bee was tugging on her hand, trying to move Esme to the stairs. She planted her feet and continued to watch Lucy. She knew that Bee knew Lucy better than she did and that if she thought Esme ought to go downstairs, it was for the best, but she still couldn't leave Luke. She wouldn't.

After what could have been hours or just a few minutes, Lucy reared up from her crouched position and threw her head back in what could have been the throes of ecstasy. Esme's skin was prickling with sudden heat. She was watching something intimate. Bee's steady presence next to her was the only comfort. Bee wouldn't let anything bad happen. Anything worse, at any rate.

Lucy squeezed Luke's sides with her thighs, she gyrated a little and her spine curved. Her hands were splayed on his chest with her fingers curved into claws that fitted into the cuts she had already made. The blood was flowing freely across Luke's skin, but he wasn't moaning or shifting any longer. He was lying unnaturally still.

As if suddenly bored, Lucy stood up on the mattress, balancing on the narrow spaces left by Luke's body. Then she jumped down lightly. Esme moved swiftly out of the way of the exit and averted her gaze as Lucy skipped past.

Bee followed her sister down the stairs and Esme ran to Luke's side. His chest wasn't bleeding as freely, but it still looked a mess. Esme begin cleaning the cuts. Tobias had brought Seren's first aid kit from the pub and Esme used antiseptic cream before applying a loose dressing across the whole area. Her hands were steady as she worked. He was a patient in need, not a male body. If a tiny part of her mind noticed that he had a very pleasant chest, one that she could imagine running her hands over with enjoyment, she didn't listen to it.

His eyes snapped open. The whites were shot with red, but he was really looking at her.

'It's okay,' she said. 'You're safe. You've been unwell, but you're on the mend.' The sentences were automatic, delivered with the professional nursing tone. Soothing. Positive. Every syllable conferring calm safety.

'Don't touch the book,' Luke said, his voice quiet and cracking. His lips were so dry they had started to flake and bleed.

The words made little sense and Esme feared the fever had returned. She placed a hand onto his forehead.

'It was the thin book. It arrived... Don't know...'

'It's all right,' Esme said. 'You're safe. Everything is all right.'

'Don't touch it.' His hand shot out and gripped Esme's wrist and his shoulders reared up from the pillow, neck muscles straining. 'Please. I know it sounds...'

'I won't. I promise.'

'Nobody.'

'I won't let anybody touch the book.' Esme was trying to arrange a pillow behind his shoulders, trying to make him comfortable. 'It's downstairs, right? I'll take care of it. You need to drink some water and…'

But he was already sinking back, as if exhausted by the speech. His eyes fluttered closed.

Esme looked at his pale face, flushes of red slashed across his cheekbones like fresh wounds. 'Get some rest,' she finished.

An hour later, Tobias arrived. 'I'll take a shift watching him. You get some rest.'

Esme stretched. She had been in the same hard chair for what felt like days, and her body was protesting. The adrenaline was fading, too, leaving a bone-deep weariness. 'I think he's out of the woods,' she said. 'He woke up for a minute, seemed lucid, but it seemed to exhaust him and he's been asleep since.'

'The body knows how to heal,' Tobias said.

She nodded her agreement. 'It seems like a more natural sleep.' She had been going to add 'since Lucy' but she found she couldn't form her mouth around the Sister's name. Too scary. It felt like it might conjure her back into the room.

The fan was off now, and the window almost shut. Esme had left it open a crack for a trickle of fresh air. The room wasn't warm and she was worried about Tobias. He always sat by his fire at home. Voicing her concerns, he waved her off. 'I'll manage.' He indicated his suit. 'Tweed is very good at retaining heat. Now, go and get some sleep. And some food. When did you last eat?'

Esme's stomach growled in response. She tried to

remember. Had it been yesterday lunchtime? She had sipped at water in the meantime and Bee had brought her a cup of tea.

'I'll be half an hour,' Esme said.

'You will not,' Tobias replied. 'Take more time.'

Rather than argue with the mayor, Esme expressed her thanks and took the stairs to the shop. Before heading to the pub to ask Seren for a takeaway meal, she went to the front room where the counter and cash register lived. Sure enough, there was a packing box open on the floor behind the counter. A pile of books sat on top of the counter and, lying in a nest of tissue paper on the top of the pile, was a slim leather journal. Esme felt an instant revulsion. She didn't know if that was because of what Luke had whispered or because she was, finally, getting some witchy intuition, but either way she wasn't going to touch the book.

She picked up the empty cardboard packing box from the floor and looked for a return address. She studied the delivery label, but it appeared standard. And then she upended the box onto the counter, covering the slim book completely so that nobody walking through would touch it by accident.

ESME DIDN'T THINK she would be able to sleep. She felt too keyed up from looking after Luke and angry that somebody had tried to hurt him. Someone had done this deliberately. She could feel malice in her bones and she didn't care that she had no evidence for it.

Whoever had sent that book had intended to cause harm. Maybe not to Luke personally, but given they had hurt him, Esme didn't much care whether they had meant it or not.

The previous Ward Witch, Madame Le Grys, hadn't

left much in the way of guidance at Strand House. There had been a ledger of past visitors to the bed-and-breakfast and neatly kept accounts, but not much information about the wards or the island or what being a Ward Witch actually entailed. Esme had figured that Bee would let her in on information over time, but now it was seven years of time and Luke was in a dangerously weakened state and Esme could feel rage overtaking her nerves.

Her painting studio was upstairs in the converted attic of the building. The light was good up there and it felt utterly private. Two things that mitigated the fact that it was chilly in the winter and roasting in the summer when the sun poured through the skylights.

She shifted some prepped canvases away from the wall to reveal the small door that led to the eaves storage. It wasn't something she had investigated before, having arrived at the island with very little in the way of personal possessions. The items she had acquired since then had all had homes in the house proper and she hadn't needed to think about extra storage space. She hadn't, she realised now, expected to still be here after seven years. Hadn't considered long-term storage in a house that she still couldn't really believe was her home.

Holding her breath, she opened the small wooden door. The air smelled of wood and whatever was being used to insulate the roof. The small attic space was entirely empty.

Backing out and shutting the door, Esme bumped into something furry and annoyed. Jet made an outraged yelp. 'Sorry, sorry,' she said hurriedly. 'I didn't know you were up here.'

Jet eyed her with disdain which, honestly, wasn't anything new.

'Why didn't Madame leave me useful books? Clues. Information.'

Jet stretched his front legs, his back curving impressively.

'I know you're better at yoga than me,' Esme said, 'there's no need to show off.'

Jet stalked from the room, tail high.

If Madame Le Grys hadn't written things down, what might she have done?

ESME OPENED the door to the bookshop. Tobias met her halfway on the stairs to Luke's rooms. 'He's asleep,' he said quietly. 'You're supposed to be resting.'

'I can't,' Esme said. 'You may as well get some sleep. I'll watch him.'

Tobias hesitated as if planning to argue, but something in her expression must have changed his mind. 'Right-oh,' he said mildly. 'Telephone me if you change your mind and I'll come back. I'm a light-sleeper.'

Esme marvelled at how healthy he looked. She had expected a night of no sleep to weigh a little heavier on his appearance, given that Tobias was older. Perhaps it was that thing of the elderly needing less sleep.

Having checked on Luke, Esme crept back downstairs and began searching the shop.

In the back room, she checked the 'esoteric' section. It seemed lighter in the corner and she found herself drifting over to that section of shelving. At eye level an ultramarine book spine caught her eye, the text stamped on the side too faded to read. She pulled it out and found herself holding a book titled 'Hexes, Curses, and All Manner of Malfeasance.'

Taking it with her upstairs, Esme settled herself in the

chair Tobias had vacated. Luke's breathing was steady and even, and she thought his colour was a little better than before. There was enough light coming from the window for Esme to read and she settled in to study the book.

An hour later, she stretched, hearing the bones in her neck and shoulders crack. She felt as if she had just had a crash course in the kinds of things that could, apparently, be done with objects. For example, with a moon-bathed crystal, a mouse bone and some poppy seeds, she could enchant a small piece of cloth to 'induce bad luck of a sort most unusual for no more than one month'. The recipe ended with the suggestion of sewing the cloth scrap into your chosen enemy's trousers while they were bathing in the river or sea.

Esme had been, briefly, a woman of science. She had poured over nursing textbooks of anatomy and chemical reactions and the physics of radiotherapy. Then she had shelved all thoughts of learning for a few years of survival. Now, she realised as she turned the pages of the book, she could feel that dormant part of her reawakening. She had been training with Bee, trying to open her mind and calm her swirling anxiety long enough to receive some kind of divine knowledge. Her intuition blossoming until she felt worthy of her title and role on the island. Now, with the information laid out in black and white (well, yellowish cream and dark grey), she saw another path open up. Study.

'Thank you,' she whispered, addressing the bookshop.

CHAPTER NINE

The light behind Luke's eyelids was painfully bright. A memory ghosted through his mind. A blazing heat scorching him from within. So hot that after a while he couldn't tell if he was freezing or burning. It was all pain. He shuddered and opened his eyes a crack.

The light stung and he blinked, wincing. Gradually, his vision cleared and he saw that he was in bed in his room above the shop. The curtains were drawn and he could see that it actually wasn't bright at all. Esme was asleep in a chair by his bed, her head lolling at an uncomfortable-looking angle.

At the same moment that he realised he was wearing boxer shorts and had nothing else, Esme stirred. He hastily grabbed the cotton sheet that was pushed to the bottom of the bed and pulled it up and over his body. The bed felt unpleasantly damp, and he was fast becoming aware that he reeked. Sweat. And he hated to think what his breath was like because his mouth felt drier than the Sahara.

Esme smiled at him. 'You're awake.'

Luke tried to reply, but his voice stuck in his throat. He was embarrassed by the weird croaking sound, but Esme didn't seem to notice. She was bustling in a professional manner. Moving his pillows and helping him to sit up. Then, blessed be to all the saints, she passed him a pint glass of blackcurrant squash with a pink bendy straw. He drained half of it before registering that it tasted weird.

'Salt,' Esme said. 'You need to replace some.'

As the liquid soothed his throat, he felt his head clearing. He felt he must have been very ill. A high temperature would have made him feel like he was burning. He grimaced at the memory of that terrible sensation. He had been boiling alive. Flesh liquefying and bubbling.

Pushing it back down, he tried to focus. 'How long?'

'Couple of days. Bee found you. Take the rest of that slowly or it will come back up.'

Luke felt hollowed out, couldn't imagine there was anything to vomit. But he didn't want to tempt it, so he lowered the glass. 'I hope I'm not contagious.' The thought was sudden. If he had the flu this badly, he didn't want Esme to get it.

A strange expression crossed her face before it was replaced with her professional calm. 'What do you remember?'

The question was a strange one. But as he rested his head on the pillows and thought, he realised that he didn't remember feeling ill. He had been downstairs. The front room of the shop. He had been reading Alvis's book. No, he had been trying to read something else. It came back to him. He had been arguing with the shop. Ignoring how weird that thought was, it had been a normal day.

He saw a stack of leather-bound books on the counter. Covers burnished and glowing in the late afternoon sunlight coming through the front window. 'There was a delivery. Really old books. And...' He could see another book. Feel the slim shape in his hands as he unwrapped the tissue paper. Panic rushed through his body, leaving an acrid taste on his tongue. He wanted to reach back in time and tell himself not to open that book.

'What?' Esme was perched on the side of the bed, her features creased in a frown.

'Don't touch the thin book.'

Her frown deepened, and she reached to put a hand on his forehead. 'You said that before.'

Luke realised that she thought he was incoherent. 'I'm not feverish. There was a book at the bottom of the box. Smaller than the others. I opened it and that's the last thing I remember.' Well, that wasn't strictly true. He remembered burning pain in every part of his body. But he wasn't going to say that to Esme. She already looked spooked enough. 'Where is it?' Sitting forward in his agitation set his head spinning and he slumped back.

'I've taken care of it,' Esme said. 'It's in a safe place.'

Her voice still had a professional tinge, and he was worried she didn't believe him. He struggled to sit straighter, to appear more lucid. She had to believe him. Had to understand. 'It's dangerous. It was the book. The thin one.'

'I won't touch it,' Esme said soothingly. 'I promise.'

He relaxed a little. 'I know it doesn't make any sense, but I really think it did this... That doesn't make sense. Does it?' He was distracted by a sharp pain in his chest. The fabric of the sheet had moved across something sore and he moved the fabric to look. A pattern of semi-circular cuts were splayed on the left side of his chest, around his heart. Five crescent moons, as if someone had dug long fingernails into his flesh.

. . .

Tobias, Bee and Esme stood by the counter of the bookshop, speaking in hushed tones.

'We should be wary of them all,' Tobias said.

'Luke wasn't affected until he touched that one,' Esme pointed at the top-most book in the pile.

They all contemplated the innocuous-looking volume. It had a pale brown leather cover that looked thin and pliable, and the pages were slightly ragged on the edges. There was probably a term for it, and Alvis would have known it.

'It looks more like a journal,' Bee said. 'I wonder if it's handwritten inside.'

'Don't touch it,' Esme said, earning herself a withering look from Bee.

'I'll try to restrain myself,' she said drily.

'He said it was wrapped in tissue paper. Maybe if we protect our skin, we will be able to move it safely. It feels wrong to leave it just sitting there.'

'I would be willing to risk it,' Tobias said, peering at the book.

'Don't you dare. That young man could have died,' Bee said severely. 'I could get my sisters.'

'We don't want to impose,' Esme said. 'Not again. Not so soon after...'

Bee could understand the witch's reluctance. It showed a healthy sense of self-preservation that she was glad to see. The woman was growing more solid. Stronger.

'More pertinent,' Tobias said. 'Is who sent this? And why?'

There was a delivery note and they all contemplated it.

'They might not have known about the killer book,' Bee said after a moment. 'If they handled it wrapped.'

'Is this normal? A delivery of books like this?'

'Not abnormal,' Tobias said. 'The bookshop keeps the lore for these islands.'

'Britain,' Bee clarified. 'The United Kingdom. Whatever it is being called at the moment. The collection of islands settled between the Atlantic Ocean and the English Channel.'

'Why didn't I know this?'

Bee looked surprised. 'Didn't Alvis tell you?'

Esme shook her head, looking dejected. 'She can't have trusted me.'

'That's not necessarily true,' Tobias said. 'She might have assumed one of us had mentioned it. Or that you knew through other means. You are our Ward Witch, after all.'

'So, we can look through her address book, see who she usually received items from. See if this place is new or whether she has had dealings with them before...' Esme trailed off at the serious expressions on the other two faces. 'What?'

'That's for the Book Keeper. We can't go rummaging through the files.'

'But he's recovering.'

Tobias shook his head gently. 'Then we must wait.'

THE CURSED BOOK was wrapped in tissue and inside a fire-safe metal box. Esme looked at the box with distrust as if it might burst into flames at any moment. Hammer had delivered the box at her request and had been unhappily tight-lipped. 'Shouldn't be your problem,' he said. And, not for the first time, offered to go out in a boat and drop the thing out at sea.

'Question is,' Esme said, ignoring Hammer's expression. 'Was this sent to kill Luke or did they not know about the danger it posed?'

Hammer grunted.

'Maybe they didn't know about it? They might have had a lucky escape. We've got to consider the possibility that it was entirely accidental. Or, they knew it was cursed, but Alvis often got things like this and knew how to handle them, so they sent it to her for safekeeping... No. That doesn't make sense. If they had known, it would have been labelled as dangerous.'

Hammer grunted again.

'But why would they want to hurt Luke? They don't know him.' She shot a warning glance at Hammer. 'Don't grunt. I'm asking for your opinion.'

Hammer scowled. 'Maybe they do know him.'

'Are you trying to be funny, because he was really hurt. It was serious. We don't even know if there will be after effects. He ought to go to hospital to get properly checked out...'

'I'm not being flippant,' Hammer broke in. 'What if whoever sent the book knew Luke would open it? And knows Luke from his previous life.' He held up his hands. 'How much do we know about Luke Taylor? I mean, really?'

'We've all got pasts,' Esme said defensively.

'I know,' Hammer said, gently enough. 'I'm just saying.'

CHAPTER TEN

The following day, Luke woke up feeling fully lucid. In place of scattered fragments, and loops of thought that refused to close, he could follow a clear narrative. He remembered the delivery guy turning up and unpacking the box of books. He remembered unwrapping the tissue from that last package. He could see the pale brown of the book's cover and feel the strangely soft and silky texture of the thin leather. He had flipped it open, the binding opening easily so that the pages splayed flat. He had been expecting blank pages and there had been a moment of surprise at the archaic typeface. And then pain.

Luke realised he needed to read more in Alvis's book. He tried not to think that if he had gotten further with her scrabbly handwriting, he might have avoided... whatever had happened to him. A book that knocked him flat for three days.

He got out of bed, his legs still a little wobbly, and opened the top drawer of the dresser to locate clean underwear, jogging bottoms and a fresh t-shirt. Wrinkling his nose as he pulled it over his head, he added 'shower' to his urgent to-do list. He was happy to be vertical and functioning, though, after so long lying down. A horrifying thought crossed his mind. He must have got out of bed to use the bathroom at some point, but he didn't remember it. He hoped he had managed it alone. The thought of Esme helping him with that side of things made him flush red with embarrassment.

Pushing that horror show to the very back of his mind, Luke concentrated on getting down the steep spiral stairs to the bookshop. That accomplished, he made it to the front room, wincing at the bright sunlight coming through the window. The leather books were packed back into the cardboard box and there was no sign of the slim volume.

Alvis's red book was sitting on his reading pile next to the armchair, though, so he fetched a glass of water and settled himself comfortably.

Flipping past the cryptic references to the 'vault', Luke found a neat list of addresses. Some had been crossed out or amended, some had asterisks next to them, others little crescent moon symbols. He paged forward and found notes for the symbols. An asterisk meant 'friendly' according to Alvis, a moon meant 'vault' and a darkly scribbled dot of ink meant 'do not use'.

There were more notes, too. A full-page screed on the 'rudeness' and 'ignorance' of somebody called Genevieve at Bookends in Truro.

All in all, Luke was building a picture of Alvis's work as both a custodian of books and slightly grumpy individual. She also seemed extremely suspicious of other people in the book world, keeping a list of 'bothersome scribes', which she had underlined several times. One of the names on this list had a note underneath which just said 'WATCH'.

He wanted to speak to Esme and to show her the book, but he also knew she was probably asleep. He didn't want to disturb her rest, so he carried on puzzling through the difficult-to-read handwriting.

Luke's eyes were getting dangerously heavy and, more than once, he had felt himself jerk awake. His drowsiness was interrupted by the bell on the shop door jangling. A moment later, the mayor appeared in front of him, looking dapper and energetic.

'You're up!' His voice was jovial, but Luke could detect concern in his eyes. 'Don't get up.'

Luke stopped his half-hearted attempt to rise from the chair. The exhaustion made his bones ache. 'I feel like death.'

'No wonder. You nearly died,' Tobias said. His voice betrayed no emotion.

Luke looked at his serious expression. 'That bad?'

'But you didn't.' Tobias broke into a gentle smile. 'And that is good news.'

Given the weight of the conversation, Luke felt a little bit petty asking, but he had to know. 'When I was ill... I don't remember much. I know Esme was there a lot, looking after me.'

Tobias's smile grew a little. 'I had to be quite stern to get her to take a break.'

'I wasn't in a state to do... anything. For myself, I mean. I was wondering whether Esme had to do full nursing.' He really didn't want to use the words 'bed pan' or 'toilet' or anything related, but Tobias's look of incomprehension was not promising.

'Ah,' Tobias said, realisation dawning. 'Don't worry about that side of things.'

'Okay,' Luke said, not feeling reassured.

'I helped you to the commode.'

Marvellous. Luke tried not to imagine his sweaty frame

leaning heavily on the elderly Tobias and all the rest of the indignities.

Tobias turned serious. 'How is your chest?'

'I have some weird cuts there. Was that...' He had been going to ask 'was that Esme?' but he knew that couldn't be right.

'Lucy. You owe her now.'

'That sounds ominous,' Luke said, trying to sound unconcerned. His chest was throbbing with remembered pain and he rubbed it with his fist.

The mayor just nodded, which wasn't reassuring. 'Bee will be along in a bit. We're all taking it in turns to check on you.'

'Thank you for the warning.'

The mayor patted the counter and left with a 'cheerio'.

Luke stayed in his reading chair and allowed himself a doze. Exactly one hour after the mayor had departed, Bee arrived. She had a small succulent in a hand-painted pot, which she placed onto the shop counter. 'For you. A get well soon present.'

'I'm all better,' Luke lied. 'But thank you.'

Bee gave him a look that told him he wasn't fooling anybody. And then hoisted a plastic bag next to the plant. 'Soup from Seren. Two minutes in the micro. There are some cheese scones in there, too.'

He opened his mouth to say another 'thank you', but Bee wasn't finished.

'She said you can pay her later.'

'Right.'

'And no skipping town before you do.'

'I'm not skipping anywhere.'

'Is that a fact?' Bee pursed her lips.

'Do you know who tidied up the books? There was one that I think... that I remember opening before I got ill.'

'You had better wear gloves when opening deliveries in the future,' Bee said. 'I think Esme's taking care of it.'

'What does that mean?'

'Making it safe if she's learned anything at all.'

Well, that made very little sense. But Luke would be the first to admit that he wasn't exactly firing on all cylinders. Bee often spoke in riddles and he wasn't about to make an enemy of one of the Three Sisters. He wasn't as addled as that.

Bee made to leave. 'Esme will be by in an hour and then Tobias after that.'

'It's very kind, but I really am fine.'

Bee shrugged.

Before she could walk out, Luke took a deep breath and spoke in a rush. 'Tobias said that your sister saved me. Lucy.'

Bee stopped. She spoke without turning around. 'She did.'

'So I owe her?'

'You do,' Bee said, finally turning to look at Luke. 'But I wouldn't rush to pay her back. If I were you, I'd keep well away. Let her forget about you.'

Well, that sounded more promising. 'Will she?'

'No,' Bee said cheerfully, 'but sometimes delaying a problem makes it disappear.'

THE LANDLINE RANG AN HOUR LATER. It was Esme, checking in. 'I'll be by in a little while, but I'm just trying to sort something.'

'You don't have to check on me,' Luke said. He wanted to see her, but he didn't want her to have to look after him.

And he had something else on his mind. 'Do you have the book?'

'I do. It's safe. I got a metal box from Hammer. It's padlocked and I've got the key in my pocket.'

'I don't like you having to deal with it. It's my responsibility.'

'I'm more interested in how you're feeling. What are you doing out of bed?'

'You called the landline,' he said defensively.

'It was a test. And you answered after three rings, which means you are downstairs.'

'All right, Columbo.'

'Go back to bed. Rest.'

'I feel fine. Better than fine. I might go for a run later.'

'Don't you dare.'

Hanging up, Luke couldn't help smiling. He didn't think Esme was entirely convinced by his breezy tone, but he felt he had done a decent job of acting normal. And well. He was neither, he could admit that to himself, but he really didn't want Esme worried. It wasn't that he didn't think Esme was strong enough, but more that he wanted to protect her. He didn't know if he was supposed to think like that. It might be toxic masculinity, a phrase he had heard and fully intended to look up the meaning of, but hadn't quite got around to. He was pretty sure the definition might just be a picture of his dad.

Instead of following Esme's orders, he searched for the delivery note that had been included with the box of books. First thing on his list was who had sent the damn thing. Second was to ask them some very pointed questions. He found the delivery slip and called the number listed with the address of the sender. A computerised voice informed him that the number he had dialled 'had not been recognised'. He tried it a couple of times to make sure he was dialling correctly, but got the same result.

Using his phone, he searched for the address. Maps showed it, the pin description matching the business name on the slip – The Shambles Book Emporium. He breathed a little easier realising that it was a real place. That the books hadn't just appeared from the ether. There were limits to what his brain could accept in any one week, and a book infecting him with a deadly virus had him at his limit. That was what he had decided. There was a pathogen on the book. A poison or a virus. Tobias had called it a curse, but that was old world suspicion. Perfectly acceptable in an old gent like Tobias, but not something that belonged in Luke's lexicon. Witch, his inner voice whispered. *Unholy Island. Wards. A magic bookshop.*

Ignoring his insolent mind, Luke focused on Google. The modern kind of magic. The sort that everybody believed in.

He used Street View to look at the outside of the building. It was a good size second-hand bookshop with an attractive display in the window and exterior woodwork painted in a smart racing green. In any other circumstances, he would put it on his mental list as a place to visit if he was ever in York. The Google results showed the business as 'closed'. He clicked on the shop's website link. It opened a Facebook page which hadn't been updated for two weeks. Which could be significant, or it could just mean that the business wasn't big on social media.

Looking back at the search page, a news story was the third result on the page. The headline showed in the link text. Beloved York institution in blazes.

He tapped the story and was greeted by a picture of a burned-out building. It was unrecognisable as the cheerful painted shop front and he felt his stomach drop at the sight and the throbbing in his chest increase. Fire. It had been burned away.

He didn't want to read the story beneath. Not after the first line: Owner perished in freak fire. Forcing himself to scan the news article, he tried to take in the details. The owner had died. Nobody else had been hurt. Investigators at scene said that the paper had acted as fuel but the accelerant was unclear 'at this time'. He could feel the burning heat, his flesh cooking and skin melting. It felt like a memory, not pure imagination and, for a very bad moment, he thought he was going to be sick. Swallowing hard, he wrapped his arms around his body and took a few breaths until the danger passed.

Scrolling, he found a picture of the owner, Graham Townsend. An unsmiling man with brown hair and black-rimmed glasses. It was clearly a posed shot, maybe for a driving licence or previous corporate job, and it had the unfortunate air of a mug shot. He stared at it and wondered whether this was the man who had sent a book to kill him.

CHAPTER ELEVEN

As much as Luke wanted to protect Esme, she was still the only person he wanted to talk to. That was another problem, but he shoved it to the side.

He called Esme. 'Can you pop round?'

'Are you okay?'

The concern in her voice was both gratifying and alarming. He didn't want to be something she had to worry about. 'I'm completely fine. Feel great.' Ignoring the lingering sensation of burning tissue, a numbness in his extremities and the kind of exhaustion that made his worst hangover seem like nothing, he was telling the truth.

Esme declined tea. She was carrying a cloth bag and seemed agitated. 'I borrowed a book,' she said. 'While you were asleep. I've brought it back, though.' She hoisted the tote.

'That's fine,' Luke said. 'You can have anything you want.' The lights flickered. 'You can borrow any books,' he amended.

'I'll keep it for a bit longer, then. If that's okay?'

He nodded absently. 'Can we go upstairs?' The sign for

the door was already flipped to 'closed' and he locked it for good measure.

Esme raised an eyebrow.

'I don't want to be disturbed.' What he didn't say was that the thought of having to jog downstairs to serve a customer was more than he could face. He was struggling to move his limbs as it was and wanted to be sat down. Ideally, for about a week.

In the bedroom, he opened the skylight to let in a stream of fresh air. Partly to cover any lingering fug from his illness and partly so that the cold draft would help him to stay awake. He sat in the upright chair closest to the window. 'I looked up the place that sent the box of books.'

He unlocked his phone and passed it to Esme. She read quickly and then looked at him with wide eyes. 'That's disturbing. The poor man.'

He nodded. There was a moment of silence as they both contemplated the ramifications. Luke had already done so, of course, but he watched the thoughts flit across Esme's face and felt as if he could read them there. The dead man could have been Luke. The island bookshop could have burned to the ground. The building they were sitting in was essentially a wooden box filled with tinder.

'I found something, too.'

He looked at the book she dug from her bag. She flipped it to a particular page and waited for him to read.

The words were archaic but easy enough to understand. He read as quickly as his pounding headache and the tiny typeface allowed. When he had finished, he didn't have to work to make his tone even. Another shift in his understanding of the world and his role in it had taken place. 'You think the book was hexed?'

'It makes sense.' Esme was looking at him beseechingly, as if willing him to listen to reason.

'Sort of,' he said. He felt the rocks of exhaustion pressing down on his head and shoulders. He was sitting, but he wanted to lie down. His brain felt sluggish, but he forced himself to keep focusing. 'I think a physical poison seems more likely. Although likely doesn't seem the right word. Why would someone be sprinkling poison onto random books? And what sort of poison makes a person feel like they are about to burst into flames?'

Esme was quiet. He had the impression she was waiting for him to work through the basic insanity of the premise until he was ready to accept reality. Fine. He could do that. He would accept the possibility that someone had placed a hex, or a hitherto-undiscovered poison, onto a book and sent it to his shop.

'Is that how you felt? I know your temperature was really high...'

'I was feverish, I know,' Luke said. He ran a hand through his hair, feeling suddenly self-conscious. 'It really felt like I was burning. I've never experienced anything like it.' He swallowed, not wanting to recall the feeling that his flesh was melting, but unable to forget it.

'And there was a fire at the shop that sent the book?' Esme confirmed. 'You think that's linked?'

He shrugged. 'It's a weird coincidence if not.'

IN HER OWN KITCHEN, a cup of calming tea cooling next to her, Esme went back to the book she had got from the bookshop. She finished the section on 'dehexing' and was now close to the end.

A word on the naturally unnatural. While many trinkets and baubles may be enchanted, naturally occurring items such as stones or plants may not. These have a form of their own and a will to remain as such.

Esme had never really thought of stone as having a will, but then, why not?

This being so, a cursed or enchanted item of this category is powerfully rare. You would be very lucky – or unlucky - indeed to happen across such a jewel and would do well to leave it where it lies. Remember that temptation is the urge that wants beyond reason. Every practitioner must cultivate their reason to guard against base urges.

The book was veering toward a preachy tone that Esme associated with organised religion. Although, she supposed that witchery was a religion of a kind and it made her smile to realise that meant she was religious. The devout foster family that had forced three-hour prayer sessions onto her when she had been a child would be proud.

Esme closed the book and stood up to stretch. Her mug of gunpowder tea had gone cold, and she took it with her to the kitchen, emptying it down the sink and filling the kettle for a fresh cup.

Her eyes were drawn to the windowsill where the lump of black sea glass sat. It was beautiful and she had placed it there as an object of art, really. With Alvis gone and unable to talk to her about it, she hadn't really known what else to do. She had considered asking Bee, but something had stopped her. Alvis had spoken to her about the glass, which made it her responsibility. If she had wanted The Three Sisters' opinion, Alvis would have gone directly to Bee herself.

The glass was sitting on the wooden sill, exactly where she had left it. Of course. It was an inanimate object. She had thought she had seen shifting colours, a swirling pattern, in its shiny surface just after she had retrieved it from Euan's bedroom, but now it was just smooth sea glass.

The kettle was whistling and she lifted it off the heat. Then, turning back to the glass, she picked it up. The weight was pleasing in her hand and the surface pleasantly smooth. It was the smoothness of a sun-warmed pebble. A piece of tumbled crystal but with the knowledge that the tumbling mechanism had been the ocean herself. She wondered how far it had travelled over its long life.

She was worried about Luke obsessing over the fire in the York bookshop. She understood that he had had a close call, but he was safe now. The police would investigate the bookshop fire and Luke needed to focus on recuperating. She hadn't liked the tiredness drawn in the lines of his face, or the pain she saw in his eyes when he thought she wasn't looking. She also didn't like the thought of his attention leading him away from the island. What if he went to the mainland and realised that he wanted to rejoin his old life?

Well, that wasn't a comforting thought. She straightened her shoulders and gave herself a pep talk. The only thing she could do was put aside her personal feelings and do what needed to be done. First of which was to attempt to denature...dehex? The book that had hurt Luke.

MATTEO WAS RESTOCKING the canned goods and trying not to think about anything else. The Book Keeper had come in earlier to buy milk, and the sight of him had served as an unwelcome reminder that Alvis was gone. And that led to memories of the man who had killed her. And been killed, in turn, by Matteo.

He knew it had been the right thing to do in the circumstances and it wasn't guilt that was eating away at his insides. More the absence of guilt. His family, the Silvers, weren't known for their morals and he was concerned that there was a cold emptiness where his conscience ought to be. Or perhaps he didn't feel guilt because it had been righteous. He had prevented Fiona from having to deal with the man who had terrorised her son. That was good. But he had taken a man's life. That was bad. And so it went, round and round, until he realised he had placed the cans of tomato soup in the place that the chickpeas lived, and that the labels didn't line up.

The door jangled and a man who had even less use for a conscience than Matteo walked into the shop. Hammer pushed the door shut against the gale outside and brushed flakes of snow from his shoulders. 'Bloody winter,' he said by way of greeting.

Matteo nodded in return, retreating behind the counter. The central strip light was making a slight buzzing noise and he made a mental note to replace the tube soon.

'I might have done something rash,' Hammer said, when he placed a lighter and packet of instant noodles onto the counter.

Matteo raised an eyebrow.

'You remember those charmers? The ones who were looking for Luke?'

The blood in Matteo's veins seemed to drop several degrees. He nodded cautiously.

'I might have followed their friends.' Hammer's hand was resting on the counter, next to the noodles. It was heavily scarred and looked like a spade next to the colourful foil packet. 'I might have found their boss and made a deal to keep an eye on Luke Taylor.'

Matteo tilted his head to indicate interest. He was well versed in non-verbal communication, but the urge to speak hadn't been this strong in years. He wanted to ask Hammer what the fuck he had been thinking.

Some of his feelings must have translated regardless as Hammer withdrew his hand, snatching up the packet and the lighter and stuffing them into his jacket pockets. 'How was I to know he was going to be our new Book Keeper? I thought he would be moving on. And it was a way to make sure Dean Fisher didn't send anyone else looking for him. If he thought I was keeping an eye, doing the job.' Hammer stopped speaking to the floor, the wall, the shelves, and met Matteo's eyes. 'It seemed like a good idea at the time.'

Matteo reached for his pad and pen. He wrote the topmost of the questions that were piling up. *You going to tell L?*

'You think I should?'

Matteo shook his head. Then changed his mind and nodded. He held out a hand and tilted it from side to side. Maybe.

'Yeah,' Hammer said. 'That was my conclusion, too. Very fucking helpful.'

Matteo deployed the eyebrow again.

ESME AND LUKE looked at the slim volume. It lay on the opened bed of tissue paper. Innocent.

'So. A cursed book. That's a thing.'

'Apparently,' Esme said. She tried to smile reassuringly. 'At least we know it's not anthrax.'

'That's the thinnest of silver linings.'

Her reassuring smile was proving hard to maintain. Truth was, she felt pretty overwhelmed herself. 'I don't know what else to tell you.'

'Right.' Luke was visibly pulling himself together. 'Hexed. It's a hexed book. So, what do we do with it?'

'Dehex it. I hope.' Esme had been devouring everything in the reference book from the shop.

'Is that okay?'

'You want to keep it? It's dangerous. Someone else could get hurt...'

'No. No, I know that. I was thinking... Isn't it evidence?'

'You calling the police?'

'No. You're right. Okay, go ahead.'

'Thank you,' Esme said drily. She didn't need his permission.

The wards required a stone, a shell, and a drop of blood. To dehex a cursed object, she needed more blood. Even if she was willing to donate it, it wouldn't work. It had to be the blood of the innocent dead. She had spoken to Bee, who had nodded and disappeared upstairs for a few minutes. When she had come back, she had told Esme that her requirement would be delivered that evening.

True to her word, Esme had found a glass milk bottle half-filled with blood, sitting on her back step.

She sank into a cross-legged position on the floor and drew the gruesome bottle out of her tapestry backpack.

'What the fuck is that?'

Esme didn't look at him. 'Take a wild guess.'

'That's not...'

'It's not human, no.' Esme sincerely hoped that was correct. Bee had said that Diana could supply what was necessary and she had chosen not to ask any further questions.

She added a stumpy pillar candle and lit it with her lighter.

Then, on a whim, she fetched the black sea glass. Alvis had thought it had something to do with denaturing. At least, Oliver had thought it might 'cure' Euan of the abilities he had inherited from his mother, Fiona.

'Don't touch it,' Luke warned again.

Esme smothered the urge to snap at him that she knew what she was doing. She was on edge. And she felt vaguely silly. She was playing at being a witch. She wasn't born to it.

Her attention was taken by the slim book lying on the floor between them. She felt as if evil was emanating from it, but that had to be suggestion. Her imagination. She heard Bee's exasperated voice in her head. Trust yourself.

Okay. So the book was evil. It was hexed. And she, the Ward Witch of Unholy Island, was going to remove the curse. She picked up the bottle of blood. The surface had congealed and the sides of the glass were gruesomely gloopy. She felt bile rise at the back of her throat and she swallowed.

With a twist of her wrist and trying not to think too much about what she was doing, Esme upended the bottle over the book. The blood flowed out, forming a stomach-churning viscous pool that immediately flooded the surface of the open book and dripped over the edges onto the plastic sheet. The smell of copper filled Esme's nostrils until she could taste it.

Luke looked unnaturally pale in the candlelight. She wondered if he was going to throw up and she hoped he had a strong stomach. 'Go if you need to,' she said, and he shook his head.

I release this evil, she thought, recalling the language from the book. There had been a variety of incantations suggested for different objects. She had opened the book to a page on removing curses from 'binding contracts, manuscripts and other written works of import'. It had a long and flowery incantation that she didn't relish reading out loud in front of Luke. All of the incantations in the book appeared to boil down to the same essential message. *Fuck off, hex.*

No sooner as the thought had resounded in her mind, the blood began to move. It flowed toward the sea glass as if magnetically drawn. The glass turned cloudy as the blood reached it, flowing up its surface and disappearing. The lump of glass seemed to be absorbing the blood. Quickly and efficiently, so that within seconds it was all gone. Finally, the clouded surface of the glass cleared until it looked just as it had before.

'What the hell?' Luke said, eyes wide.

Esme started at him, knowing her expression was a mirror of his. 'How can we check it worked?' Even as she spoke, she felt that it had. The sensation of crawling had gone from the back of her neck and when she looked at the book, now completely clear of blood apart from a couple of smudges that were already turning brown, she could no longer sense a creeping evil. Her instinct told her it was just an ordinary book.

Still. It would be sensible to be cautious.

'I think we should get rid of it,' Luke said. 'Bury it. Burn it. Throw it in the sea.'

'The sea doesn't deserve that,' Esme said.

'No. Right. I wasn't thinking... I just don't want it there.'

'It is the bookshop,' Esme said. 'I think it is the only place it can be.'

In the end, they wrapped the book in a piece of cloth and put it into the fire-safe metal box. It felt like a burial. No, an entombment.

CHAPTER TWELVE

T he next day, Luke and Esme were in the bookshop drinking tea. Esme had arrived in the morning and bustled about putting food into his fridge and making him drinks. He wasn't complaining about her company, but didn't like the fact that she was clearly still worried about him. He thought he was doing an excellent job of being fully recovered and didn't like the evidence that she could see right through his act.

'Have you taken pain killers today?' she asked, catching him rubbing the place on his chest that hadn't stopped aching. 'The wounds should be scabbing over.'

'All good,' he lied. They weren't bleeding anymore, that much was true, but they felt as if they were. And while he no longer felt as if he was burning from the inside out, his cells seemed to have retained the memory of that feeling.

She looked like she wanted to ask him something else but, after a moment of indecision, went and scrubbed the mugs in the small sink.

They had spent a companionable hour with Luke sitting in his reading chair while Esme browsed the shelves at the back of the shop. Now, they had steaming mugs of spiced tea, supplied by Esme, and a bar of Fruit & Nut chocolate, supplied by Luke by way of Matteo's shop, and they were having a well-earned break from all the relaxing.

The bell on the front door jangled and a man wearing head-to-toe black appeared from the short entrance passageway. Luke glanced at his watch, automatically checking how long before the causeway would close again for the day. Visitors often called in to ask and then left again without even glancing at the books. Luke tried not to take it personally, but it was hard, and he often found himself patting the bookshelves or the counter in hurt solidarity with the shop.

This visitor was looking around at the shelves with real interest, though. He wasn't dressed like the usual winter visitors, either, in a puffy jacket or technical waterproof. Instead, he had a long black coat that looked like something from a film. His bleach blond hair stood up in messy spikes and he had the kind of skin tone that suggested he didn't do a lot of rambling in the sunshine.

'Are you Luke?' The stranger's voice was surprisingly deep and had a rough smoker's edge. 'The owner?'

'I run the shop,' Luke said. There was a split second when he wondered if he ought to be revealing his identity to a complete stranger, but then he realised that the man didn't seem like a goon sent by Dean Fisher. His build was slim and he had a bookish goth vibe.

The man glanced at Esme, but she didn't say anything. She was sitting on a wooden stool behind the counter and she put her mug of tea down onto the surface. Luke could see tension in her shoulders and he moved next to her, providing a barrier of sorts.

'Okay, then. Good.' The man looked around again. 'I'm in the right place. I wasn't sure. You don't have a name on the shop, you know?'

Luke shrugged. 'It's the only bookshop on the island.'

The stranger didn't move for a moment, staring at Luke as if he was trying to work out whether to say something or not. Seeming to come to a conclusion, he added. 'I'm Iain.'

Luke adjusted his weight slightly. He didn't feel a threat, exactly, but he was wary. 'What can I do for you?'

'I used to deal with Jute Books in Dundee.'

'I see,' Luke said, although he didn't.

'And now I need a new place.'

'I'm sorry, I don't follow.'

'Fraser bought certain texts from me. And I bought certain texts from him. Specialist books.' Iain was watching him carefully.

Luke nodded. 'I think I know the kind of thing you mean. I don't know if I can help.'

The lights in the shop flickered.

Esme stood up as if she had been stuck with a pin. Her head whipped around as if she expected to see somebody behind her.

'I went to Campbell & Sons,' Iain was saying, 'but the owner was away. The girl there said I'd be best off coming to you. She said her boss had off-loaded most of his specialist stuff down here. To the old owner. I think the name was Alvis. Maybe Alvin? Gave me this address and your name. I've come down from Edinburgh.' There was a note of pleading in his voice. He glanced around as the lights continued to flicker. 'You got dodgy wiring?'

'Something like that,' Luke said, patting the counter gently. 'I think I spoke too hastily.' The lights stopped flickering wildly, but he could sense the bookshop listening. Waiting.

'Would you like a cup of tea?' Esme slid from the stool. She was suddenly very close to Luke, and he fought the urge to put an arm around her.

Iain looked surprised. 'All right. Yeah. Thanks.'

'We can sit down for a bit. You've had a long journey.'

'I have,' he nodded. The aggrieved note was back when he spoke again. 'There was an accident on the A1 and I don't really like crossing the border. No offence.'

Esme's back was to the man at this point, so only Luke saw her roll her eyes. He felt some of the tension leave his body at her levity. If she was comfortable enough to offer tea and make jokes with her eyes, then things must be all right.

He watched Esme head to the staff cupboard and then turned to offer the man a seat on the stool Esme had just vacated. He pulled it away from the counter so that there would be no danger of the man spilling tea onto his ledger.

'Is there somewhere private we can talk?'

Luke looked around the empty shop in a bemused manner.

Iain cut his eyes at the open door. The sound of the kettle boiling came from within.

'You can speak freely in front of Esme,' Luke said.

'Right.' He didn't look sure. 'I might look around for a moment,' he said abruptly. 'If that's okay?'

'Sure.' Luke gestured at Iain to help himself and then slipped into his usual bookseller mode. Politely ignoring the customers as they browsed the shelves but ready to help if they looked even slightly uncertain or likely to ask a question.

He also moved the stool and fetched a folding chair from the staff cupboard for a makeshift seating area.

Iain's manner had relaxed considerably by the time they gathered to drink their tea. It was the soothing effect of browsing bookshelves, Luke thought, having witnessed the phenomena many times.

'Thank you for this,' Iain said, raising his mug.

'You are very welcome.' Esme offered him a biscuit from a tin that Luke was pretty sure she had brought from her house. 'Tell us about your interest in magic.'

He went still, the oat biscuit held halfway to his mouth.

'It's all right,' Esme said. 'This is the island bookshop and Luke is Alvis's successor.' She looked at Luke encouragingly until he nodded.

'It's not in magic, as such,' Iain said. 'It's the books. I like collecting them, seeing them, touching...' He seemed to realise that he was sounding a little odd and stopped himself abruptly.

'Your interest is academic,' Esme supplied.

'You are a collector,' Luke added.

'I'm a connoisseur,' Iain corrected them somewhat fussily. He took another biscuit and dunked it into his tea. 'I can tell the good ones from the rubbish. That's why Fraser would buy from me.'

'The shop in Dundee? It's closed?'

'Aye,' Iain said. 'That's right.'

'Not permanently, I hope?' Luke asked, a horrible feeling creeping over his skin. 'There wasn't a fire?'

Iain stopped mid-dunk, his expression shocked. 'Why do you ask that?'

'There wasn't-?' Esme broke in, glancing at Luke. 'Don't say the shop burned down?'

He shook his head. 'Fraser's house. They said he was asleep. Wouldn't have known anything, but still...' Iain shuddered. 'Horrible. That's why the shop is closed. It was just him running it.'

There was a short silence. Luke didn't look at Esme. Another fire. A bookseller in his own home. The five points of pain on his chest flared and he thought, for a moment, that he could smell burning meat. He put his mug down so that nobody would see his hand shaking and took a long, slow breath.

Rubbing at his chest and feeling the pain recede to its normal ache, he heard Esme asking Iain another question and realised that she was filling in the awkward pause.

'Where do you find books for your collection?'

'Places like this,' Iain said, looking around. He turned thoughtful. 'Well, not exactly like this place. More just ordinary second-hand bookshops, sometimes charity shops, boot sales, that kind of thing.'

'That seems pretty prosaic,' Luke said. He was trying to imagine an ancient magical text hanging out on the shelf of a Red Cross Shop.

'House clearances are best,' Iain said. 'People often don't know what they've got.'

'It still doesn't seem likely. There can't be that many magical texts in the world. It must be like looking for...' He had been going to say a 'needle in a haystack' but Iain jumped in and supplied 'treasure'.

'It's a treasure hunt,' he repeated, looking truly animated for the first time.

'Okay,' Luke was still trying to get his head around the man's obsession. Luke liked books a lot, probably more than most people, but to spend his time hunting down rare volumes, sifting through thousands of Tom Clancy's in the hope of stumbling across an antique oddity, seemed extreme. 'And you make a lot of money doing this?'

The man's eyes shifted. 'Some. Sometimes. Connecting the right buyer.'

'And you just buy and sell? For profit? Do you keep some, too?'

'Yeah, I've got a small collection. But it's the finding them I like. They always move on eventually.'

That was strange phrasing. Like the books had wills of their own.

Esme brushed crumbs from her fingers. 'You're not tempted to use the books yourself?'

'Use them?'

'For magic,' she said, the word hanging in the air.

There was an awkward pause as Iain gaped at Esme like she had grown a second head. Then he gave a nervous laugh, like he had decided she was teasing him.

'Some of these books,' Luke waved a hand, 'have instructions, spells, all sorts of information.'

'Yeah, but...' Iain looked at them nervously, his eyes flicking between them. 'Magic's not real.'

CHAPTER THIRTEEN

L uke had called the Yorkshire newspaper, hoping for further details on the bookshop fire. After the brief and unsatisfying conversation, he replaced the receiver and continued to look out of the window. He felt like he should be doing something, but with the Shambles Bookshop and its owner gone, he wasn't sure what. Now there was the dead bookseller in Dundee, too, but an internet search hadn't thrown up any new information. Fraser of Jute Books didn't have much of an online footprint. He hadn't found a news story about the fire at his house, either. He wondered what books Iain would bring to sell him or ask him to source. A thought occurred to him that he should have warned Iain about the possibility of hexed books floating around. There was no reason for there to be more, but equally no reason why there *wouldn't* be more.

The jumble of books in the window hadn't been touched since he took over the shop and it suddenly hit him that they hadn't been dusted, either. He moved to the window and began retrieving the books, stacking them on top of the counter.

Once all the books were safely out of the way, he

fetched a cloth and a spray bottle of water and white vinegar and cleaned the inside of the window. It highlighted how dirty the outside was, so he filled a basin with water and went out to do the other side, too.

Then he dusted the books on the counter. Halfway through, he decided he would put some different books in the window instead. Mix things up. As he carefully wiped the books and found places to shelve them, he found himself humming quietly. He had the sudden realisation that if he looked into a mirror, he would find his face relaxed. Maybe even smiling.

He paused, his hands stilled, as he waited for the punch of guilt. He should be out looking for Lewis. He was letting his brother down. But the pain was very remote. And he was soon distracted by the task of choosing new titles to go into the window. It was January, a bleak month, but one with beauty too. He knew Esme's garden was filled with interesting pieces of driftwood, and he wondered if she would let him borrow a piece. He could use it to prop up a few books, so that their covers were better displayed. He sent her a text message and then got back to work.

Esme arrived half an hour later, carrying a large bag. 'I've been thinking about yesterday,' she announced. 'That was weird, right? Another death?'

'Very,' Luke said. 'What if both fires were caused by hexed books? And if there are cursed books in circulation, we need to find them before somebody else gets hurt.'

'That's not our responsibility,' Esme said. 'We need to focus on our community. The island-'

'It absolutely is.' Luke hated that he was right. He didn't want to worry about strangers and cursed books. He wanted to sleep. With the windows wide open so that cold air was playing across his skin the entire time, banishing the memory of the scorching fire. He opened his eyes and looked into the hazel of Esme's. Sometimes they looked brown, sometimes green, and sometimes, he could see gold in her irises. Right now, they were pale green and worried. 'What if a kid got hold of one? Or someone old or ill? They wouldn't survive ten minutes.' What he didn't add was that they would be begging for death after five. He rubbed at his aching chest. The claw marks, as he had started to think of them, were five distinct points of pain.

'It's not our business,' Esme said. 'We belong to the island. Affairs on the mainland are not our concern. My duty is to protect the island and our community. We need to stay safe and to protect this place for future generations.'

Luke waited to check that Esme had finished speaking. Her cheeks were flushed pink and her eyes were bright with what looked worryingly like tears. Esme was no longer the fearful woman he had met a few months ago, but she was still very wary. He wanted to reach out and hold her. To provide comfort instead of the question he knew he had to ask. 'If not us, then who?'

Rather than answering, Esme bent to unpack two good pieces of driftwood from her bag. 'I thought these were about the right size, but I've loads more if you want to choose your own.'

'No, these are perfect.' Luke began arranging them in the window, already imagining them surrounded by books.

She was watching him intently.

'What?'

'Hang on.' Esme was bent over her bag, pulling out other items. 'I thought these might look good twisted around the driftwood.'

She held out what looked like a coil of copper wire.

'Lights.' She held out a hand and he brought one of the pieces of wood back to the counter. She wound the wire around one end and then passed it back.

99

Luke laid and wound and twisted the wire over the two pieces of wood, hiding the battery pack behind the larger piece, and then switched it on.

'LEDs, so they stay really cool. They look good inside fishing floats, too.'

THEY WORKED COMPANIONABLY FOR AN HOUR, discussing the placement of books, and not mentioning cursed objects or burned-down shops or lost brothers.

'You could do with some height,' Esme said, surveying their efforts with her head tilted to one side. 'Either stands or something hanging from the top of the windows.'

'Next time,' Luke said. 'I'm going to start simple and work my way up.'

'Fair enough.' She smiled. 'This does look better, though.'

'It really does,' he began, and then stopped. Was there a humming sound? He listened intently for a moment. 'Can you hear that?'

He listened again, with Esme obediently tilting her head and listening, too. Silence.

'Never mind.'

'Is it me,' Esme said, looking around, 'or did it just get warmer?'

The cool chill of the shop had definitely disappeared. Luke felt pleasantly warm.

'How is this place heated, anyway? I can't see any radiators.'

'I think there's a warm air system,' Luke said absently, still half-listening for that elusive humming sound. 'There are vents at the base of some of the book-cases.' Then he heard his own words. Maybe the humming had been the heating system coming on. And that was why it had got warmer in the shop. He felt faintly ridiculous.

There were still a couple of books from the old window display on the counter. One was a book of Irish myths and legends with a sage green fabric cover and pretty foil embossed lettering. He picked it up and carried it to the back of the shop where the large mythology section lived. And then he stopped. Where there had been a single unbroken bookcase running along the wall that was shared with the building next door, was now split into two book-cases. Between them was a door that definitely hadn't been there before.

LUKE AND ESME STOOD FROZEN, staring at the new door.

'That wasn't there before, right?' Luke was the first to speak. Esme looked remarkably calm, but then she was a witch. And she had been on the island for seven years. Maybe after that length of time he would be just as chill. It's not your first new doorway, he reminded himself. The bookshop had reconfigured itself a few times, and it had taken his measure before revealing the stairs that led to the living space. It was just... still a bit discombobulating. Turned out, it took more than a few months to fully adjust to living in a magical bookshop.

'Definitely not.'

'Shall we try it?'

Esme hadn't moved, but she looked more intrigued than alarmed. It was bolstering. 'It must open into the building next door. I suppose.'

'What is next door, anyway? A house?'

'Nobody lives in it,' Esme said. 'We've got a few empty properties in the village. I don't know if anyone looks after them or...'

'Well, maybe this door opens into it.' Luke didn't really believe that. It didn't explain the magically appearing door, for one thing. And he couldn't ignore all the other strange things about the bookshop. Not if he wanted to stay sane. The stairs to the upper floor had been not here and then here, back when he had first moved into the shop. He remembered the first night in the place, camping out in the front room. There was no use pretending that this was an ordinary building. He had to accept that things were different on Unholy Island. And he had.

He reached out and brushed the door handle with his fingertips.

'Are you going to open it?'

Esme was just behind him and he could feel the warmth from her body. 'Do you think I should?'

'It's your shop. You're the Book Keeper.'

'Right. Yes.' He squared his shoulders.

The door was plain wood. Pitch pine with marks and dings as if it had always stood there. The handle was black iron and there was a keyhole. It occurred to Luke that it might be locked. He wondered if this might be the vault or repository that Alvis referred to in her book. He was prevaricating, he knew. What was the phrase? It's the hope that kills you? He wanted it to be the stockroom. The vault. He wanted a sign that the bookshop wanted him to run the place. That he belonged.

Trying to prepare himself for the disappointment of finding a cleaning cupboard or a blank wall, he grasped the handle and opened the door.

The room was dark and windowless, but a central pendant light illuminated as he stepped inside. There was a table in the middle of the room with a few large books on top and, around the four walls, floor to ceiling shelves. The simple relief was quickly followed by elation. Luke looked around and knew that he was grinning like a lunatic.

'I think you've found your stockroom,' Esme said. Her voice was a little strained.

'Are you okay?' He turned to check on her.

'Just this place,' she waved a hand, encompassing the shop and, perhaps, the whole island. 'It just keeps on surprising me.'

'I know what you mean.' He reached out a hand and touched the table, reassuring himself that it was real. 'Thought you would be used to it by now?'

She laughed, sounding more like herself. 'Not even close.'

'Thank you,' Luke said formally, addressing the shop. He had the urge to wave or do a little bow, but was self-conscious in front of Esme.

'Thank you,' Esme said, also looking around as if addressing the building itself. 'This is wonderful.'

They shared a small smile and Esme drifted over to the nearest shelves and began to look at the books that were neatly arranged. There were blocky black letter labels on the shelves, suggesting that Alvis had kept them arranged alphabetically.

The shelves along the bottom were extra deep and tall and held lidded plastic crates and thick cardboard archive boxes. In one corner there was a wooden shipping crate that looked antique. Underneath the table was a jumble of suitcases, wooden chests, and more plastic boxes. The wall shelving was broken in one place to hold a dark green metal filing cabinet that looked like a relic from the nine-teen-forties.

The room was surprisingly dust-free. There was the same scent as the rest of the shop of old paper and wood, along with ink and that distinctive 'old book' smell that was particular to bookshops and libraries. There was something else, too. Ozone. The smell of standing on the shore and breathing in the salt-tinged air of the sea.

He looked around, but there was definitely no window. Maybe there were hidden air bricks, letting in the scent of the island. Or, Luke supposed, it was just the way the air inside a magical hidden room smelled.

In addition to the piled books on the table, there was a hefty leather-bound book that must have been A3 in size. It was bound along the short edge and when Luke opened the front page, he found old-fashioned sloping handwriting in fountain pen ink. Flipping through the cream-coloured pages made something obvious. This was a shop ledger from many years ago. Opening it at the back, he found it was full and the last date was nineteen hundred and one.

Esme was crouched in front of the shelving, pulling out an enormous book from the bottom shelf. She paused, the book angled out, and glanced over her shoulder. 'May I?'

'Sure,' Luke said. 'Help yourself.'

With the large tome levered out from its place, Esme needed somewhere to put it. Luke closed the ledger and moved it over so that she could put the heavy book onto the table.

'I can't tell you how I know, but this is exactly what I need.' She was glowing with happiness and relief.

Leaving Esme to leaf ecstatically through her book, Luke drifted over to the shelving. On the bottom there was a row of Bankers Boxes filled with old paperwork. In the third one he opened, he found a stack of ledgers, each marked with a distinctive crescent moon on the cover. Looking at the most recent, a volume that minutely covered the previous five years in Alvis's distinctive sloping copper-plate, he found purchases and sales for the shop. But not the thrillers and cookery books and romances and book club hits that were fully itemised in the sales ledger that he used daily, the one kept on the counter with the cash register. This ledger listed books like 'A History of Lycanthropy' and 'Edwin Hardcastle's Diary: The Gentleman Alchemist'. As well as the date of the transaction and the price paid or received, Alvis had added details of the buyer or seller, and some extra notes. 'Nonsense' was one succinct summary. Another note was underlined three times. It said: 'Not For Resale'. The book's title wasn't written, just the author, Lyndon Blackwood, and the words 'volume three' in brackets.

Luke settled down with his own notebook and combed through the entries, collating a list of repeated names. Jute Books in Dundee was mentioned only once and Alvis had written 'Fraser is a crook'. The Shambles Book Emporium in York cropped up three times. Campbell & Sons had seven entries. Luke used Google to discover a bookshop by that name in Edinburgh's Grassmarket. He made a note of the address and telephone number. Alvis had bought from this shop on all seven occasions and the notes were mostly positive, except for one that read 'fake'. He made a mental note to visit. Iain had said the owner was away and that he had been sent to them by an employee. It could be that nothing was wrong, and the owner had just been having a day off, but his gut said otherwise.

There were a couple more regulars, one with copious notes, concluding with 'overpriced waste of time' written in red ink. Something occurred to him just as Esme shut the book she had been looking at and joined him. 'Alvis was writing this for me.' He shook his head. 'Well, not me specifically. For whoever came after. All these notes,' he swept a hand over the book, 'they're so that I can continue doing the job.'

Esme's expression said 'well, duh' and he felt like an idiot. He had been told often enough, by Bee and Tobias and Esme herself, that he was the Book Keeper. It was a role on the island. But it felt as if it was only now sinking in what that meant. This was a job that had been done for decades, maybe hundreds of years, in this exact place and in this exact way. Collecting important information and keeping it safe. He caught sight of the book that Esme was clutching to her chest as if it was her firstborn. Keeping it safe for those who need it.

If part of that job now came with danger, he had an obligation to warn others in the profession. They might not be running magical bookshops and not know the true value or importance of the books they found and traded with his shop, but they ought to know if there was a threat circulating.

CHAPTER FOURTEEN

The shop in Edinburgh was part of a picturesque row of brightly painted buildings. The young woman who greeted them had gold-rimmed round glasses that seemed far too large for her face, but in a way that was clearly a fashion choice. She had dark red hair twisted up in a bun and was wearing pink dungarees with a floral-print blouse underneath and chunky mustard-yellow boots. She introduced herself as Mona and said that they could go to the café a few doors up to chat. 'I've not seen a soul all day and I'm going stir-crazy in this place.'

They waited for Mona to flip the 'closed' sign and lock up, and then they walked the short distance to the Sunflower Café.

Luke went to the counter with their drinks order while Esme followed Mona to a table. It was covered in newspapers and Mona cleared them away, putting them back on a wall rack with a practised efficiency that Esme found very impressive.

'Thank you for speaking to us,' Esme said, as they got settled.

'No problem. Happy to help.' Mona shook her head. 'Booksellers have got to stick together, right?'

Esme wasn't sure if the woman was asking a question, but she guessed not, as Mona had already moved onto a new subject. She spoke about the café they were in and how it was a 'lifesaver' and she meant this literally. She launched into a long story about a woman having a heart attack after finishing her soup and the staff behind the counter recognised that was what was happening even though she wasn't clutching her arm or her chest or anything.

Esme nodded. 'Women's symptoms are often different.'

'Yeah,' Mona said enthusiastically. 'But it's not what we see in the media, is it? It's always old white dudes clutching their chests and falling over in films and stuff.'

'Umm,' Luke began, but Mona was on a roll.

'So this woman, right? Older lady but not old old. She's finished her soup. It was their spicy Thai veggie one which, to be fair, has a wee kick to it, but no one's blaming the soup. At least not now. So the wummin's finished and she's saying her back hurts and she just doesnae feel right.'

Mona's Scottish accent was coming out more thickly the more excited she became. Esme found she was leaning in closer, swept up in the tale.

'See Abi there?' Mona twisted in her seat and pointed to the androgynous-looking person serving behind the counter. 'They're on it. Say straight away that she doesnae look right, either. And they call an ambo straight away, no messing. Says 'I think this woman is having a heart attack' and the woman starts arguing 'am not, I feel fine, hen, dinnae make a fuss' and then she's out.'

'Out?'

'Deid to the world. Well, no *deid* deid. Unconscious. She slips over and is on the floor.'

'Awful,' Esme said, drawn in. She could imagine how scary that would be. Out in your life, not in a hospital setting or anywhere you might reasonably expect that kind of emergency.

'Did the ambulance arrive in time?' Luke asked.

'I was useless,' Mona said cheerfully. 'I froze. I think I said 'are you all right?' like the wummin was gonnae sit up and answer me.'

Abi called across the café. 'I thought you were going to pass out and all, you were that white.'

'But they come over,' Mona stabbed a finger in Abi's direction, 'cool as anything and rolls her over and checks her pulse and her breathing and then just gets on top of her and starts chest compressions. Just like that.'

'Well done,' Esme said to Abi. 'That must have been really scary.'

Abi shrugged, looking a bit pink. Esme had the impression that this wasn't the first time Mona had told the story.

'The ambo arrived and they took her away. She's fine, isn't she?' Mona looked to Abi, who nodded.

'Had a stent put in and home again.'

'It was last week,' Abi said, still seeming a bit embarrassed.

They sat for a moment, sipping their drinks and contemplating the story. When Esme felt enough time had passed to give the anecdote its fair airing, she looked at Luke for moral support.

He put his espresso cup down. 'Is it okay to ask you about the bookshop?'

'Yeah. 'Course. Sorry, I do go on sometimes. I get distracted by something and whoosh that's my heid on it. Can't help myself until I've talked it out.'

'No worries,' Luke said, smiling with a gentleness that made Esme want to lean over and hug him. Which wasn't a feeling she usually had, so it was disconcerting. Her crush seemed only to be getting worse and that was a problem. She might not still be battling Ryan's toxic litany running through her conscious mind, but she wasn't at all certain he wasn't still lurking somewhere in the depths. And she had no wish to find out.

'And you've met a few weird clients?' Luke was saying.

Esme pulled her focus away from her warm and squishy feelings and back to the interrogation. Conversation.

'Customers.' Mona confirmed. 'Loads of them. I've been running the place for Conrad since he went on his trip. Sabbatical thing.'

She had explained on the phone that Conrad, who owned Campbell and Sons, had upped and left the business three months earlier, saying that he needed an extended break. Mona, who had only been working there part-time for a year before that had found herself with a full-time managerial-and-customer-service position.

'We get all sorts. Casual readers and big-spender collectors. They like the antique stuff and the first editions. The map collection, too. That's a big hit with the scholars. And then there's the people bringing in books for us to buy. Weird stuff.'

'What sort of weird?' Luke asked.

Mona shrugged. Her loquaciousness suddenly seeming to desert her.

'Witchcraft? Satanism? Sex stuff?' Esme began listing things that Mona might class as 'weird'.

'No, not porn. I don't think, anyway. Old books.' Mona held her hands up, indicating size. 'Big ones. Like from a wizard film.'

'Or a museum,' Luke said.

'I suppose,' Mona said, not sounding sure. 'I'm not

really supposed to handle the special stock. They can be really old.'

'What did he do with them?'

Mona sat forward. 'I can tell you one thing. He took some of them home. He made a right fuss about not touching them and how valuable and rare et cetera, and then he would stroll out of there at closing with a couple in a Tesco bag.'

Esme could feel Luke looking at her, but she kept her eyes on Mona. She was thinking about Fraser from the Dundee bookshop. He had burned alive in his own home. Was that because he had taken some books home? And one of them had been hexed?

'Book people really love books,' Luke was saying. 'You don't run a bookshop in this economic climate without being a big reader.'

'Aye, it was just he made such a fuss about being careful.'

'You never heard of anything in a book hurting anyone?'

Mona frowned at Esme as if she had sprouted a second head. 'What do you mean?'

'Toxins on the cover, maybe? Someone reacting badly? We were sent a book recently that wasn't safe to touch without gloves.' This was the story she and Luke had agreed upon on their way to the city. 'Toxins' sounded more plausible than 'cursed'.

'I have to wear white gloves when I'm handling the really old stuff because oils in the skin can ruin the leather or make the pages disintegrate. But that's me damaging the books, not the other way around. They have to be packed really carefully when they're sent out, too.'

'You sell online?'

Mona looked at Luke as if he was stupid. 'I put the

customer database in. Before I arrived, Conrad was using a notebook. Writing things down by hand.' These last words as if Conrad had been carving accounts details into stone using ancient cuneiform.

'Was that still kept at the shop?'

'The ledger? Dunno.'

Luke sank back in his seat, but Esme thought he was missing the obvious. 'The database? It's in the cloud, I assume?'

'Yeah,' Mona bent down and pulled a slim laptop from her bag. 'I can show you it if you like. Well. Not customer details, of course, they're covered by data privacy, but I can show you the system if you're interested.' She glanced at Luke. 'And if you're in the market, I can do an install freelance.'

'Ours are in there, though? My shop's address, I mean. I can see that?'

Mona was concentrating on her screen, but she nodded. 'Yeah. I guess that's okay.'

The door to the café opened and a couple of women came in. One had a sleeping baby in a sling.

'Got it,' Mona said and turned the laptop around to show Luke and Esme.

The database had tabs along the bottom, but the screen was filled with an open window showing a single entry. It gave Esme a prickling sensation in her palms to see Unholy Island's address in black and white type on a stranger's screen.

'You said you've worked there for a year or so?'

Mona nodded. 'Owner wanted to step back. He hadn't been so well, I think, and wanted to take more time. He's in New Zealand, now, I think I said on the phone...'

'You did,' Luke confirmed.

'I've got a note that you're interested in magical texts.

What's that? Like Wiccan stuff?' Mona didn't pause to let them answer. 'I'm not great at the sourcing, I'll admit. The folk who want to offload stuff are irritating as hell. They want wads of cash and don't seem to understand the margins in this business.' She raised an eyebrow at Luke. 'You get it, right?'

'Do you hear from the other shops on this list?' Luke angled his phone so that Mona could see the file.

'Mebbe. Probably. Conrad dealt with that stuff.'

'But you're running the place now,' Esme said, trying to sound encouraging.

'Until I've saved up enough for my own trip,' Mona said.

'Have you had any deliveries from a shop in York? The Shambles Emporium?'

'Mebbe,' Mona said again. She sat back. 'I'll be honest with you guys, I've kind of been a wee bit overwhelmed. Since Conrad took off. There have been a few stock deliveries and I just bunged them out the back.'

'Do you mind if we take a look?' Esme asked.

'I was expecting something from the York shop and wondered if it got sent to you by mistake,' Luke said. He smiled winningly at Mona, who straightened up in response.

'You're welcome to take a look.' She looked at her watch and sighed. 'I should probably get back there, anyway.'

CAMPBELL & SONS was a traditional second-hand bookshop with floor to ceiling shelves and narrow corridors formed from multiple bookcases. It also clearly carried high-end, antiquarian stock, as the shelves were distinctly lacking in blockbuster thrillers or brightly covered romcoms. Instead, the shelves were lined with clothbound spines, the kind that you saw in the libraries of stately homes, oversized art books with colourful plates, and an impressive collection of antique maps.

Luke would have happily spent a few hours browsing, but he stayed on mission. He wasn't sure if Mona would baulk at letting a complete stranger look through the shop's deliveries, but he was relieved that she hadn't unpacked anything recently. The hexed book had been sent from the Shambles Emporium and that meant there was a possibility – however small – that something dangerous might have been sent here, as well.

'Conrad deserved a wee break, that's true. He's been running this place for sixty years, but I wish he had given me some notice. He just upped and went. Didn't even say goodbye, just left me a note saying that I was in charge while he was away and that I could leave the place closed on my days off. That means it's only open half the week and it's no like the margins are exactly huge to start with.'

Sixty years. Luke imagined a frail old man opening a book like the one that had floored him. The guy would be dead in hours. Maybe minutes.

Mona led the way through to the back of the shop. There was a flimsy-looking door marked 'staff' and she pushed it open to reveal a large cupboard. There was metal shelving along one wall and a narrow table at the back and, at one time, you could probably have got a couple of people comfortably inside the remaining space. Now, however, it was filled with packaging materials and unopened boxes.

'Conrad handled all of this. I wasn't even supposed to come in here. I don't know what he wants me to do now. He hasn't said and I haven't exactly been badgering him for extra work.'

'Fair enough,' Luke said. He was scanning the visible

address labels on the first boxes. 'I assume the ones closest will be the most recent? Do you mind if I...'

'Knock yourself out,' Mona said.

Esme asked Mona about living in Edinburgh, leading her a few steps away from the open cupboard, so that Luke could look at the boxes.

It didn't take long. 'I've got it,' he said, appearing with a cardboard box the size of a decent dictionary. He had ripped open the plastic bag stuck to the outside of the package and was holding it up as evidence. 'This was sent from the Shambles two weeks ago. It's got the contents listed, along with the value.'

He passed the paper to Mona, who glanced at it quickly. 'And you want it?' She read the title of the book. 'A Complete History of the Scottish Witch Trials, 1590-1662' and then raised her eyes to Esme. 'Jeezy peeps. That's gonnae be a depressing read.'

Esme nodded her agreement, but her focus was on Luke. He looked shaken, and she understood how he felt. Neither of them had truly expected to find another delivery from the bookshop in York. Especially now that they knew it had burned down. She wondered if they ought to tell Mona about the fire.

'It's got twenty-five quid listed as the value,' Mona said, still looking at the delivery note. 'I don't know if that was what Conrad had agreed to pay or whether he's already transferred the money. I can look through the accounts...'

'Don't go to any trouble,' Luke said. 'How about I give you forty quid for it now? Cash.'

Mona's eyes lit up. 'Works for me.'

Luke handed over two twenties and they made to leave.

'You don't want to open the box and check it?' Mona

hesitated with the cash in her hand, as if suddenly realising how oddly they were behaving.

'Happy to take the chance,' Luke said cheerfully, hustling toward the door.

'He likes to live dangerously,' Esme said. 'Thanks so much for your time. We'll let you get on.'

As Mona walked with them to the front of the shop, Esme asked: 'What will happen to this place if you go?'

Mona shrugged. 'I don't know whether he cares anymore.'

'Conrad is very hands off, then. Now he's on his big trip?'

'Haven't heard a thing,' Mona said cheerfully enough.

LEAVING the old bookshop felt like breaking the surface of a warm pool, the cold air slapping her skin. Esme looked at the cobbled street that curved away, the brightly painted shop fronts and the wide pavement filled with so many people. She was dizzy with the varying faces and bodies, so many strangers, flowing around and past and away from her all at once. A sea without a shore. A sea without the ordering regularity of waves and tide. Her head spun a little, and she dropped her gaze to the grey slabs of the pavement.

A touch on her arm brought her back to reality. Luke's face was peering down from his great height and the sight of something known and safe cleared her head. The buzzing receded and she managed a smile.

'Are you all right?'

She realised it wasn't the first time he had spoken. 'Just dizzy for a second.' She gestured with one hand, her fingers fluttering.

His smile widened in understanding, enthusiasm radiating. 'It's a bit different to the island.' He inhaled deeply, as if trying to assimilate the city into himself.

Esme's stomach was cold and hard with the realisation that he loved this place. He loved this bustle and noise, these tall buildings, these crowds.

On the way home, Esme stared out of the window and wondered whether they had done enough to warn Mona. She felt protective of the young woman, and a little envious of her seemingly boundless energy. Had Esme ever been that vibrant? Mona couldn't be more than six or seven years younger than Esme, but she made her feel tired and old. Had Ryan sucked up her life force? Made her old before her time?

'Are you okay?'

Luke was driving the way he had on the way up to Edinburgh: eyes on the road and with focused attention. Esme liked this about him. She didn't know if he was always a conscientious driver, but either way she appreciated it. Safety was an underrated quality in her opinion.

'I can hear you thinking,' he said now, hitting the stick to make the wipers work faster. The noise seemed louder than it should have done and Esme was suddenly aware of the small space they were occupying. With the rain pouring down the glass and the half-light of the early dusk. It was dark in the car and it felt like a cocoon for the two of them. Inside in the warm and dry, with the noise of the wipers and the heater blowing hot air onto their feet. 'Just wondering what we can do next.'

He rolled his shoulders as if they felt stiff. 'I'm looking forward to a beer and a bath.'

'With bubbles?' She had meant to be teasing, but now she was imagining a naked Luke lying in a scented bubble bath, and that wasn't helpful for making conversation. Or sense. Thanking all the goddesses it was dark in the car and Luke wouldn't see her flaming face even if he did look away from the road, Esme tried to steer the conversation onto firmer ground. 'I meant about the hexed book. We know the Shambles Bookshop sent something to the Edinburgh shop as well as us. I mean, it might not be hexed, but it's a bit of a coincidence.'

'We'll check it,' Esme said. 'Carefully.'

'It does point us straight back to the Shambles Bookshop. Which is gone. Along with the owner.' He frowned. 'It feels like we need to find out more about him and what he had going on. But we can't exactly phone up the police and ask for information.'

'A clue,' Esme agreed. 'We could use one of those.'

'If we assume that whoever sent the book knows what they are doing, then it follows they know about magic stuff. Do you know any other witches?'

'I didn't know they existed until I arrived on the island. And since then, I haven't been a social butterfly.'

'Butterflies are overrated,' he said. 'Although it would be handy now, if you had an address book full of likely suspects.'

'This is very surreal,' Esme mused. 'Suspects. Clues.'

'Magic,' Luke said, and she could see the corners of his mouth lift.

She took his point. There were more surreal things in their lives on a daily basis. 'Somehow, I accept everything when I'm home. It's just reality. It feels a bit weird seen from this perspective.'

'You think the wards have an effect on our brains?'

'I don't know. Or just the atmosphere of the island. Or maybe it's because it's all there. Our minds don't bother worrying about it being odd or unusual because it's happening. I don't know if that makes any sense...'

'It does. There would be no point freaking out because it is what it is.' The wipers' rhythmic movement was soothing. 'It is what it is,' he repeated, as if testing whether the phrase worked.

'And now we're here, in...' Esme peered ahead looking for a handy sign, 'wherever we are, it's hitting me how weird the island truly is.'

'Northumberland,' Luke said. 'We crossed the border ten minutes ago.'

Esme checked the time. 'We're cutting it fine for the causeway.' It occurred to her that if they missed the window, they would be stuck on the mainland for the night. The thought of having to find a bed-and-breakfast, of their day trip being forcibly extended, held a pleasant charge of excitement.

'We'll make it,' Luke said, sounding determined and confident.

Esme's hopes that he might have also been harbouring secret hopes of being stuck out for longer deflated.

CHAPTER FIFTEEN

Having crossed the causeway in the last few minutes before the official timing, Luke had been very aware of the black water creeping toward the road surface. It wasn't close, of course, not really. The official crossing times gave plenty of leeway to ensure that casual visitors weren't caught out. The reasoning went, if you say it's safe to cross until half past six, there will always be an idiot who tries their luck at six-forty-five. Which meant that locals knew that there was wiggle room around the official times. But also to respect the sea. The tide could move with ferocious speed, swallowing the sand faster than the mind could believe.

As usual, he left his car in the car park at the edge of the island. The night was crisp, but not entirely dry. The island air had its usual dash of salt water, and the scent of ozone that made him think of wide-open skies that Luke now knew was particular to the place.

He and Esme chatted easily enough on the way back to Strand House, but he felt the difference as soon as they had left the car. Or, maybe even as they had crossed the causeway and landed on familiar land.

He wondered what would have happened if they had been too late to cross. A cosy dinner in a restaurant and a night in a hotel might have been the time together needed for them to move things forward. He wanted to know if Esme felt the same way about him as he felt about her, but he also knew that she was very cautious.

The islanders weren't gossips, but he had picked up enough to know that Esme had been in a bad relationship in the past. And that was on top of her time in the foster system. He didn't have to be the king of sensitivity to know that Esme was gun-shy.

Speaking to Mona had been like the times he had interviewed people in his search for Lewis. Searching for hints of his brother's whereabouts. But it had been different, too. Being with Esme, part of a team rather than alone, had been surprisingly pleasant.

He was distracted from his thoughts by Esme gasping. They were almost at Strand House, but Esme's gaze was directed down the lane that led toward the bay. A four-by-four was parked outside the wrecked cottages.

Without conferring, Esme walked past her house, heading for the mayor's.

'It will be a mistake,' Luke said. 'A visitor will have left their car there by accident.'

Esme didn't answer. She couldn't have explained to Luke why she was certain she would find Kate Foster in Tobias's living room.

She knocked and then opened the door, not waiting for Tobias. 'May I come in?' She called as she stepped over the threshold. Esme had always been polite and would never have dreamed of walking into the mayor's home like this before. She didn't know what had gotten into her, only that energy was fizzing through her veins and her body seemed to have a mind of its own and that mind was propelling her to the living room door.

'Esme,' Tobias said as she walked in. 'And Luke. You're just in time to meet our new resident.'

Luke frowned but stuck his hand out. 'Hello.'

Kate Foster was standing near the fireplace, looking just as perfect as she had on her last visit to the island. Her hair, if anything, was even more glossy and luscious than before and her eyes were lined with the thickest, darkest eyelashes that Esme had ever seen in real life.

Kate licked her lips as she took in the sight of Luke Taylor. Esme didn't blame her, of course, the woman was only human, but she also wanted to throw up. *Of course* Kate Foster liked what she saw. And no doubt the feeling would be mutual.

'I run the bookshop,' Luke was saying, seemingly oblivious to the new woman who was shamelessly looking him up and down.

'And you remember Esme,' Tobias said, ever the gentleman.

Kate's gaze flicked briefly in Esme's direction and then returned to ogling Luke.

'So, it appears that the cottages were available for sale,' Tobias added.

'What?' Esme asked, only trusting herself with single words.

'The deeds were held in trust. I found the executor of the trust, the beneficiary has long since passed away, and paid cash. As the sum offered was market value it was considered in the best interests of the trust, so all above board.'

Esme's confusion must have shown on her face, as Tobias explained. 'Trustees have an obligation to protect the trust and must act accordingly when evaluating changes.' He frowned at Kate. 'I'm surprised there wasn't a stipulation in the will that the cottages and land could not be sold.'

'I haven't bought the land.' For the first time, Kate looked annoyed. 'Just a one-hundred-year leasehold on the cottages themselves.'

'Why?' Tobias's voice was very calm and Esme didn't know how he managed it.

'I like a project.'

'But why here? You've never been here before. You don't know the place at all.'

'I told you, my friend came here for a walk and he told me...'

'That doesn't make any sense.' Esme found she couldn't stop speaking, even though Tobias was frowning slightly. She knew her voice had become higher, and that she was in danger of sounding panicked. 'Nobody buys property just like that.'

'Some people clearly do,' Tobias said mildly. 'I assume that Ms Foster-'

'Kate, please.'

'That Kate has financial resources that enable her to take on a renovation project while not needing to live in the project or require it to produce income. At least not in,' he coughed delicately, 'physical reality. Strictly speaking.'

'I don't understand.' Esme was pleased her voice was back at its usual pitch. She was the island's witch and it was unseemly to display anxiety in front of a complete stranger.

'He thinks I'm buying a tax write-off. Or something to launder cash.' Her lips were pursed and there was a light in her eyes. Esme wasn't sure if she was offended or amused.

Tobias shrugged. 'Forgive me. If you live for as long as I

have, you see all kinds of things.' He paused before speaking again. 'And, I notice, you haven't denied it.'

Kate smiled thinly. 'I don't think my financial affairs are any of your business. Mayor.' The air quotes were loud and clear.

'Quite.' Tobias clapped his hands together. 'Who would like a cup of tea? Or something stronger, perhaps.'

After Kate had left, saying that she was going to take stock of the situation in her new property, Esme turned to Tobias. Her heart was hammering and she hated her reaction. She had been given sanctuary on the island. She ought not deny it to another person. Especially a woman. Who knew what pain or fear Kate was hiding beneath her shiny exterior?

'How could she have purchased the cottages?'

'The leasehold? I don't know.'

'I thought... I don't know what I thought. But it's the island.' Esme was struggling to articulate what she felt instinctively. 'Who could she have bought the cottages *from*?'

'She brought paperwork. Apparently, the deeds for the cottages were held in a trust. I didn't recognise the names, but it had been left to the trust in a bequest over three hundred years ago. The executor of the trust is the solicitor handling the estate.'

'Did you know about it? The trust?'

Tobias shook his head, clearly uncomfortable. 'I haven't always tracked every little detail.'

Ownership of buildings on the island didn't seem like little details to Esme, but she kept her mouth closed. Tobias looked miserable enough.

'There have been times when I have been tired or even

asleep,' he was saying, gazing into the fire and not meeting Esme's eye. 'There are many things I have missed over the years.'

After a short pause, Esme spoke, injecting as much lightness into her tone as possible. 'She might still forget all about her plans. Perhaps she'll go home, wherever that is, and mislay the paperwork.'

Tobias gave her a small grateful smile. 'Maybe.'

'Unholy Island is a special place. It's not like just anybody can buy a piece of it.' Esme hoped that was true.

CHAPTER SIXTEEN

When Esme opened her door the next morning, she didn't expect to see Fiona standing on her step. She felt a rush of happiness at the sight of the older woman, along with confusion. Fiona was holding a small child in her arms. A baby, really. Esme didn't have much experience with infants, but he couldn't be much more than a year old.

'I just wanted to let you know we're back.'

They weren't huggers, neither woman being big on physical contact, but Esme put as much warmth into her voice as she could. 'Who is this?'

'Hamish.'

'Hello, Hamish.' Esme smiled and hoped the child wouldn't start crying. She had always had bad luck with small children in the past, but Hamish twisted in Fiona's arms and stared frankly at her. His expression was serious, but he wasn't crying, so that was a start.

'He's my niece's boy. And he's here for a lovely holiday.' She jiggled the boy in her arms. 'Aren't you, Hamish?'

'Did you want to come in for tea?'

'Better not. Euan's gone on to the cottage and I don't want him on his own there.'

First time seeing the place where his stepfather had attacked him. Esme nodded her understanding. 'How is he doing?'

Fiona pulled a face. 'I don't know. He doesn't seem upset at all about Oliver, which is pretty worrying. I don't want him to bottle it all up. He won't talk about it, though. I know it's partly his age... This is a tricky time for... People like us.'

'I don't know anything about it,' Esme said. 'But I'm happy to learn. And I'm always here to listen.'

'Thank you.' Fiona nodded briskly. 'I'd better go. Will you spread the word for me? Tell everyone not to make a fuss?'

'Of course. Goodbye, Hamish.'

The boy's face crumpled and Esme thought he was going to start crying.

Fiona jiggled him again until he looked at her.

'But first, we're going to see Seren and see if she can find us some biscuits.'

The boy brightened and he pointed over Fiona's shoulder.

'Yes, that way. Clever wee man.'

'See you later?' She said to Esme, distracted.

'Of course. Do you need anything?'

'No, we're good.' Fiona was already walking away.

'Welcome home,' Esme called after her.

Once Fiona had gone, Esme called around the villagers and passed on the message. Everyone was to act completely normal, as if she and Euan hadn't been away. Esme added her own instruction - that nobody was to mention Oliver.

. . .

Luke hadn't slept well. It wasn't just the presence of the package from Campbell & Sons. He had stored the maybe-hexed-book in the fire-safe metal box along with the dehexed book that had done its best to kill him, and there was no logical reason to believe it would suddenly 'activate' or whatever the right word was, but he still felt uneasy. Plus, there was the upset of the newcomer, Kate Foster, and the nagging feeling that he had messed up with Esme somehow. He had enjoyed being in Edinburgh with her and thought they had got on well, but something seemed to change when they came back from the mainland. He had become distracted with thoughts of Lewis, he knew that, but then Esme had seemed distant, too, and he hadn't known how to bring back the easy intimacy they had enjoyed while interviewing Mona.

Now, he stood in the doorway of Bee's house and asked about the supplies for dehexing the new book.

'How do you know it's hexed?'

'We don't. But Esme said that if we did the ritual and it worked, we would know it had been hexed. And we would have fixed it at the same time. Two stones, one...'

'It takes blood,' Bee said. Her silver hair had plaits running along the sides of her head with the back loose. It was the style that made her look like a warrior or goddess from Norse mythology and her expression at this moment matched perfectly. 'That's not something to be done lightly.'

'No.'

Bee pursed her lips. 'We'll take a look at it first and then decide what to do.'

Having instructed them to meet her at the northern end of Coire Bay, Luke passed the message to Esme. An hour later, they stood together at the rocks of the beach ward, feeling a little like children who were about to be told off. 'Did she seem angry?' Esme asked, not for the first time.

'You know Bee,' Luke said. 'She can be quite scary. She's probably just concerned.'

They watched the figure approach. In deference to the cold weather, Bee had added a thick woollen jumper underneath her ubiquitous denim dungarees and was wearing black wellington boots and a knitted hat.

'What were you thinking?' She asked Esme the moment she came close. 'Bringing problems from the mainland?'

'It was my idea,' Luke said. 'I didn't want anyone else to get hurt the way I did. I know I'm lucky to be alive.'

Bee ignored him. 'We are a place of sanctuary. We don't go looking for trouble.'

'Alvis traded with other bookshops, it's part of being the Book Keeper. Luke needs to do the same and he can't do that if all the other shops have been burned to the ground.'

Luke looked at her in surprise. He felt like he wanted to curl up in the face of Bee's disapproval, but Esme was holding her gaze steadily.

After a moment, Bee nodded. 'Well, then. Let's take a look.'

'I'll do it,' Luke said.

'No.' Esme pulled a pair of rubber gloves out of her coat pocket. 'I will. Find me a stick.'

Bee nodded her approval as Esme unlocked the metal box. 'Do you know why I told you to come here?'

'Less likely to start a wildfire on the beach?' Luke said. He passed a stick to Esme, worn smooth from the sea.

'The ward,' Esme said. 'For protection.'

'Exactly so,' Bee nodded. She dropped into a squat and peered at the package.

Esme opened the cardboard box, revealing a hardback text book that looked like it came from the sixties or seventies. It had lurid colour-printing on a glossy cover that had faded to a strange orangey-tinge.

'Careful,' Luke said.

Esme didn't look up from her task. She hadn't touched the book itself, yet, only the cardboard packaging. Now she straightened up and used the stick to flick open the front cover. The sea breeze riffled the edge of the pages as if trying to turn them.

Bee was watching Esme intently. 'Now look. Just like we've practised.'

Esme closed her eyes. When she opened them, she looked the same to Luke, but her body had gone very still. He could feel her concentrating as she stared at the book.

'I'm not sure,' Esme said after a long moment.

'Don't think. Just look.'

'Pestilence,' Esme said immediately.

Bee nodded in approval. 'The witch has spoken.'

'It's hexed?' Luke's mouth was suddenly dry. A gull screeched up above as if voicing his own discomfort.

'It looked like tiny black flies. Just for a second.'

'We can assume it's cursed,' Bee said. 'So, we need to lock that box and make sure nobody stumbles across it. I have a cellar.'

'I will keep it in the stockroom of the shop. It's not going to burst into flames spontaneously.'

'As far as we know. That seems dangerous.'

'He's right,' Bee said. 'And I'm not asking Diana for another blood sacrifice. Not when I would have to explain

that you two fools brought the damn thing to our doorstep.'
But she smiled as she spoke and Luke felt the knots of
tension in his neck loosen.

CHAPTER SEVENTEEN

Esme would not admit to herself that she was nervous to see Euan. Walking along the shore, she saw his familiar figure and she continued on her course. The shock at his appearance was hard to hide. Euan's soft young features had been transformed into something angular. More jarring than the accelerated puberty, however, were his eyes. With no white visible at all, the boy's eyes looked entirely a dark polished brown. The sun went behind a cloud and his eyes looked black. Esme realised she had taken a step back in shock.

'It's me,' Euan said.

His sweet, uncertain smile completely disarmed Esme. She couldn't remember seeing the boy smile before and she wondered if it was the effect of the physical changes or being free of his stepfather. 'Welcome home,' she said. 'Did you have a good trip?'

He ducked his head. 'We saw where mum grew up. On Orkney.'

Esme was about to ask about seeing family but she stopped herself. She knew all too well that family could be a touchy subject. She would wait to see if Euan mentioned them spontaneously. 'Cool,' she said instead. And then wanted to smack her forehead. She was acting the quintessential awkward adult.

'We went into the water at the Sands of Evie.' Euan's expression was dreamy and he turned his head to stare out at the sea, as if unable to look away from it for long.

'Well, we're happy you're both back.'

When Euan didn't seem about to respond, Esme set off again. 'See you later.'

He glanced back, his eyes looking more normal again, and Esme wondered if it was something under his control. She had never seen Fiona's eyes change, so perhaps it was something that happened when their kind were young.

'You are nice,' he said.

'I hope so,' Esme replied. She wanted to say something more significant. Something that encompassed everything he had gone through, something to let him know that she was available if he ever wanted to talk. But he had already turned back to the sea and the words wouldn't come.

ISLAND MEETINGS TOOK place at The Rising Moon, which meant that everyone had just eaten a good dinner. Luke didn't know what this meeting was about and hadn't had time to ask anybody beforehand. He had spent the day contacting bookshops listed in the secret 'crescent moon' ledger and trying to work out whether there was anything that linked them, other than being bookshops.

His mind had been running over his research and the gnawing guilt that he had swapped his obsession with finding his brother for a new project. And that he wasn't feeling anywhere near bad enough about it. Tobias was standing and talking for a few minutes before Luke properly tuned into the subject. Kate Foster. The woman who had visited the island a couple of weeks ago and asked about the dilapidated cottages near to Esme's place, had returned.

'She proposes to renovate the cottage on the end in the first instance, but has plans for the other two later on. They are in an even worse state, but she intends to rent out the renovated cottage to summer visitors to raise the capital to renovate the others.'

'Well, that's not going to work,' Seren said. 'What about the two-night rule?'

Tobias nodded and then looked around the room. 'Any more thoughts? The floor is open.'

Luke wasn't going to open his mouth. He was still a newcomer, he knew, and he wasn't about to rock the boat.

'How does she even remember the island?'

It was the question that everyone was thinking, but Esme was the one to voice it.

Tobias shook his head. 'I have no idea, I'm afraid. We,' he indicated Bee, 'had hoped that you might have some thoughts.'

Esme's cheeks flushed and she shook her head.

'The cottages are a wreck,' Fiona said. 'It might not be a bad thing to have them looked after.' Hamish was sitting on her lap, gazing around the room with wide eyes, one hand firmly wedged into his mouth and a trail of dribble running off his chin. 'We might need some more accommodation in the future. If our community expands.'

'Euan might want his own place one day,' Esme said. 'We want him to be able to find that on the island.'

Fiona smiled at the other woman and nodded.

Matteo wrote on his pad and slid it across to Seren, who read it and passed it on. When it got to Luke, he read: *Is it just business? Does she plan to move here?*

After Tobias had seen the question, he said, 'I believe

she wishes to use one of the cottages as a holiday home.' He pulled a wry smile.

Seren tapped the table. 'We don't need to worry about any of that. She will forget about this idea, about the island soon enough. People say things all the time.' She looked around, challenging somebody to argue with her assessment. 'I serve visitors and they often say stuff like 'it's so peaceful I could stay a week' or 'we must come back', but they never do.'

'What do you think?' Tobias looked at Esme. 'You're our Ward Witch. Do you have any... sense about this new person?'

Esme looked uncomfortable 'Nothing concrete,' she said after a few moments. 'Perhaps if I speak to her again?'

That seemed to pretty much end the discussion. Luke and Esme walked out with Fiona, who wanted to get Hamish home for bed.

'Thank you,' Fiona said. 'For thinking about Euan's future.'

'It's only right he should have a place of his own,' Esme said. 'It's strange to think of him growing up, though. Must be even weirder for you.'

'It is and it isn't. On one hand, he'll always be my baby,' she hefted Hamish a little higher in her arms as she spoke, 'but he's also a person. And so clearly growing up that it's impossible not to see him as he is. If that makes sense.'

'It does,' Esme said. 'You just have to hold more than one idea of him in your mind at all times.'

'Exactly.' Fiona laughed. 'I was worried I was babbling nonsense. I'm a bit sleep deprived.'

'How is his mum doing?' Luke asked.

'Good,' Fiona said. 'She's out of hospital and recovering well.' Her face had fallen, though, and Luke felt like he had put his foot in it.

. . .

AFTER THE MEETING had adjourned and the islanders dispersed, and Seren had disappeared into the kitchen to clear up, Bee turned to Tobias. There was something weighing on her conscience. Lucy had told her something was coming to the island and she hadn't stopped it. The Book Keeper had been hexed, he had almost died. People did die, of course, but this wouldn't have been a natural death. 'What do you think?'

'About the renovations or the woman?'

'Kate Foster. How does she remember the island? We know Esme has been keeping the wards.'

'Our Book Keeper was close to crossing over,' Tobias said. 'Very close.'

'You think the island got confused? Opened up a vacancy and then Luke recovered?'

'Not confused, but maybe cautious.'

'Allowed Kate Foster to remember us as a backup to fill the role of Book Keeper, you mean? Like an understudy?'

He shrugged. 'She does seem very drawn to the bookshop.'

Bee allowed herself a wry smile. 'Perhaps that's got something to do with the god-like man behind the counter?'

'God-like?' Tobias looked both confused and affronted.

'My deepest apologies,' Bee said. 'Too much time on the road. I meant fine-looking. Pleasing on the eye. Good husband material.'

'I see,' Tobias's face had cleared. He nodded thoughtfully. 'I do tend to overlook those kinds of things. It's good you see more clearly.'

'Most of the time,' Bee said, taking the compliment. It didn't soothe her feeling of being off-kilter, though. 'I haven't made as much progress with Esme as I had hoped. And I didn't see the evil that came for our Book Keeper.'

'Didn't see or didn't look?'

Bee nodded to accept the fairness of the question. 'The latter,' she admitted.

'That's all right, then,' Tobias said, patting her hand. 'Just because you are capable of something doesn't mean you have a moral obligation to do it.'

'Even if it could save lives?' Bee hadn't meant to say the words, but Alvis's death was still weighing on her mind. Guilt was an entirely new and unwelcome addition to her repertoire. Too much time around humanity.

'You know that's not true. Not in the end,' Tobias said. 'Everybody dies. Even us.'

She caught a heavy undercurrent to his words. 'Are you feeling well?'

'Perfectly.' His eyes flicked to Winter, sleeping in front of the pub fire. The dog's sides were shuddering as if his breathing was laboured.

Bee didn't know what to say. She knew that Tobias had been alive for a very long time and the wits to know how deeply lonely such an existence must be. But she also didn't know how a being like Tobias suffered frailties like loneliness or grief. Perhaps, like her, he had spent too much time with the human islanders.

She was saved from deep conversational waters by Tobias clapping his hands together. 'Tea,' he said. 'If you'd like to join me back at the house? I do believe I have half a fruit cake in the tin.'

CHAPTER EIGHTEEN

Nothing had been decided in the meeting, but the fact remained that Kate Foster had purchased the cottages and her large vehicle was now parked outside them for all the island to see.

Seren reported to Fiona and Esme that she had seen Kate unload supplies from her car, including a Calor gas stove, a sleeping bag, and several suitcases.

'I wonder if there's even electricity to the place,' Esme said. 'I didn't see any lights this morning on my way over here.'

Euan had joined them from the back room, where Esme presumed he had been having a reunion with the ancient Space Invaders machine. Instead, he was carrying Hamish in his arms and looking every part the responsible adult. She still couldn't get over how much he seemed to have grown up in the time he had been away with Fiona. She wondered if it was just the way growth spurts always worked, or whether it was a kind of physiological response to no longer living in misery.

The baby was holding a plastic giraffe in one small fist.

He raised it to his mouth and gave it a good chew while staring around the room.

'What a poppet,' Seren said, running her hand over Hamish's hair. 'Can I hold him?'

Euan looked at Fiona, who nodded. Then he transferred Hamish to Seren, looking a little bereft to have lost his companion.

Hamish took one look at Seren and opened his mouth to wail, his face flushing red. He dropped his giraffe and Euan bent to retrieve the toy.

'Oops,' Seren said. 'You'd better have him back.' She passed the incensed Hamish back to Euan and he instantly stopped crying.

'You've got the magic touch,' Seren said to Euan.

'He likes me,' Euan said, and there was a touch of wonder in his voice that made Esme's heart clench.

'What can I get you? Do you need anything for the wee man?'

'Could you warm this up?' Fiona passed across a plastic tub. 'Just a minute in the micro.'

'I think I can manage that.' Seren shot a longing glance at Hamish. 'Maybe if I provide food, he'll decide I'm not the Antichrist.'

Fiona laughed. 'He's at the attachment stage. Don't take it personally.'

'I'm going to show him the invaders again,' Euan said, carrying Hamish away to the back room.

Fiona watched them go before asking: 'So, what else have I missed?'

'All the usual excitements,' Esme said lightly. She didn't want to talk about Luke's brush with death or think about hexed books. And Fiona had said she didn't want to talk about Oliver, but Esme wanted there to be space in the conversation in case she changed her mind. 'Tobias wore a dark green tweed on Sunday.'

Seren joined in, picking up on Esme's cue to keep it breezy. 'Never thought I would see the man forsake his trusty brown, but there you go, just shows you never really know anybody...' She trailed off as if realising the awkwardness of that statement in front of Fiona.

'It's all right, hen,' Fiona said. 'Pour us a whisky and we'll toast my ex. Then we'll not speak of him again.'

Seren went behind the bar as Esme and Fiona took seats on the stools. She pulled out the good stuff and poured small measures. Esme was relieved as she hadn't eaten since an early breakfast and would be in danger of getting instantly drunk.

Fiona lifted her glass and, making eye contact with Esme and then Seren, she said: 'Good riddance, Oliver. Don't haste ye back.'

With thoughts of Hallows Eve and restless spirits returning to the world when the veil was thin, Esme had to hide a shudder by taking a bigger mouthful than she had intended. Any tension was broken as the other two women laughed and thumped her back while she coughed and spluttered.

ESME WALKED BACK to Strand House with the pleasant buzz of the alcohol warming her chest and stomach. The weather was turning, the sea looking blacker by the second. She was just approaching her front door when a voice hailed her from the path. Kate Foster. The woman who ought to have forgotten all about the island the moment she returned to the mainland.

'I keep getting turned around in this place,' Kate said, pushing a strand of honey blonde hair out of her eyes.

Her smile was crooked, a little uncertain. It was endearing, but something about it made Esme think she was working at being endearing. She shoved the uncharitable thought down and smiled back at the woman. 'We don't get many visitors at this time of year.' She gestured at the darkening sky. 'It's not very inviting.'

'I'm not a visitor anymore. I'm going to live here.'

'The cottages don't seem to be very habitable,' Esme said. It was the most neutral thing she could think of to say. Her mind still couldn't accept that Kate Foster had wandered into their community so easily. She had already checked the wards, but she vowed she would go out and check them again. Weather be damned.

'That's why I'm renovating,' Kate said. She gave a fake little chuckle.

'Right. Yes.' The sky was the colour of iron, now, and a stiff breeze was buffeting them both where they stood.

'I know it's a big job and I will probably have to live off site while the roof is being replaced. Perhaps I'll stay at your little B and B.'

Esme wanted to say 'like hell you will'. But that was unwelcoming. Just because Kate Foster was beautiful and confident and had, somehow, thwarted the island's wards, didn't mean Esme had to be hostile. She remembered Bee's teachings. The island provided sanctuary, so perhaps Kate Foster needed it. Her surface confidence could be just that. Surface. Who knew what she was suffering underneath? She forced a smile. 'Would you like to come in for a cup of tea?'

'That's kind, but I don't want to be any trouble.'

'It's no trouble.' Esme's face felt stiff with the effort of forming the polite phrase.

'Maybe another time,' Kate said, her expression

suddenly serious. 'I need to get my steps in.' She flashed her wrist to reveal a bulky smartwatch.

'I wouldn't if I were you,' Esme said. 'Bad weather's coming in.'

Kate flashed a wide smile, showing the kind of even white teeth that belonged on a film poster or toothpaste advert. 'I'm stronger than I look.'

Having gone inside and gathered her supplies, Esme plucked her waterproof from the hook by the door and changed her trainers for walking boots. She took her time, wanting to make sure she wasn't going to instantly bump into Kate Foster again.

She walked her usual route, checking each of the wards carefully. Halfway around the island, the gale force wind was joined with lashing rain. By the time she made it back to the far end of the village, the visibility was atrocious. Winter dark fell fast, and with the dense cloud and driving rain, it was plain miserable.

The lights were on in the bookshop. A warm and inviting glow that spilled onto the wet cobbles of the wynd. Any port in a storm, Esme thought, pushing down the awareness that she must look half-drowned. An image of Kate Foster's stylish clothes and swishy hair flashed into her mind and she pushed that down, too.

The door of the bookshop opened easily, but the wind fought Esme as she tried to close it.

Luke appeared behind her, expressing his dismay. 'Bloody hell, you're soaked.'

Now that she was inside, the warmth making her skin tingle and sting, and the roaring of the wind was turned down a notch, Esme realised just how cold and tired she was. 'It wasn't this bad when I set out.'

'Hang on,' Luke disappeared and she heard his footsteps on the stairs. He returned with a couple of navy-blue towels. 'You need to take your wet stuff off.' He averted his gaze, his cheeks reddening. 'You won't warm up otherwise.'

Trying not to think about it, Esme stripped off her sodden outerwear. The sensible part of her knew that Luke was right. Hypothermia was no joke and her teeth were clattering together unpleasantly. She tried to make a joke about him getting his own back on her, but her voice wouldn't come out steadily.

Luke stepped past her and locked the door. The wind howled in frustration, rattling the glass at the front of the shop.

Esme dried her hands and face and then wrapped the towel around her hair and squeezed. The cotton top she was wearing underneath her jumper was mercifully only a little damp.

Luke disappeared again and she heard the tap go on in the tiny kitchen space. When he returned with a steaming mug, Esme took it gratefully, but the liquid slopped over the edge with a particularly big spasm. He took the mug back and put it onto the counter.

'You're shivering,' he said. 'Come here.'

She took a step toward him as he grabbed a large towel. With one movement, he had wrapped it around her and was rubbing her arms. It wasn't exactly comfortable, but all she could think about was how close they were, and that his hands were on her body. Through layers of clothes and towel, but still. It was possibly the most intimate contact she had experienced with a man for years.

'Better?' He dipped his head to look into her eyes.

She nodded. The shivering had subsided, although she still felt frozen through. He was still very close, his hands on her arms, holding her enveloped in the towel. She took another step closer, feeling the heat coming from his skin. 'Luke...' She didn't know how to follow that and fell quiet. Her voice had sounded strange to her own ears. Husky and full of need.

He lifted his hands from her arms, letting the towel drop to the floor. And then his fingertips were on her face, tracing her cold skin. They sent a trail of fire wherever they touched. Esme knew exactly the last time a man had touched her bare skin in a loving caress, but she couldn't remember a time when it had felt like this. Safe and exciting, all tangled together. She leaned into his touch and he cupped her cheek with his large palm.

He was going to kiss her. She knew it. She could have sworn that the atmosphere between them was actually electric, that there was a faint humming sound at the edge of her hearing. She could feel the heat from his body, see the lines of muscle on his bare arms, the tiny hairs poking through his skin on his jaw and cheeks. Everything was hyperreal and detailed. Very much like the moments before she had a panic attack. Her chest was tight like a panic attack, too, but she didn't think this was fear. Or not just fear.

She wanted him to kiss her. Tilted her head a little in invitation.

He leaned closer, his eyes flicking from her eyes to her lips and back, a questioning look of longing that made her breath stop all together.

And then his lips brushed hers. The gentlest of touches that set every nerve in her body buzzing. She leaned into him, into the kiss, wanting more.

This time, their lips met and it was indescribable. His hand moved from her cheek to the back of her neck, cradling her head, and she felt the size of him. His body was so much larger than hers. His hands could crush her skull.

The thought was intrusive. Unwanted. And definitely unwarranted. Luke was a good man. He would not hurt her.

He pulled back a little. His eyes were filled with desire and happiness, but seeing her expression they changed to concern. His eyebrows drew down, but before he could form a question, Esme was stepping back. His hands slipped from her skin and she was alone in her bubble once again. The cool air forming a barrier around her.

'I'm sorry,' Esme said. Her voice sounded strange. Broken. 'I have to go.'

She turned and fled.

'Wait,' Luke said, following her to the door. 'The weather...'

Esme didn't stop long enough to hear the end of his sentence. She wrenched the door to the bookshop, setting the bell jangling, and rushed into the howling wind.

CHAPTER NINETEEN

Gusts threatened to blow Esme from her feet as she ran, but she made it back to Strand House without incident. Her heart pounded and her breathing felt constricted, but she was safe in her home. She closed the back door and leaned against it, willing her mind to still. She had left her coat at the bookshop and was shivering violently. The combination of freezing air, copious rain and a wicked wind had worked frighteningly quickly.

Her clothes were cold and wet and she knew she needed to change out of them. Jet appeared from underneath the table, tail high in the air and an expression of misery on his face. She dropped to her knees, instantly filled with guilt. Jet hated storms and she had deserted him. She was a terrible cat mother. A terrible terrible person.

Her eyes were stinging from the wind and she didn't realise she was crying until she felt the hot tears on her cold cheeks. She put her face to the soft fur on Jet's head and stroked the length of his back to his tail. 'I'm sorry I wasn't here.'

Jet didn't yowl at her. It was almost as if he knew she

was already at breaking point. Instead, he pressed his head into her cold cheek.

When Esme woke up the next day, the humiliation was just as fresh. The thing she had been longing for had happened. The Viking had kissed her. She hadn't been imagining the way he looked at her, the spark between them, like a lovesick teenager. But that was all ruined now. She had run away from him as if burned. Worse, as if he had done something wrong.

The weather had blown through and sunlight illuminated the pale blue curtains at the bedroom window. Jet was curled up halfway down the bed, fast asleep.

She touched her lips. Luke's lips on hers hadn't been a dream.

Downstairs, swaddled in a dressing gown, she checked her phone. There was a message from Luke. *Are you okay?*

She was relieved he hadn't apologised. He had nothing to be sorry for and it would have made her feel a million times worse. In the light of a new day, she could feel that maybe it was salvageable. After all, they were both adults. She had bolted like a frightened fawn, but she could explain. They could try again, perhaps. She waited for the fear to return, but it didn't. Probably because she was just imagining kissing Luke Taylor and that seemed completely fine in the safety of her own mind. It was the real-life three-dimensional version of the event that sent her into a panic attack. She tapped a quick reply.

I'm fine. Sorry about yesterday.

Then she paused. She pressed the key that would delete the last three words. She was sorry she had run away, but she wasn't sorry they had kissed, and she didn't want him to get the wrong impression. Written words were difficult. Once you had put them down, they were immutable. And subject to misinterpretation. She would let him know she was fine and then go and speak to him in person. She added: *speak later?* And sent the message. Her whole body tingled with an electric charge. Nerves and excitement. Hope and fear.

THE WINTER SUN shone over the water, picking out sparkles amongst the dark grey waves. The sky was a dirty white, and black seabirds stood out against it like type on a manuscript.

Luke huffed in the salt air and stared at the horizon. He was wearing an insulated jacket and felt perfectly comfortable, although the breeze on his face was icy. It had been two weeks since he had been ill and they were no further in their investigation. He had phoned about half of the bookshops in Alvis's journal, but he had lost the will. Without knowing what to ask, the conversations were brief and unhelpful. And many just didn't answer at all, leaving him wondering if they had closed or burned down.

He wanted to stay outside and to keep moving. Needed to work off some energy. The main thing on his mind wasn't the hexed book or the thought of theoretical danger stalking other booksellers. Although he would usually take the route west past Esme's house and onto Coire Bay, he turned east. He didn't want to risk Esme looking out of her window and seeing him. She might feel pressured. If his attention was unwanted, it would be upsetting. He had no wish to act like a stalker. The thought that he might cause her discomfort was physically repellent. He had kissed her and she couldn't have got away from him fast enough. He had crossed a line and broken her trust.

She leaned in, his mind supplied. He had lost count of the number of times he had replayed the scene. She had leaned in. She had stepped closer to him. He knew he hadn't imagined any of that. And he would swear on his life that her eyes had held desire. But none of that mattered. Not when he had clearly moved too quickly. Not when he had done the one thing he had sworn he wouldn't do. His guts twisted in pure misery as he remembered the speed of her leaving. Esme had *run* from him.

He walked to the end of Shell Bay and carried along the coastal path toward the castle, moving at a pace that had him sweating under his jacket.

He had been thinking so deeply that it took him a moment to realise that there was a figure walking towards him.

Kate Foster was dressed in a slim-fitting coat which flared out at the hips, leather gloves, and riding boots. She looked like she had stepped off the front cover of a glossy magazine. 'Morning,' Luke said. He moved to the side of the path to give her plenty of room to pass by, not wanting to appear threatening. He was acutely aware that she was a lone woman in the middle of nowhere and he was a man.

She slowed as she approached and then stepped off the path to join him. 'You're up early.'

'You, too,' Luke said. And then felt, inexplicably, as if he had said something intimate.

'I like to exercise in the morning.' She smiled and maintained eye contact until Luke felt the urge to glance away. 'Sets me up for the day. And this,' she swept an arm indicating the sea view, 'beats the gym.'

'I'll let you get on,' he said and made to move away.

She moved with him. Her hand was on his arm and when he looked down, she was gazing up at him, eyes wide. He didn't consider himself especially arrogant, but he knew when somebody was showing an interest. If they had been in a bar on the mainland, he would think she was coming on to him.

'Did you want to join me for breakfast?'

'I'm walking,' Luke said. Then, knowing he had sounded abrupt, tried to soften it. 'The residents often eat at The Rising Moon. If you want company, there will probably be someone there at lunchtime.' He had been going to say 'or dinner', but he didn't know if Kate was staying on the island. And if she was, how popular that would be with the islanders.

'Will you be there at lunch?' Kate asked, her head tilted and eyes wide.

'I'm working,' he said, instantly scuppering plans for a midday pint.

'Shame,' she said. 'Maybe later, then.'

LUKE WAS STILL WORRYING about Esme, but thoughts of his brother had joined the mix. He felt that he could hear his twin's voice in his head asking why the fuck he was obsessing over Esme Gray. Lewis's message had told him to stop looking, but that didn't let him off the hook. He walked down to the car park, wrestling with his options. One plus side of taking a trip to the mainland would mean he wouldn't bump into Kate Foster again for a few hours.

'You planning a road trip?'

Luke jumped at the sound of Hammer's voice. He turned to find the man glowering at him from the path that led from the car park to the village. 'How the fuck did you know I was here? Do you have me tagged or something?'

Hammer didn't smile as he approached. 'Another attempt at a suicide mission? Not that I care, you understand, but I do like to know what's going on.'

Luke didn't feel like explaining himself to Hammer, but he also didn't have the time or inclination for a physical confrontation. He still didn't feel one hundred per cent from being almost burned to death. And even if he had, he wasn't too proud to concede that Hammer could probably beat him to a pulp and barely break a sweat.

He leaned against his car, facing Hammer. 'I'm trying to find out who sent the cursed book to the shop. I know it sounds mad, but Esme is sure...'

'Cursed book. Made you all sweaty. I heard.'

Luke set his jaw.

'And you want revenge?'

'No.' Luke was surprised to find he was speaking the truth. 'I want to make sure nobody else gets hurt. There was a fire, a bookshop in York burned down.'

'Not our concern,' Hammer said promptly.

'That's what Esme said at first,' Luke replied.

'Well, then. She's got her head screwed on.'

'But I convinced her. It's not like the police will know what to look for. It's our duty.'

'Fuck that,' Hammer said, but the phrase lacked his usual conviction.

'You are welcome to join me if you don't believe me,' Luke said insouciantly and breathed easier when Hammer shook his head.

'Just make sure you don't bring any more shit back here. Right?'

'That's part of it. If I don't find out who sent the book, what's to stop them doing it again? What if next time the shop burns down? I know you don't give a shit if I become a human flare, but Esme and Tobias and Bee would prefer the bookshop stayed intact.'

Hammer paused. His face didn't betray any emotion and for a moment, Luke wasn't sure if he was going to change his mind and accompany him or take a swing. Or maybe a nap. The man had a good line in blank expressions, he had to hand it to him.

'You heard anything else from your brother?'

Luke swallowed. The guilt, never far from the surface, bubbled up in a toxic brew that scalded his insides. 'No.'

Hammer didn't say anything for a long moment. 'You stopped looking.'

'I looked for eighteen months.' Luke wasn't trying to defend himself, but he did, suddenly, want to make Hammer understand. 'I didn't care what happened to me. Not really. It's not like Lewis and I were even close anymore, but I felt like it was my duty. And I didn't have anything else to lose. I do now. I don't want to bring attention here. I don't want to bring trouble here any more than you do.'

Another long pause.

Finally, Hammer spoke. 'Give me your phone.'

'Why?'

'The message. Let me see it.'

Luke unlocked the screen and navigated to the WhatsApp conversation before passing it across.

Hammer read it quickly and then began typing.

'I've tried ringing the number,' Luke said. 'It's never answered. And you can see my reply hasn't been read.'

Hammer shrugged, handing the phone back. 'I need to tell you something. I told Dean Fisher I would keep an eye on you.'

'What?'

153

'I didn't want him sending any more of his people to take a look around.'

Luke wasn't sure how annoyed he was at this revelation. Not very, he decided. He could understand Hammer's reasoning.

'Now you've sent the kind of message they understand.'

Luke unlocked the screen again and read Hammer's reply to Lewis. Or whoever had Lewis's phone.

Send sign of life.

IT TURNED out that walking to the car park and speaking to Hammer about everything he now stood to lose was enough activity to sap Luke's energy. He hated to admit that he still wasn't back to full health, but the pressing exhaustion that had crept over him at the thought of the long drive to York didn't lie. He had walked back to the shop and napped for half an hour to try to clear his pounding headache before opening the shop.

Thankfully, it was a quiet morning. Luke wasn't surprised as the weather had turned from a crisp dawn to a grey and grim day. He remembered days like this from the mainland, when the sky felt as if it was hugging the earth, pressing down. It was different on the island with the ever-changing water and the far horizon, but the lowering cloud was obliterating much of the view and Luke was happy to be inside with the warmth of the shop and the lights gently illuminating the wooden shelves and the colours of the books.

His stomach growled, telling him it was lunchtime. With a brief thought of the venison pie and chips he had promised himself, he went into the tiny room that held a fridge and kettle.

He made a packet soup in a mug and broke off a hunk of cheese from the block of cheddar in the fridge. He had run out of bread, but there was a box of crackers upstairs that would do for now. He nipped upstairs to retrieve them and heard the front door open as he headed back down the stairs.

Kate Foster was walking through the shop, and he paused on the stairs.

'Hello, again,' she smiled up at him, as if he were the best thing she had seen in a week.

He took the last few steps and then crossed to close the door to the back room. Realising he should have put the crackers inside, he turned, feeling self-conscious. He was clearly out of practice to be so thrown by one woman. She was objectively attractive and appeared to be interested in him, which would, historically, have instantly increased her appeal. Now, he felt nothing but irritation at having his lunch delayed and a vague unease.

'Feel free to browse,' he said. 'Unless there's something in particular you're looking for?'

She licked her lips. 'This is a bit awkward, but I was hoping to persuade you to have lunch with me.'

'I'm working,' he gestured to the shop. 'I'm sorry, I thought I said...'

'You did,' she smiled. 'But I hate eating alone and there's no one in the pub. I've been in the cottage all morning and it's a bit overwhelming. I may have bitten off more than I can chew and I'd really appreciate some friendly company.'

He wanted to say 'call a friend'. He didn't know her. She was causing consternation on the island. But he also felt guilty. She hadn't done anything wrong. And he remembered how he had felt when he had arrived on the island and been met with suspicion and hostility.

She hoisted her leather bag. 'I brought sandwiches.'

He had a flash of memory. Esme bringing him food. They had eaten upstairs in his flat. He wasn't taking Kate upstairs, that was for sure.

'There's nowhere for two people to sit,' he said, gesturing around at the packed shelves and narrow corridors. 'And I don't allow eating in the bookshop.' He realised his statement was undercut by the box of crackers in his hand. In his defence, it hadn't really come up with customers before. He ate in the shop often, but that was different. Surely. 'Sorry. I really do have to work.'

He really thought that would do it. He was braced for her to look disappointed. Maybe even a little hurt. Instead, she shook her head. 'That won't do. You run this place, yes? That means you're the boss. You can take a lunch break. Shut the shop, there's no one here anyway. We can eat here or we can go to the pub. I'm not taking no for an answer.'

Kate walked to the front room of the shop and hoisted her bag onto the counter next to the register. The ledger that kept track of sales, purchases and exchanges got shoved onto the floor and she rounded the counter to pick it up.

At that moment, the front door opened and Esme walked in. Luke was standing in the passage that led to the front door and it gave him a perfect view of Esme closing the door behind her and turning to smile at him. 'Do you have time for a chat?'

'Yes,' he said, shooting a glance toward the front room where Kate was no longer visible. She was still behind the counter retrieving the ledger, and he didn't know why it was taking so long. Her big squashy leather bag filled the countertop like it was claiming space.

'Good.' Esme's smile widened as she walked toward him. 'Did you want to eat? I thought we could go over to...'

'Got it,' Kate said, popping up from behind the counter. She moved her bag, revealing a bakery box and two cans of Dr Pepper. 'Do you want to start with savoury or sweet? I know it's supposed to be sweet after, but we could be naughty.' She stopped a second too late for it to seem natural. 'Oh, hi. Esme, right?'

Luke saw Esme stiffen and her face flush. He could see how it looked. Kate was standing behind the counter, in his domain, as if invited. As if she *belonged*.

He wanted to walk behind the counter and force Kate to move, but what if she didn't? Then the two of them would be standing very close together, the counter a barrier between them and Esme, with Esme on the wrong side.

'Sorry,' Kate said, leaning on the counter as if she had been there for hours. 'We were just about to have lunch. Did you need help with something?'

'No,' Esme said. 'I was just... popping in.'

'Lunch would be good,' Luke said, trying to get control of the conversation.

'I don't know if we've quite enough for three, but I'm sure we can make it stretch. I don't eat much, honestly.'

There wasn't anything wrong with her tone, nothing specifically unwelcoming, but Luke could see Esme's expression get even more closed. He knew he was missing something. It was like girls in high school. They had seemed to have their own language.

'Thank you,' Esme said carefully. 'Kind of you, but I need to get on.' She barely looked in Luke's direction before turning and leaving. 'See you later.'

CHAPTER TWENTY

id you need help with something? Esme replayed the words in utter fury. Okay, so you could argue that it was a reasonable question. But not in that tone. And not with that face. And not while standing behind the counter of Luke's shop like she owned the place.

This is what you get for being so pathetic, Esme told herself severely. This is what happens when you sit around waiting for something to happen. And then running away like a frightened rabbit when it finally does. She had been scared, she knew that, but now that Luke was no longer a possibility, now that it was clear he was interested in someone else and she was in no danger of him making any kind of romantic move, she found she could admit to herself that that was what she wanted. Truly. Deeply. She wanted Luke to look at her in that soul-searching way he had, his full attention trained on her as if she was fascinating and funny. As if she mattered. She wanted him to lean across the space between them and to touch his lips to hers. She wanted to put her hands into his scruffy hair and pull his head close, so feel his hands on her waist, her neck, her face.

She was crying. That was annoying. The view of the beach was blurred.

Hammer was outside his boathouse, chopping wood with a small hand axe. She wiped at her eyes and tried to adjust her face into something normal.

He put down his axe and walked a few steps in her direction.

'What's wrong?' Hammer was in front of her. He lifted a hand as if he was going to pat her, but let it drop. 'What did he do?'

'Nothing,' Esme forced a wobbly smile. 'I'm okay.'

'You're not,' Hammer said. Then he turned abruptly and walked away. The door to his boat house swung shut and Esme concentrated on mopping up her face. She would go home. She would have some tea and snuggle with Jet if he was in a friendly mood. She would eat something very sweet and probably not enjoy it. *I don't eat much, honestly.*

She pictured Kate Foster's clear, smooth skin and her long slim legs. She looked like an Instagram filter in real life. Of course Luke would be interested. They matched.

The door opened again and Hammer was back. He was glowering and on any other man it would have sent her heart rate into the danger zone, but she knew that was just Hammer's face. From the moment she had arrived on the island, he had represented safety and always would.

'Kettle's on,' he said gruffly. 'You need a sit down.'

She followed him into the boathouse. It smelled of wood smoke, linseed and cedar, with a tinge of engine oil. There was wood piled against one wall and a handmade shelf filled with his carved animals on the other.

There was only one proper chair and Hammer gestured for her to take it. He moved around the crowded space with surprising grace, filling two enamel mugs with tea and finding a stool to sit on while they drank.

Esme opened her mouth to lie to Hammer. She was going to say 'it's not Luke' but, instead, a question popped out. 'Are you ever lonely?'

He looked at his mug for a long moment before answering. 'Sometimes.'

She nodded. 'I wasn't. Not for years. I've been perfectly content. Happier than I ever thought possible.'

'But now?'

She felt the tears threaten again and took a sip of the hot tea.

Hammer drank from his own mug, not saying anything. It was something that Esme appreciated, the way that he could sit in silence and not feel the need to fill it. With some people it could feel manipulative, like they were making you do the work, or awkward, as if there was simply nothing to say, but with Hammer she never felt either of those things. From the first moment they had met, he had made her feel accepted. Flaws and all. She took a deep breath. 'I don't like her.'

'Who?'

That was another thing about Hammer. He didn't make assumptions or act like he knew what you were talking about if he didn't. 'Kate Foster. Our new resident. And I feel bad because she hasn't done anything wrong. I'm a terrible person.'

Instead of reassuring her that she wasn't a bad human being, Hammer simply said, 'I don't trust her.'

Grateful for the support, Esme managed a watery smile. 'You don't trust anyone.'

Hammer nodded. 'That's fair.'

'But why don't I trust her?' Esme rubbed at her face

with one hand. 'I don't know. I think I'm just being petty. Or it's the patriarchy.'

Hammer, wisely, stayed quiet.

'I'm threatened by her.'

He tensed.

'Not like that.' Esme gripped her warm mug more tightly and found that she couldn't meet Hammer's gaze. 'It's more... she is here to take my place.' With Luke. And, she realised, without having to say the words out loud, on the island. Which was daft. Kate Foster wasn't a witch.

Hammer was frowning, deep in thought. Eventually he mumbled something about not understanding how the island stuff worked, but that Esme would always have a place. 'This is your home.'

Esme wanted that to be true more than anything, but she had realised that she wanted something more... for Luke to make Unholy Island his home, too.

HAVING GOT RID of Kate Foster as quickly and politely as possible, Luke turned the sign to 'closed' and locked the front door. His mood had plummeted and he didn't feel up to any more visitors. The lights in the shop stayed steady, which he assumed meant that the shop didn't mind his taking the rest of the afternoon off. He picked at the food he had in the fridge and tried not to think about how things must have looked to Esme. He would explain later, he told himself, it would be better done in person.

But Esme didn't show up to the pub for dinner that evening. His heart leapt every time the door opened, but The Rising Moon remained stubbornly Esme-free.

Hammer called in briefly and picked up a takeaway order from the bar, and Tobias was sitting with Bee at one of the smaller tables. There was no sign of Fiona, and he guessed she must be at home with the baby. He was very relieved that there was no Kate Foster, either. He didn't know if she was staying at the cottage or whether she had headed back over the causeway. The last thing he wanted was for Esme to arrive at the pub and to assume he had invited Kate out for dinner.

Matteo joined Luke halfway through his venison casserole and asked him whether he had seen the '*weirdo in black*'. Luke tried to stop watching the door to focus on the conversation. Matteo was tapping his written question and had his eyebrows raised.

'No. Not today. You get hassle?'

Matteo shook his head. Then wrote his reply: *Nerdy. Goth? Very intense.*

Luke understood why Matteo was surprised. At this time of year, Tobias had told him that there were few visitors and they tended to be the outdoorsy hiking type. Then the description struck him. The guy from Edinburgh, Iain, had worn a long black coat. He had probably come to visit the bookshop again, and had found it closed.

Once he had finished eating, he stretched out his single pint. Still no Esme and Seren would be closing the kitchen at any moment. She really wasn't coming in for dinner. He tapped a text message letting her know he was at the pub and asking if she was okay. They had spent so much time together recently, he was hoping she would respond with an invitation to swing by Strand House.

Twenty minutes later, his pint long-since-drained, his mobile finally pinged with a response from Esme.

Fine, thanks.

His heart sank at the brief politeness of the message, and he went back to sleep at the bookshop with a heaviness pressing down across his shoulders.

. . .

THE NEXT AFTERNOON, Luke locked the bookshop with a feeling of guilt. Not just for leaving it closed another day, but for walking down to the car park alone and driving away from the island without Esme. She would come with him, he knew. At least, she would have. He wasn't sure where they stood now, and part of him didn't want to find out for sure. *Coward.* Yes, he knew it was fear. But he told himself that he was just giving Esme space. Letting her come to him so that he wasn't in danger of hassling her. Of going too fast. *Coward*, his wise-ass inner voice said again, but he ignored it.

The causeway was passable from one o'clock and, as he made his way to the car park, Luke wondered whether Hammer would stop him from leaving the island on his own, as he had before. If he saw Luke leaving, he might assume that Luke was going to pick up his search for his brother, to speak to Dean Fisher or one of his dangerous associates. The nagging guilt that he felt since the WhatsApp message was still present, but he had grown used to it in a way. It was no longer the loudest song in the soundtrack of his life.

DRIVING AWAY from Unholy Island felt like a physical wrench, as if the place had a magnetic pull. He had felt it driving to Edinburgh with Esme, but it was worse when he was alone in the car without a companion to distract him. That thought led to Esme and the way her expression had shut down when she had seen Kate Foster in the bookshop. He forced his mind away from that particular path and focused on his plan for the day.

. . .

GRAHAM TOWNSEND HAD RUN the Shambles Book Emporium for ten years. Having found two hexed books that had been sent from the shop before it had burned down, Luke had renewed his research into the place. What had seemed like a literal dead end had opened up with the funeral notice going into the local paper. It had listed the names of Graham Townsend's surviving relatives. After that, it hadn't been too difficult to find the right Valerie Townsend and her Facebook profile. He sent a friend request and was surprised when it was accepted.

Now, Graham's mother agreed to meet Graham's 'old friend' in a Costa in York centre as he 'happened to be passing and wanted to pay his respects, being sadly unable to attend the funeral due to being out of the country'. Luke didn't dwell on how easy he found the deception. He had learned plenty from his father and brother. He comforted himself that, at least, he wasn't crashing the funeral itself.

He wasn't looking forward to meeting a bereaved and grieving mother, but he thought that the greater good justified the intrusion. At least two people were dead and he should have made a third. Something was killing bookshop owners and he had a duty to try and stop it. It wasn't as if he could go to the police with a tale of a hexed book and how he suspected it caused spontaneous combustion.

Valerie Townsend arrived bang on time. Luke stood up when she walked into the coffee shop, recognising her distinctive black bobbed hair from her Facebook profile picture, and waved her over to the table he had acquired. 'What can I get for you?'

'Uh, a latte. Thanks.'

'Anything to eat?'

She shook her head, gaze taking him in with frank assessment.

He didn't know what he had been expecting, but

Valerie's sharp eyes and well-cut grey suit both spoke of somebody successful and pulled together. The poor woman may well be a puddle of grief inside, but she was presenting an excellent front to the world. He admired her fortitude and was selfishly grateful that she appeared strong enough for the conversation ahead.

Once they had drinks and had dispensed with a little small talk, the coldness of the day, Luke's journey, Valerie got to the point. 'What is it you want?'

Luke began to say something about paying his respects, but he caught understanding in Valerie's eyes. Knowing he might be making a mistake, he decided to be honest. 'I'm looking into the circumstances of your son's death.'

Valerie tilted her head. 'You're not an old friend of Graham's?'

'No,' Luke said. 'I apologise for lying to you.'

'And you're not police.' It wasn't a question.

'I run a bookshop,' Luke said. 'And there have been a few fires in bookshops. Including the one in which Graham...'

'Died. Yes. They say it was suicide.'

'The police?'

She nodded, lips compressed so hard they disappeared. 'Graham didn't kill himself.'

Luke kept quiet.

'I'm not saying it's impossible that he was suicidal. He didn't seem depressed, but I know these things aren't always apparent from the outside. I'm not in denial.' A pointed look as if daring Luke to disagree. He kept silent, not wanting to say the wrong thing or to derail her thoughts.

'But he wouldn't have done it that way. Setting fire to himself? Not exactly a painless way to go. He wasn't a fool. He wasn't deranged. If he was going to kill himself, he would have done it differently.' She nodded as if having won an argument, and he wondered how many times she had said the same words. Who had she been trying to convince? He realised how she was getting through each moment in her fresh grief. She was furious.

'Have the police found the accelerant?' The newspaper article had said not, but Luke didn't know how much information was being shared with the press.

'No. They have decided suicide. Officially. I got the impression that they thought...' She trailed off.

'What?'

Her lips thinned again. 'That he botched an insurance job, but couldn't prove it so went with the suicide angle. Death by misadventure.'

'Burning the place down for a pay-out?'

'It was insured and they acted like that was suspicious. Everyone has buildings insurance. It's ridiculous.'

'And there's nothing else that leads them in that direction?'

'Just that they don't see how it would have happened accidentally and they haven't found any suspects. It's like a diagnosis by elimination, but they don't have actual proof that he did it himself. It's just easier for them if he did.'

Luke didn't know how justified Valerie's cynicism was, but he knew the police were stretched thin and if the case didn't have any obvious leads, then he could imagine it falling to the bottom of the pile. It made him feel a little better about asking his next question. 'Do you have any ideas about what happened? Did Graham have any enemies?'

'No.' A shake of the head. 'He wasn't the kind of man who inspired hatred. I love him, he's my son, but he wasn't... exciting. He didn't have grand passions in his life or relationships. The closest thing to him was his shop.

He was obsessive about that. He'd always loved collections. He was that stereotypical little boy who had collections of gaming cards, and fossils, and toys. All sorts. But he really focused down onto books in his teens and stayed there. Graphic novels, first editions, out-of-print ephemera.'

None of this was shocking. Or helpful. The picture of Graham was beginning to sound reclusive and obsessive and maybe a little lonely. Not exactly the image to steer the police away from their suicide verdict. 'It doesn't sound as if he would willingly damage a shop full of books.'

'No. Definitely not. And that's not all. He had just taken somebody new on, to help out in the shop, give him more time for reading and research. Why would he do that if he was planning to end it all?'

THINKING about the conversation on his way back to his car, Luke wished that Valerie had asked her son more questions when he had been alive. It wasn't fair, of course, and if Lewis showed up dead, everyone would no doubt be shocked by how little he knew about his own brother, but it would have made things easier now. Valerie hadn't known who Graham had hired as an assistant, and hadn't even been completely sure of their gender, although she 'thought female'. It wasn't enough. He had thoroughly Googled Graham's life, and Valerie had been his only way in. He stopped walking and fought the urge to smack himself in the forehead. The bookshop had been described as 'an institution'. And it was situated on a busy street in a popular city.

'Why should I care?' Esme asked Jet, and not for the first time. He jumped onto the kitchen table and eyeballed her disdainfully.

'It was just lunch. Could be just a shared meal between friends. Nothing to it.' No reason to jump to conclusions. Just because Luke and Kate looked unfathomably right standing together behind the counter of the bookshop, both winners in the genetic lottery, didn't mean they were going to fall in love.

Jet meowed in a tone that suggested he thought Esme was being pathetic. Or he was hungry.

After feeding Jet some shredded cold chicken, Esme distracted herself by scrubbing the house from top to bottom. She started in the bedrooms, opening the windows to the freezing day to change the air, and vacuuming the carpets, wiping down the skirting boards and doors with a bucket of hot soapy water and a clean cloth, and changing her bed linen. The letting rooms hadn't been slept in since she last changed them and they were covered in counterpanes, so she left them be.

She took a handheld brush and swept the stairs, before vacuuming them for good measure, wiped the wooden banisters and spindles, and went through the downstairs rooms in a similar fashion. By the time she had reached the kitchen, she had been working for two hours and felt she deserved a cup of tea and a sit down. But ended up sipping at her tea and taking bites of fruit cake in between cleaning the sink and stove, tidying and dusting the open shelves and watering her plants.

Sylvie, the art nouveau-style French stove, squatted in the living room with a hurt air of neglect and fury, so she swept the ash and re-laid kindling, before giving the blue enamel exterior a gentle polish with a chamois until it gleamed.

Then, still fired up with an energy that she couldn't seem to discharge, she wax-polished the dented pine coffee table and dusted the bookcase.

With the whole house gleaming and scented with fresh air, beeswax, and the amber candle she had lit in the living room, Esme felt a little of her tension ease. But, as was always the case with cleaning, the more she did, the more corners she noticed to clean. One bright sweep of dusted wood simply highlighted the grubbiness of the piece next to it. Her mood dipped as she contemplated the futility of her actions. There was always more to do. It was then that she realised that cleaning wasn't going to cut it. This was a problem that required direct action. She would go to see Luke. Clear the air. Apologise for running away when he had kissed her and see if he was interested in another go at the whole thing. And if not, if he had turned his attention to Kate Foster, she would, at least, know where she stood.

Esme stared at the closed sign on the bookshop door and knocked for the third time. The shop remained quiet and dark, no lights showing. After waiting for a few more minutes, Esme walked to the car park. Luke's car wasn't there. He had gone to the mainland without her. Maybe he had found a new investigative partner. The thought burned all the way down to her stomach.

CHAPTER TWENTY-ONE

Luke had no trouble finding the area of York known as the shambles. There was plentiful signage in the city centre and they all seemed keen to direct him to the cobbled shopping street. It was easy to see why it was a tourist draw. The beautifully-preserved medieval buildings and attractive shop fronts were picturesque as hell. It was also simple to find the place where the Shambles Book Emporium had stood. What wasn't easy to understand was how the police hadn't marked the fire as 'highly fucking suspicious'. The space where the bookshop had stood was a boarded-up space, but the buildings on either side looked essentially untouched. Luke didn't know enough about fires to know for sure, but it seemed weird that it hadn't spread. Especially in old structures. Perhaps fire-safety measures had been installed over the years. There was also still a distinct smell of charred wood and soot in the air.

Further up the cobbled street, past a fudge shop and a place that sold handmade miniature statues of ghosts, he found a pub. Inside the tavern, which wasn't just 'ye olde style' but 'actually extremely old, thank you very much', was inviting. It had gleaming brass fixtures, a polished bar, and a large wood burner. If he hadn't been on a mission, he could have happily hunkered down for the evening and worked his way through the forty-two craft beers they listed on a large chalkboard. Instead, he ordered an alcohol-free pint and asked the man who served him about the bookshop. Small talk wasn't Luke's strongest suit, but he had developed a few techniques while looking for his brother. He leaned against the bar and asked: 'How's business this time of year?'

'Not bad,' the guy replied. He had a neatly tended short beard and was wearing a t-shirt with a picture of a velociraptor and the words 'clever girl' underneath.

'Shame about that fire. The bookshop. You can still smell the smoke out there.'

'Yeah.' The guy shook his head. 'Makes you think. The place was full of paper, but still. Wouldn't have thought it would have gone up like that.' He looked around the wood-filled room and the fire leaping merrily in the burner. 'Makes you think.'

'Do they know who did it?'

'Oh, man. You didn't hear?'

Luke shook his head.

He lowered his voice. 'Guy killed himself.'

Luke played dumb. 'Really? Doesn't seem like a good way to go... Not that there's a good way, but you know what I mean.'

'Pills or something? I don't know.' He shrugged. 'Can I get you anything else?'

'Do you do food?' Luke asked, purely to prolong the conversation.

The man fetched a menu and slid it across the bar. Luke sat on a stool and scanned it while the barman served a couple.

When he came back, Luke asked for a packet of dry

roast peanuts from the display behind the bar. 'Did you know the guy?'

'Graham? A bit. York's not that big. And all the businesses along here keep in touch. We run group promotions and stuff like that. Graham's heart wasn't in it over the last few months, though.'

'Is that why you think he did it? You'd noticed he was down?'

'He wasn't just down, he was distressed.' The man leaned his elbows on the bar. 'One of his regular customers topped himself. He took it really badly.'

'God,' Luke said. 'That's rough. Do you know the man who died?'

'Not really. I recognised him when I saw it in the paper. He was one of the mental ones. Not supposed to say that, now, are we? He was weird, though. Intense guy.'

'And you think Graham was really upset about this customer dying?'

'That's why he did himself in. It was the last straw, I reckon. Graham had been down for a while, like I said, but that business must have just tipped him over.'

Sitting in The Rising Moon with Fiona, Esme was reminded that her own problems were petty and inconsequential. Fiona had been in a bad marriage. Her husband had terrorised her son and she would carry the guilt for that for the rest of her life. Esme knew fine well how that felt. She had often counted her blessings that she hadn't fallen pregnant while with Ryan.

'He's going to be okay,' she said. 'He's got you.'

Fiona nodded briskly. The conversation had clearly got too touchy-feely for her practical nature and she looked ready to change the subject.

'And me,' Esme added. Keen to get it in before they moved on.

She smiled at that. 'Thank you.'

Seren stopped by their table on her way back to the kitchen. 'Anything else?'

'Has she been in today?'

Seren shook her head. 'Not so far.'

The door opened, letting in a blast of cold air. Tobias entered, Winter close on his heels. There were general greetings and a burst of conversation. Esme was almost too distracted to notice when Kate Foster arrived. Almost. She felt a rush of energy at the realisation that she wasn't with Luke. Wherever he had gone, it wasn't with her. And that was something.

'What can I get for you?' Seren asked the newcomer. 'It's butternut squash and chilli soup or venison pie.'

'Or both,' Tobias said, patting his flat stomach. Winter was pressed against his side and Tobias shooed him toward his usual spot in front of the large fireplace. The dog seemed reluctant to leave his master, whining pitifully until Tobias walked over to the fire with him. Winter's gait was staggered and he collapsed rather than lying down.

'I've already eaten, I'm afraid,' Kate Foster replied. 'More's the pity. It smells amazing in here.'

Seren smiled, pleased. 'Drink?'

'Is it too early for a G and T?'

'We don't judge around here,' Seren said.

'Join us,' Fiona said and Esme felt her chest tighten.

She chided herself for being unfriendly. It wasn't Kate's fault that Luke liked her. It wasn't her fault that she looked like the perfect example of modern womanhood. That she exuded youthful beauty and spoke with the kind of careless confidence that made you think she was smarter than she was.

174

Now, that's not kind, Esme chided herself again. She might be just as smart as she sounded. Or smarter. Just because a woman happened to be beautiful didn't mean she deserved judgement. Esme was a feminist. She believed in the sisterhood. She was not going to allow petty jealousy and years of social conditioning by the patriarchy twist her into bitterness or force her to see other women as rivals. That was misogynist bollocks and she was better than that.

'I love your outfit.' Kate chose that moment to speak.

It took Esme a second to realise that she was addressing her. 'Thanks.'

'It's so cute.'

And there it was. The unmistakable note of derision under the words. Kate Foster obviously hadn't heard the sisterhood pep talk.

'We dress for comfort here,' Fiona said, seemingly oblivious to Kate Foster's Mean Girls impression. 'Or I do, at any rate.'

'Very sensible,' Kate said, making it sound like an insult.

Esme blinked. She knew that tone. Had encountered it at school and in group homes. She knew the technique. But she was an adult now. And Fiona was her friend. 'When you're as naturally stunning as Fi, you don't have to make an effort,' she said, smiling warmly at Fiona. 'It's not fair.'

Fiona looked uncertain and her cheeks pinked. 'Don't make fun.'

'I'm not,' Esme said airily. 'More's the pity. You have luminous skin and eyes to drown in.' Too late, she realised that was possibly an unfortunate turn of phrase, given Fiona's true nature.

Fiona was laughing, though. Delighted. 'Too right,' she said with a tinge of satisfaction.

Kate Foster was watching the exchange with a small furrow between her perfectly shaped brows.

'You've got great skin, too,' Esme said generously to the newcomer. 'Honestly, it looks airbrushed. But in real life.'

Kate nodded, still slightly stunned. 'Thank you.' She looked at Seren, who had just arrived to take Esme and Fiona's plates. 'And you have incredible eyebrows. You must give me the name of your person.'

Seren shook her head. 'I do them myself.' She piled the plates and placed the cutlery on top. 'And I'm not taking on clients. I've got enough to bloody do with the pub.'

'Fair enough,' Kate said, looking genuinely disappointed.

Once Seren had left, Fiona asked Esme whether she had any spare paper and pencils. 'Not your good stuff, obviously. I just wanted some around for Euan. He mentioned some YouTube person who did painting tutorials.'

'I'll put a box together. I've got some acrylic paint and brushes, pastels...'

'Not your good stuff,' Fiona repeated, looking alarmed. 'Just some bits to start him off. I don't even know if he will want to. He might just like watching them.'

'Like Bob Ross.'

'Exactly.'

'Happy to encourage him having a go,' Esme said. 'And I've way more supplies than I'll ever use. I always over-order.'

'You paint?' Kate asked, and Esme braced herself for the putdown.

'Just for fun,' she said. It was a lie. She painted because she felt compelled to do so. The enjoyment was part of it, but that came in flashes and usually after having painted. Not during.

176

'Interesting,' Kate said and pursed her lips. 'You're a dark horse.'

Fiona left at the same time as Esme. They paused by the door, pulling on coats and hats for their short walks home.

'Euan's babysitting, I don't want to be late,' Fiona was saying.

Esme was only half-listening as she was watching Kate Foster out of the corner of her eye. She was at the bar, chatting to Seren. The older woman was usually too busy at this time of the evening, but she had paused in her tasks to give Kate her full attention. There was something magnetic about Kate, Esme supposed. Magnetic, beautiful, interesting. That had to be why she couldn't stop looking. She pushed down the feeling of foreboding.

'Where's Luke tonight?' Fiona asked as they pushed out of the warmth of the pub and into the cold smack of the evening air.

'I'm not sure, but I would guess York. There have been fires in bookshops and he's investigating.' They had been investigating, she thought. Together.

'Investigating?' Fiona paused. 'That sounds very formal.'

'You know what happened with the book? He doesn't want it to happen to anybody else. He's trying to work out where it came from.'

'It'll be a freak occurrence, surely? Just a mistake. One dangerous book amongst thousands that are fine.'

Fiona seemed so sure it was tempting to accept that version of events. 'I don't know. Maybe.'

'I've got to go,' Fiona said apologetically. 'You're welcome to come with?'

'Are you sure?' Esme said. 'I'm afraid I won't be good company this evening.'

Fiona waved off this objection and they began the short walk together. 'There's something else I have been meaning to say... about Euan.' She spoke quickly, as if wanting to get the words out before they reached her home.

'Is he all right?'

Fiona smiled at her concern. 'Just a friendly warning. Don't approach him when he's near the sea. Wait to see if he greets you.'

'Okay,' Esme said, thinking guiltily of the previous night when she had walked up to talk to Euan on the beach.

'He might be about to change, and that's a dangerous time. Until he's got used to it, anyway. And then he'll choose when it happens. Until then, it's not so controlled and his instincts will be all over the place. The animal part of him might perceive company as a threat and that wouldn't be good.'

'No. Right. Got it.'

Fiona's smile was strained. 'I don't want you to be frightened of him. He would never intentionally hurt anybody.'

'I know that,' Esme said. 'We need to protect him.'

Fiona's smile softened. 'That's exactly it.'

CHAPTER TWENTY-TWO

It was only a short walk to Fiona's house, but Esme's hands were frozen and she was glad to get inside. Euan was in his bedroom and Esme sipped her tea in the living room while Fiona checked on Hamish. The room was essentially the same as when Oliver had lived here, but it was also completely altered. There were rectangles of discoloured paint where two framed photographs had hung, one of Fiona and Oliver holding a sword to cut their wedding cake, and the other a professional family portrait with, as Esme remembered it, Euan looking uncomfortable in a shirt and tie. There were additions, as well as gaps. A brightly coloured woollen throw lay on the arm of the sofa and there was a cheerful clutter of handmade pottery arranged in the fireplace. More significant, however, was the overall energy. Everything just had a more relaxed air, with little bits of household stuff lying around, where before there had been only regimented cleanliness. It wasn't that the room was messy now, but it did look more lived in. There was a pile of graphic novels stacked on the floor next to the easy chair. Esme wondered if Euan had heard her arriving and cleared out to his room.

Fiona walked in, her face soft in the gentle lighting. 'I think he's down,' she said with satisfaction. 'I thought it would be harder, with this all being new for him, but he seems to have gone off...' She smiled, looking happier than Esme could ever remember. 'Listen to me, jinxing it. We'll see how he goes tonight. I might be less smug at three in the morning.' Her forehead furrowed. 'And I'm a bit out of practise.'

'Fingers crossed he's tired out with the travel.'

Fiona shook her head gently. 'That's not how wee ones work, sadly. The more tired they are, the worse they sleep. They go past it.'

'Well, that sounds inconvenient.'

Fiona laughed. 'It's only temporary, so I'm going to enjoy every moment.' She sat on the other end of the sofa and picked up her mug. The tea had to be cold by now, but she took a sip anyway.

'Do you know how long he'll be with you?'

Fiona shook her head. 'Eilidh should be out of hospital by the end of the week, but she'll need at least a week to recover.'

'I didn't know you had family.' She regretted the words as soon as they came out. 'I meant, I don't think you've mentioned your niece before. Sorry.'

'It's okay,' Fiona said. 'Oliver wasn't a fan of my family, so we didn't spend much time with them before. I stopped talking about them because it only caused rows and I must have got out of the habit.'

Esme knew well the controlling type. Her ex, Ryan, had set about isolating her from her friends and her nursing course. She nodded her understanding, but kept her lips compressed shut. This wasn't the time to jump in with her own experiences.

'I'm a little bit worried,' Fiona said. Her lips compressed as if resisting opening up.

Esme waited. It had taken seven years of island life for Fiona to call her a friend, she wasn't one to rush. And now Esme knew that part of that had been Oliver's influence, but she knew that some of it was just Fiona's way. Growing up in the human world as a supernatural creature probably added to the instinct to be insular.

'I just...' Fiona stopped, looking down at her mug. 'When Euan was a baby, I couldn't have been away from him for a couple of weeks. I know Eilidh has no choice about the surgery, but I'm surprised she wants me to have Hamish for so long. After, I mean.'

'You think there's something else going on?'

'We're all different,' Fiona said slowly. 'I know that. And it's not easy being on your own with a wee one.'

Esme wasn't sure when Oliver had arrived in Fiona's life or for how long she had been a single mum to Euan.

'But I can't help worrying that there's something more she's not telling me. I offered to stay and help out, but she was adamant I should bring Hamish home with me instead. I can't imagine choosing to have my baby so far away, not when there was another option.' She stopped speaking abruptly, as if having said more than she intended.

Esme nodded her understanding, but didn't speak. She could sense that Fiona had more to say and she wanted to give her the space to do so. There was a silence, broken only by the ticking of the clock on the mantle and the wind testing the window frames.

Finally, Fiona looked at Esme. 'It's a minor op, apparently, but she wouldn't tell me more. Just brushed it off. But she said she wanted to rest after so that she recovered properly and was back to full speed. Not just muddle through and then be half-fixed for months.'

'That sounds very sensible.'

'It does.' Fiona still didn't look sure. 'Do you think she was playing it down?'

'The surgery?'

'What if it's more serious than she's letting on?'

Esme didn't have an answer for that. She pulled a sympathetic face. 'You're doing everything you can. You're looking after Hamish and that'll be a big help.'

Fiona brightened. 'I'm going to take him to Seal Point tomorrow.' She turned slightly self-conscious. 'See who we can wave at.'

Esme woke up with a painful sensation in her chest. She opened her eyes to find two green eyes close to her own.

'What's wrong, Jet?' She felt stupid as soon as the words had croaked past her parched throat. Jet wasn't Lassie. He wasn't about to lead her to a lost child down a well.

Seeing that she was awake, Jet jumped from her chest and settled himself on the pillow next to her head. She rubbed her chest where he had been standing, easing the ache, then reached out a hand from underneath the covers and stroked Jet's smooth fur. He began a deep rhythmic purr, as if very happy with the world.

The moon was shining through the curtains and Esme felt a rush of energy, the sleep clearing from her mind. She got out of bed, Jet opening an eye and glaring as if she had disturbed his deep slumber and not the other way around.

Knowing that she was going to stand in the moonlight and that it was freezing outside, she pulled on clothes, layering a woolly jumper over her PJ top and choosing her thickest socks. By the back door, she added a coat, hat and scarf, even though her whole body was vibrating with excitement, making her fingers clumsy as she fumbled with the zip and buttons on her coat. The silvery moon visible through the kitchen window seemed to be calling to her, impatient.

Outside, the wind had dropped and the air was unnaturally still. There was a tingle in the atmosphere that was nothing to do with the cold. It was as if the island was holding its breath. The moon was even more beautiful seen through the clear night air and she stood still for a moment, just drinking in the sight. The air was so still and quiet that she could make out the sound of the sea from her garden, just faintly. It seemed to be getting a little louder, as if it wanted to be heard. She swept her gaze over the garden and the lane beyond, seeing the familiar environment anew. All was bathed in moonglow and it was intoxicating.

Following an instinct she didn't want to examine too closely, Esme walked out of the quiet garden and down the lane where it met the path. She could turn right and walk to Coire Bay, or left along the coast path toward the harbour. The full moon was low in the sky, large and bright, and it seemed to illuminate the path to the right more than the left. It lit Esme's steps and the marram grass that led over the dunes to the sweeping curve of Coire Bay.

As soon as Esme could see the sea rolling onto the sand with its soothing regularity, she felt the tension in her chest loosen. There was a wild happiness running through her body that was pure and uncomplicated. The delight of her animal soul at being alive and well fed and in good clean air under the moonlight. She wondered if this was how Fiona felt when she shifted.

The sand was silvery and the moon blazed a glowing path across the waves. It looked as if you could follow it to the horizon and, for one mad moment, Esme imagined stepping into the water and doing just that. The word lunacy came to mind. Luna from moon, people sent crazy by the pull of the moon. It was probably misogynistic, too, like so many things from the past were. The idea of women's cycles being linked to the phases of the moon leading to ideas of madness. Like the wandering womb of hysteria.

Her mind was wandering now, and she increased her pace across the sand. She would walk to the far point of the bay, to the ward, and then back again and home. It was an easy forty-minute round trip, and she was perfectly warm in her substantial layers.

The motion of her footsteps on the compacted sand and the slight breeze from the sea quieted her mind so that by the time she was nearing the furthest edge of the bay, the place that Alvis had died, she felt calm and clear.

She licked her lips and tasted salt, and it was comforting that if she were to feel like crying, her tears would taste like the sea and the island air. Bee had said she belonged to the island, that she was part of it, and at this moment she could feel that was true. Another wave of exhilaration ran through her. She had never belonged before. Never been someone's or something's.

Clouds scudded across the moon and the beach was plunged into shadow. Esme had a torch in her coat pocket but didn't feel the need to reach for it. She picked her way a little further along, wanting to reach the rocks of the ward before turning back.

The rocks led to a promontory that sliced out to sea, marking the furthest point of the bay. After the large rocks, there was a scrubby portion of land, skirted by the coastal path that led around the headland and along the northern edge of the island toward the castle. Just before turning around to head for home, the clouds shifted and the scene was bathed once again in bright moonlight.

Silhouetted against the deep blue sky, there was a shape that didn't belong. A figure.

CHAPTER TWENTY-THREE

Her heart in her mouth, Esme stood completely still. She didn't know if the figure could see her, but as she was close to the rocks and down on the beach, with no light directly behind her, she thought there was a good chance that the other person could only see dark shadows from where they were standing.

The figure was moving along the promontory and then it disappeared. They must have moved below on the other side or around the headland. Who the hell was out at this time of night? Of course, she was, Esme admitted. But she was the Ward Witch. And this was her island.

Esme ignored the route up the rocks at the back of the bay. She would need to use her torch to navigate them safely, and the path was close enough. Once she had skirted the promontory from behind, she might be able to see where the figure had headed and follow.

As she took the path, another thought crossed her mind. The figure could be doubling back and be about to walk into her. Or they might be waiting on the promontory, crouched behind one of the large boulders and ready to leap out and attack.

Breathing in cold air through her nose, Esme straightened her shoulders and rubbed her sternum firmly. She was not going to give into fear. The old Esme would have run by now. The old Esme would be overwhelmed with anxiety, hyperventilating through a panic attack. This was her home. And, besides, the figure had been small and, Esme thought, female.

Stepping as softly as possible, Esme made her way along the path. After a few minutes, the path curved around and she saw a light up ahead. Whoever she had seen was walking along the path toward the castle and they had switched on a torch.

AT THE CASTLE RUINS, the breeze picked up. The cold air sliced Esme's cheeks and she was glad of her thick coat and layers of clothes. The breeze carried more than cold. The smell of wood smoke set Esme's heart racing. Whoever was out in the middle of the night had now set a fire in the ruins of the castle. This was more than a mere midnight stroll, the action of an insomniac. This was intent.

Esme crept toward the low wall of the castle. She could see the glow of firelight, bright in the winter darkness, and hear the crackle of burning sticks. Who was setting a fire at the castle ward in the middle of the night? Who would dare?

She felt her heart hammering but, for once, it was anger and not fear. Or not just fear. So that was a step forward. Holding her breath, Esme listened and then heard a low singing voice. Female. It wasn't Fiona or Seren or Bee. Before her brain had finished working it out, the singing stopped and a loud clear voice said: 'It's warmer closer to the fire.' A pause. 'Come on, Esme. I won't bite.'

Straightening up, Esme saw Kate Foster crouched by a

188

circle of stones. She fed a stick to the small fire contained within the circle and looked up as Esme approached. The fire was properly contained and they were within stone ruins, but still she felt a sense of outrage. What was this woman doing setting a fire here? And, with her stomach dropping, she asked herself why she hadn't done it before herself? With the firelight leaping up the ruined walls, illuminating the worn and broken edges, the castle seemed to be more alive than before. Esme felt the island approve.

'I'm glad you're here,' Kate said. Her voice carried clearly in the still night.

'What are you doing?' Esme's voice felt rusty in her mouth.

'Paying homage to this old place. You can feel its spirit, can't you?'

'Who are you?'

Kate cocked her head to one side as if giving the question serious consideration. After a moment, she turned back to the fire. 'You know my name.'

Esme looked at the scrubby ground between the ruined walls. There were a few low flat stones, maybe the remains of another inner wall, that would have been perfect to sit on. The flames danced in the darkness, illuminating Kate Foster's face as she fed another, larger stick to the fire. 'I read a book once, it was ever so interesting,' Kate said conversationally. 'There are ancient lines of power criss-crossing all over the land. You can find them if you know how to look. It's like divining water.'

'That sounds like an unusual book,' Esme said.

Kate didn't look away from the fire. She fed it another piece of wood. 'Please. Someone has been doing a ritual around here. Maybe for protection, something like that. I'm guessing it's not the barmaid.' She shot a look at Esme.

Esme didn't answer and she hoped that her expression

was neutral. She waited until Kate was satisfied and had moved back from the fire, taking a seat on a stone. Esme had always been good at waiting. She wasn't sure, in this moment, what she was waiting for exactly. But she felt as if she couldn't walk away.

'Are you going to sit?' Kate smiled up at Esme, white teeth flashing in the light from the fire. 'I didn't bring marshmallows, I'm afraid. I didn't know I was going to have company. I do have this, though.' She produced a silver flask from her coat pocket and tilted it invitingly.

Esme felt as if she was standing on the edge of a cliff. Or in the space between two worlds. On one side, she had happened upon her eccentric new neighbour enjoying a midnight ramble, and on the other she could see a beautiful and powerful woman, blood pumping beneath her skin while she conjured fire, warming the ancient bones in the castle ward. Waking something up.

She told herself that she was imagining the feeling that something was stirring beneath her feet. And the creeping sensation across her skin was just the cool night air. The other voice, which sounded very much like Bee, told her sharply to look out. To mind her instincts. To trust her intuition. Normal folk had gut feelings, instincts they used for self-preservation and to avert catastrophe. Witches had gut and head and heart feelings, all working together with the extra sight that was there for the using if only she had the wit to do so. That was Bee, again. Her voice was insistent and Esme knew it was important she listen.

The two sides of her vision opened and, for a single instant, Esme saw something else sitting by the fire in place of Kate Foster. Instead of a woman with long, lustrous hair and smooth young skin, she saw a wrinkled creature. Small, hunched and with skin the colour of ash. Unnaturally large eyes gazed up, a skinny arm that was more bone than flesh, reaching out and holding the silver flask in offering. Another instant and the image was gone. Kate Foster was back. A beautiful woman clothed in cashmere and leather.

Esme swallowed very carefully and shook her head. 'Not for me.'

The woman shrugged and unscrewed the lid, taking a long swallow. Esme watched the muscles of Kate's throat move and tried not to show that her own skin was crawling. She was registering her base terror, but it felt disconnected. Her mind was working clearly and it was instructing her in very certain tones that she needed to make sure the creature that was Kate Foster had no idea that she had just seen her true shape. That if she suspected, she would kill her. 'You're out late,' she heard herself say. Her voice was normal. A little too normal for a woman finding another making a fire in the middle of the night. She added a little self-conscious laugh. 'I thought I was the only lunatic around here. I like walking at night, but Fiona and Seren think I'm mad.' Invoking their names felt protective, somehow. As if just by saying them they might appear.

A split second and then Kate smiled warmly. 'I won't tell if you won't.' She glanced around. 'They don't know what they're missing. It's so peaceful at night.'

Peaceful was another word for deserted.

'I won't gate crash,' she said, forcing a smile. 'And I've got to be up early, anyway.' She placed a foot behind her. A single step that unlocked her limbs. She wanted to turn and flee. Every instinct was screaming at her to run, while her brain told her that she had to appear calm. Unconcerned. That she couldn't let the creature know she was scared.

'Fair enough,' Kate Foster said. She held Esme's gaze for a few more seconds and Esme felt herself being assessed.

Then, thankfully, Kate turned back to the fire. 'Watch your step.'

'Sorry?'

Another quick smile. 'On the path. You should use a torch.'

'Right. Yes.' Esme turned and fled.

Esme didn't know if Luke was back from his solo trip to the mainland, but she wasn't going to ask him for help with this. He might think she was being jealous. He might already have feelings for Kate Foster that would cloud his judgement. There was only one person she knew would be on her side without question.

She knocked lightly on the door of the boathouse. She couldn't hear any movement inside and had raised her hand to knock again when the door flew open. Hammer was towering over her in an instant, a snarl on his face.

She let out an involuntary squeak and took a step back.

'Shit, sorry.' Hammer's face instantly softened. 'What's wrong?'

Esme realised he was mostly naked and that he had a hammer in one hand.

He looked down and seemed to realise that he was wearing jersey shorts. A split second later, he casually dropped his weapon. It hit the floor with a dull thunk.

Hammer's body was solid with muscle, and his skin was a patchwork of scars. The moonlight caught the silvery tracing and Esme forced herself not to stare.

His expression had gone stony. 'What did he do? I'll fucking kill him.'

'It's not Luke.'

Esme wasn't sure if he would believe her instinct. Or, more accurately, whether he would take her instinct as enough of a reason to go tramping about in the darkness, but Hammer was pulling clothes on before she had even finished explaining.

'I just want to make sure the fire is properly out,' she said. It sounded silly out loud. There was nothing for the fire to catch in the middle of the ruin. And it was winter. The rain would no doubt smother it.

'We should see what else she had done,' Hammer said.

Esme felt the relief that he was listening to her, taking her seriously. Then she chided herself. When had Hammer ever done anything else? She had to stop expecting people to act in the way that Ryan had. He was long gone. And she had friends, now.

Hammer put on a head torch and handed another to Esme.

She could see the sense in keeping her hands free, so she tightened the band and pulled it over her head.

Hammer was quiet as they picked their way over the sand toward the coastal path. She wondered if he was embarrassed by her seeing his body. Or whether he felt exposed by his fast reactions. He had been her friend since the moment she had arrived on the island, but there was a reserve about him. Hammer was a private man, and she didn't want him to feel uncomfortable.

'I'm sorry to disturb you like this,' she said, keeping her voice low.

He held out a hand and took her arm. 'Watch. There's a hole.'

After steering her around the trip hazard, he lapsed back into silence.

The walls of the castle stood out deepest black against the purplish-blue of the night sky.

Hammer's footsteps were so quiet that Esme couldn't

imagine anything hearing him. She felt like a clumsy toddler next to him.

When they got close to the castle, Esme slowed down. Hammer widened the gap between them as he kept moving at the same quiet, deceptively swift pace. Watching him was like seeing a predator in the wild, and she felt a wave of gratitude that he was on her side.

The moon moved from behind a cloud and illuminated the ruins just as Esme joined Hammer. He had traversed the west side of the ruin, approaching it where the wall was highest and using the intact window to check the inside. Keeping to the edge of the opening, with one arm reaching out to hold Esme in place, he scanned the inside for a long moment. Esme saw some of the tension leave his body and then he turned and shook his head at her. She didn't speak, not wanting to do the wrong thing.

He moved his head and took another, longer look, before moving quietly to the side. He leaned in very close and whispered into her ear. 'Stay.'

Watching Hammer creep around the ruined wall and into the place she had seen Kate Foster ought to have been mildly comical. He was such a big man it should have been impossible, but in the moonlit darkness with his soft tread and the way he moved along the wall, so close as to be almost a part of it, meant he seemed to blend into the shadows. She wondered where he had learned to stalk like that. And shivered.

Hammer disappeared from view and, after a minute or so, just when she was starting to wonder if she ought to follow, he reappeared. 'She's gone,' he said quietly. 'We should head back.'

He didn't want her to look inside the castle. The realisation hit Esme with the weight of certainty. He was already moving away down the path, expecting her to follow. She didn't move. 'What's wrong?'

'We should head back. It's freezing.'

Before he'd even finished not answering her question, Esme had stepped around the broken wall of the castle.

SHE SAW INSTANTLY why Hammer hadn't wanted her to look. There was white paint daubed on a stretch of intact castle wall and the sheer vandalism of it took Esme's breath away. How dare she? The stones of the castle were not the most ancient part of the island, but they had stood in place since the Middle Ages and they ought to be shown respect.

It was a rough circle with symbols that Esme didn't recognise drawn at four places, like compass points. She stepped closer in order to examine it, the familiar feelings of inadequacy and frustration rising up. She didn't know what it was supposed to be, but it definitely looked like part of a ritual of some kind. Which begged the question: what was the ritual supposed to do?

Hammer had joined her and was picking at the paint with a fingernail. 'I can clean this up, easy.'

'I'll know it was here,' Esme said miserably. The mix of anger and sadness was swirling in her stomach, and she didn't know which was going to win. She was the Ward Witch. If anyone ought to be doing arcane rituals, it was her.

CHAPTER TWENTY-FOUR

As they walked back toward their respective homes, Hammer and Esme were mostly quiet. Esme was watching her feet and mourning the loss of the electric atmosphere she had felt on her way out to the bay. Clouds scudded across the sky, intermittently hiding the glorious moon, but it wasn't the only change. Whether it was the adrenaline rush and subsequent anger, or whether it was because she now had company, she could no longer feel the sea and the moon in the same way. They had seemed sentient In a way she could barely put into words.

It was almost three in the morning, and they had a brief conversation about whether they should wake Tobias up or meet in the morning.

'I'll clean the wall first thing,' Hammer said. He had already offered, but Esme had said she wanted to help.

'I'll meet you there. Is nine too early?'

He nodded in agreement. 'First, we need to tell Tobias. He'll know what to do. But he might want to see the paint first.'

Esme didn't disagree. And what was the point in having a mayor if you didn't take your problems to him?

Tobias opened the door looking slightly rumpled in a dressing gown and slippers. He still looked glowingly healthy, especially for a man of his years, but there was a distracted sadness around him. He waved away their apologies for disturbing him in the middle of the night. 'I don't sleep much this time of the year. What's happened?'

Hammer bulldozed straight onto the topic in hand.

'Let me put the kettle on,' Tobias said. 'Or I have whisky if you want something warming.'

'Whisky,' Hammer said at the same time as Esme said that she was fine.

In Tobias's cosy living room, the fire crackling in the grate and the frost patterns traced across the inside of the windows, she could see that Tobias hadn't, in fact, been in bed. There was a tartan blanket over his favourite chair, his reading glasses on the side table, and Winter was in front of the fire.

Hammer walked over to the sideboard where the whisky decanter and glasses sat and Tobias picked up the blanket, folding it up neatly and offering Esme a seat.

Winter lifted his head. He tried to get up and greet Esme, but his legs buckled and he lay back down.

'I don't know what's wrong,' Tobias said sadly, stroking the dog's head.

Esme knew the answer was probably 'old age' but there was no cure for that and very little comfort, so she didn't say the words. Instead, she asked about whether he was eating and drinking and all the usual calming but useless queries we make when we just need to make some soothing noise, to show that we care and to fill the awful silence.

'He's not a young dog,' Tobias said. 'But I thought I would have more time.'

And that, in a nutshell, was life. Esme felt a pool of deep sadness well up beneath her. It dragged at her ankles, and she knew it could pull her under. Life was passing her by. She had been so focused on staying safe that she had stopped paying attention to anything else. She was furious that Kate Foster had defaced the castle walls, but another part of her was jealous. Not for defiling the stonework, but for the freedom and excitement and curiosity that Kate Foster represented.

Pulling her mind back to Winter, she joined Tobias in stroking the dog. He turned his eyes up to her and gave a soft whine. There were tears in Esme's eyes but she wasn't sure if they were for Winter, Tobias, herself or all three.

'Now, START AGAIN,' Tobias said, accepting a glass from Hammer. 'What's this about Kate Foster?'

Hammer sat on the floor, his back against the sofa and legs stretched out. 'She defaced the castle', he said. 'With paint.'

Tobias frowned.

The heavy cut-glass tumbler was comforting in Esme's hand. She wasn't a big drinker, but the slightly medicinal smell felt appropriate. 'And I know why she has been able to stay on the island.'

Tobias raised his eyebrows, turning to give Esme his full attention.

'She's not human,' she said.

He nodded, his expression smoothing out. 'That makes sense.'

'Does it?' Esme felt the wild urge to laugh bubble up inside. She clamped down on it. 'Right. Well. What do we do?'

'About what?'

'Her. I saw her tonight. She had a fire at the castle. She turned into something in front of me. Before I left. And that's when she must have used the spray paint. Symbols on the walls, some of them looked pagan.'

'She shifted form?' Tobias's tone was calm, like he was inquiring after somebody's hair colour or accent.

Esme took a beat to regroup. She took a breath before replying, trying to calm herself. 'No. Not exactly. She looked different for a moment. But I don't know if that was me seeing things or her physically changing. If it was the latter, it was very quick. And then she changed back again.'

'I see.'

'You don't seem very shocked.'

'Don't I?' Tobias steepled his fingers together.

All of the retorts that Esme had lined up dissolved on her tongue. His reaction was perfectly reasonable. It wasn't really shocking. Fiona was a selkie and shifted into the form of a seal. Her son, Euan, was probably the same. She was a witch. The bookshop produced the book you wanted, but only if you asked it nicely.

'The question,' Tobias said, 'is what do we do as a community? I had considered the possibility that Ms Foster was able to stay more than two nights because the island wanted her to take up a position here. Like it did for Luke.'

Esme frowned. 'But what position?'

'Perhaps when Luke was ill, the island opened the door for a replacement.' Tobias shook his head. 'But that doesn't quite work. Ms Foster had already shown an interest in the cottages before Luke was hexed.'

'Luke didn't die,' Esme said. 'He's the Book Keeper.'

'Indeed. Which is why your supposition that Ms Foster isn't human makes the most sense at this point. We have been a sanctuary for the more unusual members of society for centuries. But this is a community decision. I won't impose my will on the group.'

'You want her to stay?'

'I want her to be able to stay. If that is what she needs.'

Esme wanted to say that Kate's true form had looked evil, but she realised that could be prejudice. There were more things in this world than she had ever dreamed possible and some of those things might look alarming, while being perfectly benign. Or not. That was the small voice at the back of her mind, the one that had kept her safe during a turbulent life.

AFTER HAMMER and the young witch had left, Tobias returned to his chair by the fire. Winter struggled to his feet and leaned heavily against his legs. His tail thumped the floor with a couple of half-hearted movements.

'I know,' Tobias said. He felt tired. This was his most energised time of the year, but it was one more turn of the wheel and he felt the creak of it in his bones. It would keep on turning, he supposed. Until the sun exploded or whatever the latest prediction from science suggested. He remembered when the prevailing wisdom said that the giant world snake would devour the earth. Throughout time, there had always been the awareness that existence would end eventually. Even for him.

He stroked the soft fur on Winter's head and sent a prayer to the gods that had long since died. His old playmates from the long-ago beginning. The time before the island was an island, and before he stood between the earth and the sky and felt the sting of the salt air. The time that, in truth, had grown hazy even for him. He knew that Winter was an animal and that his ending would come before Tobias's final sleep, but he prayed now, with a burst of fervent energy. *Not yet.*

· · ·

THE NEXT MORNING, Esme was still furious. Painting the ruins was disrespectful. And she was frightened, too. But Tobias was right. This was a place of sanctuary. And just because Kate Foster's true form, or her spirit or whatever, had looked pretty terrifying, didn't mean she was a bad person. Creature. Whatever.

The fact remained. The island had allowed her to stay for more than two nights. She had left the place and remembered it enough to come back. The wards were all intact, but still Kate Foster was here. That had to mean the island was welcoming her. And if the island welcomed her, then Esme, the Ward Witch, ought to do the same.

She shoved her personal feelings down. The churning jealousy at the thought of her spending more time with Luke and the fear that he would fall for her obvious charms. You weren't going to do anything anyway, she told herself sharply.

A screeching meow broke the peaceful quiet of the kitchen. Jet was glaring at her and she went to the fridge to get him some cooked chicken. 'Spoiled beast,' she said as she pulled apart a few small pieces and put them onto a saucer on the floor.

Jet fell upon the food as if he had been starved for a week. He made the growling noises of satisfaction as he ate and Esme wished, for a moment, that she was a cat. Simple life. Simple pleasures. That made her think of Luke leaning slightly toward her as if he was considering kissing her. Which brought with it the crushing sense of failure. She had missed her chance, been too slow and too nervous.

And now Kate Foster had arrived. Luke was a confident man. And he looked like a Viking god. Kate was a whole and healthy woman, one who wasn't terrified of men. Soon, they would be making naked, beautiful, confident love.

She felt sick.

'This is unworthy of you,' she said out loud.

Jet, who was licking the saucer so that it scooted across the tiled floor, didn't look up.

'And that is unworthy of you.' She picked up the saucer and dumped it into the washing-up bowl. Jet sat back on his haunches and began an ungainly wash-session. Esme couldn't help feel it was directed at her.

It was wet and windy outside, so she layered up with a waterproof coat and slipped a small pebble from her collection into her pocket. She often picked up interesting stones on her beach walks and kept them around the house. Her latest borrow from the bookshop had a section on charms and she thought there was no harm in trying a couple. She would have thought it absolute nonsense in the past, witch or not, but now that she had dehexed a book, she felt differently.

The wind smacked into her body as she rounded the corner of Strand House. The cottages weren't far away and Esme could already hear the loud snapping of the tarps lashed around the roof and windows. Kate had presumably discovered that the old building wasn't weather-tight, and Esme couldn't help being impressed by her practicality.

Satisfied that she wasn't going to be interrupting a group of builders, but questioning whether Kate could really be staying in the cottage in this state, she knocked on the front door. There was no answer, which wasn't a surprise. She was pretty sure that the sound of her knuckles on the painted wooden door had been swallowed by the flapping tarp and the howl of the wind.

It ought to be different for a person inside, she

reasoned, so she tried again, hammering with the side of her fist this time.

She waited for a minute, listening intently for sounds from within. Caught in a moment of indecision, she scanned the front of the cottages. It was a short row of three. The first was in the state of renovation, and that was why she had chosen to knock on its door. Next door was in the condition it had always been. Dilapidated. The roof sagging and the windows blank. The one next to that was even worse. The roof was bowed inward and tiles that had long since given up the fight lay on the ground around the exterior walls. The front door was boarded up and had been since Esme could remember.

She crossed the small front garden to the middle cottage and knocked on that door. When there was no answer there, she put her hands up to the glass in the downstairs window and peered inside. Although there were no curtains up, it was still hard to see anything. It certainly didn't appear inhabited.

Although, on second look, there were candles in the middle of the room. And a camping stove. Esme tried knocking on the door one last time.

Kate clearly wasn't home and she ought to come back later. Esme hesitated, wrestling with her desire to see the woman. Part of her wanted to face the creature she had seen at the castle, to confirm for her own mind that there was something wrong. Another part of her wanted to welcome Kate Foster to the island, to try to forge a connection. The island had allowed Kate to stay. That had to mean something.

She tried the door. It wasn't locked and opened easily. There was an inner door that was ajar. Closing the outer door behind her, she pushed through and into the main living space. 'Hello?' She called out. 'Anybody home?'

The cottage was all on one level. There was an attic space with a hatch for access, but the living quarters comprised a tiny vestibule, which mainly provided a double door system for warmth and shelter from the weather, the second door opening into the living room. It was a good size and you could place a small dining table at one end and still have room for a sofa and a couple of comfy chairs. The original chimney and fireplace were extant, but in clear need of renovation. A hall led away from the living room, and there was a small bathroom and a double bedroom off it. At the end, a compact kitchen that hadn't been touched since the nineteen sixties. It still had the original Formica surfaces, sliding door cabinets and a tall cabinet with thick ribbed glass doors. Esme knew she had little excuse for looking around the cottage, but she felt a compulsion she didn't want to examine too closely.

It was even colder in the kitchen and Esme could hear something scurrying under the units. She could see how lovely it could be with a bit of care and attention, though, and she understood what Kate had seen. It was a shame to let a home fall to ruin like this. With people in the world without a roof over their head, it was downright immoral.

With a new perspective on Kate Foster's role on the island, Esme took a notebook and pen from her bag, intending to leave a note for the other woman. She would leave her number and hopefully Kate would call. They could clear the air.

Next to the kitchen there was another door and Esme opened it, expecting a linen press. Instead, it was another bedroom. This one was much smaller than the first and it was completely devoid of furniture, except for a single blow-up mattress on the floor.

It also contained a dead body.

CHAPTER TWENTY-FIVE

The smell hit Esme at the same time as her brain caught up to the fact that she wasn't just seeing a rumpled sleeping bag underneath a pile of clothes, but she was actually seeing a lifeless corpse. She put her hand over her mouth and nose, gagging.

It was a man. He was wearing a black shirt and jeans and had spiky white-blond hair. There was a long black leather coat thrown casually to the right of the sleeping bag and the leather gleamed in the half-light as if it was wet. The corpse's skin had the waxy appearance of the very dead.

The recognition started with the leather coat and then washed over her in a single wave. It was the man who had visited the bookshop. The one who didn't believe in magic, but liked collecting books about it anyway. The man she and Luke had smiled about, had considered a harmless enthusiast. Iain.

She took a step closer to the pile of clothes, part of her brain still hoping that perhaps she was mistaken. That the smell was due to rotting food, not a person. Perhaps Kate Foster was just a really bad housekeeper and not, as it appeared, a deranged murderer. The urge to laugh bubbled up and Esme recognised the impulse as hysteria. There wasn't time for that now. She was a healer. Almost a trained nurse. She ought to check for signs of life.

Esme opened her mouth to ask if the man was all right, but more of the smell got in the moment she parted her lips and she couldn't help retching. She swallowed hard and covered her mouth with her hand, knowing enough from television that she really shouldn't vomit all over a crime scene. She also knew that a smell like that meant decomposition. The man was definitely past saving.

Esme couldn't move for a moment. She couldn't be a nurse or a helper, there was nothing to heal, and in that absence she froze. There was a dead man in this sad little room and nothing she did would change that fact.

She couldn't stop staring at the collar of the black shirt. It was open at the base of Iain's neck and the fabric was shiny around the button where someone had used too hot an iron. She could see flakes of dry skin, sprinkled white on the material. At once, she could imagine Iain picking the shirt from his wardrobe and putting it on. She could see him brushing those flakes away, maybe even worrying about them being visible. The vulnerability of it made her lose her breath. The thought that this man had got dressed one day, with no idea that his life would drain away a few hours later. It was the sheer random mundanity of it that made her head spin.

As she stared at the shirt collar, she saw something move. It was a flash of creamy white wriggling at the edge of the black fabric.

Bile was already rising, Esme's instincts knowing this was very wrong before her conscious mind caught up. With another step, her gaze locked onto the gruesome sight and unable to look away even as she felt her revulsion growing, she comprehended what was underneath the shirt. Maggots.

Finally, her muscles remembered how to move. She took a step back. She had to get out. Kate Foster could return at any moment. Esme hadn't imagined the creature at the castle. She wasn't going crazy or being deceived by jealousy. Either Kate Foster was something other than human, or she was seriously unhinged.

LUKE WAS POTTERING about in the bookshop, refilling some gaps in the shelves with books from the stockroom. If somebody had quizzed him on why, exactly, he had picked up a volume of folk herbal remedies and placed it with the books on military history, he couldn't have told them, but he felt the bookshop hum with satisfaction so knew it was right.

He had tea in his favourite mug and a piece of fruit-cake, delivered by Fiona that morning. In return, she had gone away with a handful of board books for Hamish. Luke hadn't even been aware that the shop stocked books for toddlers, but Hamish had crawled through the stacked shelves until they appeared.

The shop wasn't the only one humming. He realised, with a second of shock, that he had been doing the same. Humming with a contented happiness and calm that would have seemed impossible to the Luke of a few months earlier. If his father and brother could see him now, they wouldn't recognise him. The thought brought a pang of guilt, but it was too small to puncture the bubble of satisfaction. He had always been the quiet, bookish one in his small family, it was just the bar for that label had been so incredibly low and it had been so thoroughly ridiculed, that he had feared he would never be anything other than a carbon copy of his dear old dad. A macho archetype who used his size and strength to get his own way. Violent. Angry. And filled with a raging grief that was a fire that would never burn out.

THE LANDLINE RANG and he answered. It was Mona, the woman from the Edinburgh bookshop.

'Do you want to buy a shitload of stock?' She sounded upset.

'What's wrong?'

'Conrad called from New Zealand. He's decided to make his sabbatical permanent and he says he's closing the place. He doesn't want me to run it anymore. So that's me out of a job.'

'I'm sorry,' Luke said.

'Me too,' Mona said, sounding pissed off. 'So, do you want stock? You're welcome to come up and have a look at it all. Conrad said to call a house clearance place, which is basically paying somebody to take all the books. It's his money he's burning, but it still isnae right. I don't know why he's suddenly in such a hurry. I do the accounts and place is solvent, even with paying me and the rates going up last year. I don't understand. What if he's having a wee moment and then he comes to his senses and regrets it?'

Luke listened to Mona vent, his own mind whirring. 'Did something happen?'

'Not that I know of,' she said. Adding quickly, 'I didn't do anything wrong.'

'Of course not,' Luke tried to be soothing.

'Conrad said it was too dangerous, which is pretty doolally. Right?'

'Maybe not so crazy. You know I said about toxins on books? I got hurt by some really badly. Have you received any strange deliveries? Books from other shops that you weren't expecting?' Having found the hexed book from the Shambles, Luke was pretty sure that was the only source, but he didn't want to take any chances. He didn't want a nice kid like Mona getting hurt.

'Nothing like that,' Mona said. 'It's been business as usual. Better than usual, really. I put us on Insta and I'm getting some traction. There are collectors all over the world and they love the thought of buying from a wee place in bonnie Scotland. Especially the Americans.'

'So it's definitely not a financial decision. Something has spooked him?'

'Sales are up. Accounts are healthy. Which I pointed out. Speaking of sales, look out for a guy called Iain. I sent him your way.'

'I met him,' Luke said. 'Matrix coat.'

'Aye,' Mona laughed, sounding more like herself. 'He's a wee character. But, hang on... you met him?'

'He came to the shop. Told us you had recommended us.'

'He was in here on Monday, asking after the same stuff and he went all vague when I mentioned your place. I assumed he hadn't made the trip.'

He had probably forgotten, Luke thought. The wards protected the island and tended to make people forget about it once they left.

'I gave him your address again, though. He said he was gonnae visit.'

'Thanks,' Luke said. 'And good luck with whatever you do next. I'm sorry about the shop.'

'Me, too,' Mona said. 'It's a wee shame.'

· · ·

Luke couldn't settle to work or reading after Mona's phone call. His first instinct had been to call Esme. He realised that she was always the person he wanted to speak to. About this or anything in his life.

He prowled to the fridge, hoping to distract himself with some food. His stomach growled as soon as he thought about eating and he realised he hadn't had lunch. The fridge was empty apart from a half a pint of milk and a sliver of cheddar. He stared at the uninspiring offerings without really seeing them, still thinking about Esme. He wasn't just attracted to her, he was man enough to admit it. It was something far deeper and far more terrifying than that. Unable to work out what to do with that information, he went with the more straightforward problem to solve. He would go to the pub for an early dinner.

He was the only customer at The Rising Moon, which suited him just fine. Seren kept decent Wi-Fi for customers and he used his phone to browse the newspaper archive for the York area. Mona's call had reminded him of something the barman in the Shambles had said about Graham. Mona had said that Conrad had told her running the Edinburgh shop was too dangerous. Had somebody threatened him? Or had he heard that somebody connected with the shop had died and decided that it was, somehow, his fault?

The barman in York had said that Graham had been really upset by the death of one of his regular customers. He had said it had been suicide, which might not make the news, but it seemed worth a look. If the customer had been a regular, he might have been local to York and therefore of interest to the local news. And at least Luke had a fairly small time period to check, just a month or two before the Shambles Book Emporium burned.

On the second page of results, he was rewarded by a headline dated a couple of weeks before the fire in the bookshop: Man falls to death from city walls. Clicking on the story, Luke read that the man's body had been found in the early hours of the morning and the death was being considered 'suspicious'. There was a picture of the spot next to the ancient York walls, worn stone steps visible in one corner of the image. The police were appealing for witnesses. A follow-up article was linked at the bottom of the story, below a panel of adverts. Dated a week later, the article named the deceased as Nicholas Jones, and that police were no longer treating the death as suspicious. The man was known to have been suffering from an illness and they asked that the family's wishes for privacy be respected at this difficult time. There was a picture of Nicholas Jones in presumably happier times. It showed a hipster-ish man wearing a waistcoat, shirt and jeans. He had long dark hair and the cheekbones and colouring that Luke associated with native Americans. His arm was slung around a young woman who was gazing up at him adoringly. The expression of love wasn't the only striking thing about the photograph, however. He recognised her.

CHAPTER TWENTY-SIX

Head spinning, Luke left The Rising Moon and walked the short distance back to the bookshop. He wanted to check the ledger from the stockroom and see if he could find the name Nicholas – or Elin – Jones.

He had barely started looking when he heard the shop bell. He put down the ledger and went to greet the visitor, closing the stockroom door behind him.

Kate Foster was browsing the shelves at the front of the shop.

He managed a normal-sounding 'hello'. Seeing her in person reinforced the fact that she was the woman from the news article. He was in no doubt that she was the woman from the picture, that he hadn't been mistaken. Which meant that the woman calling herself Kate Foster had been married to Nicholas Jones, erstwhile customer of the Shambles Book Emporium. The place that had sent at least two hexed books to other shops. Now, that bookshop had burned to the ground, and she was here, on the island, and was using a new name. He didn't know what these facts meant. Perhaps she had wanted the freshest of fresh starts. Perhaps there were financial difficulties that had contributed to her husband's suicide and she was running from them. The possibilities flickered through his mind, and he felt off-balance. One thing he was very sure of, though, was that he fervently hoped that this was a genuine visit to buy a book and not another attempt at asking him out. He manoeuvred behind the counter, wanting to put some furniture between them and to formalise their roles. Customer. Proprietor.

That was when he noticed her suitcase. It was the compact sort with wheels and looked expensive. She was carrying it by the retracted handle, the wheels off the ground. Either she was planning to buy a lot of books or she was on her way off the island. He hoped it was the latter. And the sooner the better.

'We know each other, now,' she began, flashing him a gleaming white smile, 'don't we?'

He nodded. He didn't agree, but politeness dictated one possible response. And he was a shop proprietor. Part of the job was being polite to customers. Although, now that he thought about it, Alvis's instruction book hadn't said anything about that. Maybe he could use his own judgement.

'I want to see the books.'

Luke gestured at the shop. 'Help yourself. If there's something in particular you're looking for, let me know.'

'No.' Kate's smile was slick with red lipstick. It made her mouth look like a warning sign. 'The books that aren't on display. The special books.'

'I don't know what you mean.' Luke forced himself not to look toward the stockroom door.

The smile disappeared. A second later, it was replaced with something altogether more sultry. She placed her forearms onto the counter and leaned forward, affording him a view of smooth tanned skin dipping below the neckline of

216

her soft cream jumper. Her eyes were hooded and her voice dropped low. 'I thought we were friends. Don't you trust me?'

Luke realised that he couldn't hear the shop humming anymore. He understood something else: he didn't trust Kate Foster and the shop didn't either.

A little pout. 'I know they're here. This isn't an ordinary bookshop. It's like the Shambles Emporium.'

He went still. 'The place in York?'

She straightened up. 'I used to shop there. With my husband.'

'You're married?' Luke decided it wouldn't be wise to let her know he already knew this, or that he had been investigating the hexed books.

She nodded. Not smiling or looking sultry. Suddenly, in fact, looking furious. 'Forever.'

Several questions were jostling Luke's mind, but his hindbrain was telling him not to get distracted. This woman had been married to a regular customer of the Shambles Bookshop. She might even have been the female assistant at the shop that Graham's mother had mentioned. And if that guess was right, it meant she had ample opportunity to send hexed books from the Shambles. Which would make her... magic?

'We do stock some more unusual titles,' he said cautiously. 'Rare books. Specialist subjects. It would help if you could let me know the area you are interested in.'

She smiled thinly. 'Magical lore. Supernatural history. Practical spellcasting. Divination. Summoning.'

Floored, Luke struggled for an appropriate response. 'I didn't know you were... a scholar.' He had been fishing, but he hadn't expected her to say it outright. Her openness was new and it set alarm bells ringing. From his research, he knew that there were plenty of enthusiasts interested in the arcane and occult, but where, exactly, did the line blur between academics and those who took a more practical interest?

'It's not something I advertise,' Kate continued. 'But I would very much like to see your collection.'

Luke led Kate to the back of the shop, to the esoteric section. It wasn't always in the same place and sometimes didn't seem to be there at all. He wasn't all that surprised to find that the shop was playing hide and seek again.

'It's usually here,' he said, waving at the bookshelves that lined the back wall. 'Between cookery and psychology, but we don't seem to have anything in stock at the moment. Was there something in particular you were looking for?'

When he turned to speak, he found Kate uncomfortably close. He took a step back and felt the bookshelves against his back.

'I'm sure you can find some books for me to look at,' Kate said. 'Maybe you haven't got all your stock on display. It would make sense to keep some things away from the general public. I'm happy to wait while you fetch them.'

Wanting nothing more than an excuse to get further away from the woman, Luke nodded. 'I'll look in the stockroom. Give me a minute.'

'Sure.' She turned her attention to the cookery section and he made his way to the front of the shop. He would use the landline while she was distracted at the back of the shop. Hammer would be the obvious choice, he was the island's enforcer and muscle. Instead, he called Esme. Her phone rang and rang. No answer.

CHAPTER TWENTY-SEVEN

Esme opened the door to the bookshop and walked inside. The doorbell, that was usually a gentle chime alerting the Book Keeper that a visitor had arrived, was a crashing discordant noise. An alarm.

It wasn't the only thing that was wrong. Kate Foster was sitting on the floor in the biggest room of the shop, a can of spray paint in one hand and a wheelie case open to reveal several plastic bottles of liquid. She had pushed back the kilim rug and was in the middle of desecrating the ancient oak floorboards with squiggly symbols.

Esme kicked herself. Instead of following her heart and coming directly to warn Luke, she ought to have called Bee and Tobias. She had texted Hammer to tell him she was coming to the bookshop rather than meeting him at the castle, but now that seemed nowhere near enough. Belatedly, she realised that her first call should have been to the police. This woman, shiny and perfect as she looked, had most likely murdered Iain. It was too late for recriminations, though. She was standing a few feet from a killer.

'You don't look all that surprised to see me,' Kate said conversationally as she finished spraying a little more paint onto her design. It was a circle, like the one painted on the castle wall. Instead of symbols on the outside of the circle at the four compass points, the symbols were drawn inside.

'What on earth do you think you are doing?' Esme knew she needed to turn around and get the hell out, but she also didn't see Luke. *Where was Luke?*

'A little renovation. I told you all.' A little smile, pleased and cruel, played at the corners of her mouth.

'I was looking for you,' Esme said, her voice sounding hoarse. All of her saliva seemed to have dried up. 'At your house.'

Kate's eyes narrowed. 'You went inside?'

'I did.' Esme forced herself to maintain eye contact. There was a chance that Kate hadn't seen Luke and that he was hiding somewhere. If she kept Kate focused on her, he could get out, go and get help.

'You're looking for Luke, I presume.' She gave Esme a knowing look. 'He ran off, I believe. Wise of him. You're staying, I assume?'

'Why do you say that?' Esme's fingers were tingling and her chest felt tight. She wasn't getting enough oxygen and she reminded herself to take a breath.

'Curiosity killed the cat.' Kate gestured to the symbols on the floor. 'And witches are always so curious. We want to know everything, and it's always our downfall. Makes you wonder how many of us would have been burned at the stake if we had just behaved ourselves?'

'I can't tell if you're joking.' Every part of Esme wanted to turn and flee, but she didn't know where Luke was and she didn't want to leave this maniac alone in the bookshop. Her eyes flicked to the bottles of liquid in the open case.

'I never joke about witchcraft.'

The door to the stockroom was wide open, light spilling out into the corridor. And there was a strange buzzing sensation in the atmosphere, like static or the feeling in the atmosphere before a lightning storm. It made the hairs on Esme's skin stand up.

'What is that?' Esme pointed to the circle. 'It's like the one you drew at the castle.'

Kate shook her head. 'Don't pretend you don't know. Circle of protection. Basic stuff.' She moved so that she was standing inside the circle, dragging the open case close enough so that she could reach the bottles. She picked one up and began unscrewing the lid.

Esme moved forwards, intent on grabbing the case, or maybe Kate herself, but a muffled thump came from inside the stockroom, distracting her. Luke appeared in the doorway. His lip was bleeding and he looked a little dazed.

Kate glanced over her shoulder, a look of surprised irritation crossing her face. 'Hello, sleepyhead. I must admit, I thought that would knock you out more permanently. Not another step, please.' She turned and splashed liquid over the floor, splashing over Esme at the same time. The smell was unmistakable. Petrol.

'You hit me,' Luke said, staring at Kate Foster in disbelief. 'What did you hit me with?' He shook his head as if trying to clear it.

'Just a little spell of my own devising.' She gave them both a wide smile that had no warmth in it. 'Amazing what you can learn from books, isn't it?'

'Elin Jones,' Luke said, his voice slurring very slightly. Esme wondered what magic Kate had used and whether it had caused permanent damage. The image of Iain's decomposing corpse swam to the front of her mind and her head span dizzily.

Kate Foster raised her eyebrows. 'Am I supposed to be impressed?' She had another bottle open and was dousing the floor around her, and then squeezing the bottle to widen her radius.

'That's your name, isn't it?' Luke said. He took another step toward Kate, but Esme could see he was unsteady on his feet. His skin was very white, the blood from his lip stark against his complexion. He didn't seem to be noticing that Kate was splashing petrol around, soaking the books, wooden floor and shelves, her own clothes. The smell was pungent and hit the back of Esme's throat, making her cough.

'It was,' she said, bending to the case again. 'I go by Kate, now.'

Esme lunged for Kate, trying to stop her from opening a third bottle. Her hands bounced off an invisible barrier, one that made her whole body spasm in a single instant of agonising shock. Esme had never stuck her fingers into an electrical socket, but this was exactly how she had imagined it would feel. She checked her clothes to see if she had wet herself, as it had felt as if she had lost all control of her body for a few seconds, and was momentarily relieved that her front was already soaked with petrol which would hide a urine stain. Then her mind came fully back online, and she remembered why being covered in petrol was a more terrible, frightening thing. Especially now that the woman inside the circle was on her last bottle of petrol and Esme had to assume that wasn't the end of her trick.

'Why are you doing this?' Luke was holding his head as in pain, and he still seemed woozy. He staggered as he came closer to the circle and Kate and Esme wondered if he was acting, trying to get Kate to lower her guard. 'Don't touch her!' She warned him. 'The circle hurts. It gave me an electric shock.' She shook her hands, fingers still tingling painfully.

'I came to see why my little gift didn't work. This

place,' Kate waved a hand, 'is supposed to be a pile of ashes.'

'You sent the hexed book,' Esme said.

'Ding ding ding.' Kate pointed a finger. 'She's got it.'

'But why?'

The look that Kate shot at Esme was part mocking amusement and part simmering rage. 'You're all the same.' The words spat like a curse. 'You think you're so special. You're not special. And I'm going to prove it. You'll burn just the same as anybody else.'

Esme couldn't process the words. 'What have we done to you? Why would you-'

'Your husband died,' Luke said quietly. 'Nicholas.'

Kate whipped around. 'Don't say his name.'

'The paper said it was an illness, but the word in the Shambles is that he topped himself.'

Luke wasn't looking at Esme and she realised he was trying to hold Kate's attention. He probably wanted her to take the chance to run away. But she wasn't going to leave him.

'Those people,' Kate was saying. 'They didn't care who they hurt. Dealing in information they don't understand. They had to be stopped. You lot are even worse. I think you might know a thing or two, especially you,' she looked at Esme, 'and you're still buying and selling like it's nothing.'

'Not like it's nothing,' Luke said. 'We look after the information. We keep it safe.'

'You sent the book,' Esme said, trying to catch up. Her own fury was building. 'Luke nearly died.'

The smile that crossed Kate Foster's face was a twitch of muscles, nothing warm or happy about it. 'It was meant to burn down the bookshop. I had to come here to find out why that hadn't happened and I found you. And Tobias. And now Fiona and those freak children of hers. All of you. There is something very wrong with this place and I am going to clean it up.'

The wrongness of the woman hadn't been imaginary. Later she might feel some pride in that fact, but right now Esme was consumed with the danger she represented. Every hair was standing up on her arms and her instinct to freeze or flee was trying to override her system. She fought it. 'What have we done to you?'

'You're all the same. Dangerous. Don't care who you hurt...'

'That's not true.' Esme interrupted, her fury gaining ground on her fear. This was the woman who had tried to kill Luke. She had killed Iain and, apparently, Graham at the York bookshop, too. The evil of it was staggering.

'You don't know what you're doing,' Kate said, eyes blazing with barely controlled fury. 'Ordinary people get hurt.'

'Ordinary people like Iain. What had he done to you?'

Luke frowned at Esme, his expression questioning.

Kate waved a hand airily. 'He was dabbling in something he didn't understand. Supplying the demand for the information, even if he didn't know what he was dealing with. He would have started using eventually. And if not, he was still part of the problem.'

'Besides,' Esme said, her voice grim, 'you needed human blood for your little spells. That's why he died, wasn't it? Your convenience. Your desires. It wasn't anything high-minded. You're just a murderer.'

Esme was hoping to use Luke's trick. If she could keep Kate's eyes on her, Luke would have a chance at getting outside and phoning for help. The big lug wasn't leaving, though. At least she didn't think so, she didn't want to shift her gaze to where he was standing in case Kate followed suit.

'Hardly little spells. I'm protecting people. Innocent people,' Kate spat. 'My husband stumbled into your world and he didn't stand a chance. I'm going to stop that from happening to anybody else.'

'I don't understand. I've never met your husband.'

'It seduced him. Both of us, really. I loved it, too. In the beginning we were so excited.' Her eyes were shining. 'We could do so many things. Things that shouldn't be possible. Fairy tales, but in real life.'

Fairy tales were gruesome as far as Esme remembered, but she kept her thoughts to herself.

'It doesn't matter now,' Kate said, the light in her eyes dimming. 'He's gone.'

'We can help you,' Esme said. 'You don't have to do this. You shouldn't mess with magic. It's making you sick.' Esme found it hard to believe that the woman couldn't feel the damage she was doing. If she looked carefully, she thought she could see a dark miasma surrounding Kate's body, as if she herself had become cursed.

A short laugh cut the air. 'Like you care.'

'There's been enough death. Surely.'

'Not nearly enough. Nicholas is gone.' She threw the empty bottle of petrol to one side and produced a metal lighter from her pocket. 'And we are going to join him.'

CHAPTER TWENTY-EIGHT

The smell of petrol was clogging the back of Esme's throat, but her fear, her ever-present companion, seemed to have left the building. She felt nothing except a pure, clear rage. How dare this woman put petrol on the books? How dare she threaten Luke? The shop. The island.

'You are wrong,' she said, her voice conversational. 'I would say I'm sorry for you, but it would be a lie. I understand your grief, but you are hurting people. Deliberately. There's no excuse. In fact, you've taken the memory of your husband and twisted it into something evil. You have destroyed whatever good he stood for, too.' Esme had no idea if Nicholas had stood for good. She didn't much care. He was probably like the rest of them, a little bit good, a little bit bad, often confused and sometimes lazy. What she cared about was that while they were talking about Nicholas, Kate Foster wasn't flicking the lighter in her hand.

'He would be proud of me.'

'I doubt that's true. I think he would be horrified.'

Kate's face spasmed. 'You don't know him.'

'No. Thank Goddess. If he would be proud of you becoming a homicidal hypocrite, I'm glad I never had the pleasure.'

Kate's face suddenly cleared. 'You're trying to distract me. You're trying to provoke an argument so that I forget my purpose. Delay the inevitable. It won't help. There's nobody coming. Or if they are, they'll be too late.'

Kate flicked the lighter open and used her thumb to produce a flame. Esme closed her eyes instinctively, expecting there to be enough fumes in the air for the place to go up even before the flame touched the petrol-soaked books.

She opened them again to see Kate flicking at the lighter repeatedly and the flame stubbornly refusing to appear. A small, deranged part of Esme had the urge to offer her a light. She almost wanted the inevitable to be over. The unbearable tension of waiting to die a fiery death.

'Don't you care about the good things you are destroying?' She tried. 'The cures for illnesses. There could be a cure for cancer in this place. How do you think you'll be judged?'

Kate didn't look convinced, but she paused in the business of flicking the lighter. 'If one of these books says it can cure cancer, it will be a lie. Or there will be a price that nobody would want to pay. That's how they get you. They offer the world. Offer whatever you want and no consequences, but it's a lie. All of it.'

'There's always a price,' Esme said. 'I would never say otherwise, but that doesn't mean there aren't useful exchanges to be made. It doesn't make it all bad.'

'You sound like Nicholas,' Kate said, her mouth twisting. 'And look what happened to him.'

'What did happen?'

She let out a choking sound. 'He got so sick...' She stopped speaking. 'No. You're not going to...' She tried flicking the lighter again.

Luke was close behind Kate, had been moving slowly and quietly while Esme had been talking. She could see him in her peripheral vision and she forced herself not to focus on him, not to betray him with a movement in her gaze. She kept her eyes firmly on Kate and the hand that was holding the lighter.

'Let's go outside, get some fresh air, talk this over. You don't have to do this.'

Flick. Flick. Flick.

Esme wondered what would happen when Luke tackled Kate. Would he be fast enough to be able to wrestle the lighter away from her grasp? Or would Kate have enough time to flick it once more, maybe lighting it? She could torch them all, and the shop with its centuries of magical knowledge, with one tiny movement of her thumb. 'You don't want to do this,' she said, just saying whatever came into her head, trying to keep Kate's attention firmly fixed forward. Luke was physically stronger than her, even in his currently weakened state. Maybe he would be able to withstand the electrical shock of the magical barrier long enough to grab Kate and pull her out of the circle. 'You don't want to die.'

Kate hesitated. Some of the manic energy seemed to have dissipated and Esme could see her thinking. Maybe the reality of setting fire to the shop while she was inside it was beginning to dawn. Maybe she was remembering the charred remains of the other shops, imagining what it had been like for the booksellers trapped inside as they felt the intense heat, their skin bubbling and charring and the smell of their own flesh cooking filling the air. Or maybe the circle would protect her. Did she intend to stand unscathed in the centre of an inferno?

'How do you know that will protect you from the flames? Or the fumes? You will die along with us.'

'I'm ready for it. The cleansing fire. They knew what they were doing in the trials, you know? Fire is the only way to eradicate the evil of witchcraft. You deserve to die and so do I. This circle is my insurance. It means nobody can stop me or pull me out.' She cocked her head. 'I don't hear fire engines, though, so I hardly needed to worry.'

Luke lunged for Kate, and Esme saw him thrown back as he hit the invisible barrier of the circle. He crumpled to the floor, moaning.

'Luke!'

He lifted his head and she could see pain etched across his features. He tried a reassuring smile, but it was a grimace. She could see the sheen of sweat on his forehead.

Kate raised the lighter again, her thumb poised.

Esme knew she could make a break for the door, try to get out before Kate flicked the lighter and set them all on fire. But she was covered in petrol and probably wouldn't make it in time. Besides, she wasn't about to leave Luke. Or the bookshop. It didn't make logical sense, but Esme couldn't help that.

There wasn't time for Luke to get out now, either. Even if he was willing to leave her. Esme had to fix this. Had to find a way out for them both.

She tried to relax enough to see clearly. She didn't know how seeing Kate's true nature would help, but it was her only witchy power. She could renew the island wards, but that was performing a ritual and giving a drop or two of her blood, nothing she actually *did*. No super power. No spells. She had cleared the hex from the book, but that had been knowledge from the book. It occurred to her that the low sound she had been putting down to tinnitus, brought on my supreme stress, was, in fact, a real sound. Or real to her, at any rate. She didn't know if the others could hear it, but it was a low keening sound coming from the shop itself. Her misery increased as her heart broke a little for the bookshop. And then it hit her.

She was standing in the middle of a magical shop.

CHAPTER TWENTY-NINE

What was being a witch? Really, when you came down to it, it meant having knowledge that others didn't possess. And, if Bee was to be believed, the strength to see things how they really were. And she was the witch for Unholy Island. The Ward Witch. Bee had said that her blood worked because she belonged to the island. Looked at clearly, that meant the island belonged to her, too.

'I know you're in pain,' she said out loud, addressing the shop. 'It's abominable. But I think I can clean the books. I will find a way, if such a way exists.' She wanted to reach out and pat the nearest shelf, but didn't want to waste time. Kate had just tried her lighter again. There were perhaps seconds before she was successful.

Esme had one weapon of her own. The small penknife that she used for the ward ritual. She drew it from her skirt pocket.

Kate's eyes widened in something close to amusement. 'Are you going to stab me, Esme? I would like to see you try.'

Esme kept the blade sharp. As a much younger, more troubled woman, she had struggled with self-harm. Cutting herself had been a relief and a way to escape her reality, but not, ultimately, a very effective one. Now, she felt the same rush of calm energy that she had always felt before preparing to slice into her skin. The feeling of having a purpose and a path. When she had been self-harming, living in a group home and struggling to cope with the misery of her day-to-day existence, cutting her skin had provided a path. A route she could follow with the promise of euphoric release, however brief, that was free and available and entirely under her own control.

Long before beginning training as a nurse, she had developed the skill of cutting into skin. She knew the angle to hold the blade and how much pressure to apply for the perfect depth of cut. She looked at Kate, knowing that her blade was sharp and that, despite what Kate thought, she probably could do some decent damage, if it wasn't for the powerful circle of protection. It wasn't the size of the blade, after all, that made the difference. With a slice to the artery in Kate Foster's neck or thigh, she could do real damage.

Instead, she opened her left hand and sliced quickly across the palm. It was exactly the right place. Wrist was too dangerous, too much blood, and a shallow cut on the hand would heal more quickly than on other parts of the body. At the same time, she sank to the floor, onto her knees, and pressed her bloodied hand to the floor.

Esme didn't know if she was saying the words out loud or just inside her head. Either way, they were loud and sure. She called on the shop to wake up and protect itself. She called on the island, her island, to protect her. She didn't know if the pulse she could feel was her own, thundering in the line of fire and pain that ran across her palm or from the ancient oak boards of the shop's floor. She hoped it was the latter and repeated her supplication. And then again.

The doors blew open and the front window shattered, letting in blessed fresh air. It cut through the petrol fumes but would also provide extra oxygen for a fire. Then the walls began to shake, books were shuddering on the shaking shelves, some falling. The lights flickered wildly.

Esme looked up in time to see Kate Foster's face with an almost comical expression of surprise. The floorboards were lifting around where Esme had her hands pressed down. They wrenched upward with a ripping and splintering, the cracking wood loud as gunshot. The solid planks jutted up, breaking the painted circle. Kate cried out in pain as jagged pieces of wood flew, embedding into the arms she had thrown in front of her face to protect herself.

The circle was broken and Luke was on his feet. He lunged at Kate and connected. His arms wrapped around her from behind and was shaking the hand holding the lighter, forcing her to drop it. He lifted her bodily and began moving to the front door.

Books were flying from the shelves now, and the wind inside the shop was wild. It roared and swirled with far more force than could be expected from the openings, the air moving as if with purpose.

Trying to stand up was more difficult than Esme expected. Her hand felt stuck to the floor and pulling it away took every ounce of her strength. Her forehead broke out in sweat and her whole body felt clammy as she stumbled back. Her whole hand was a ball of pain, now, and it radiated up her arm. She doubled over with the force of it.

Kate wanted to bathe them in fire, to burn away their knowledge. She had heard about all of those poor women through the years, being persecuted for their vision and know-how, their strength and their differences. She had learned entirely the wrong lesson. She could still feel the pulse in her palm, but it felt like it was the pulse of the shop, maybe even the island. All she knew was that she wanted to put her hand back onto the floor, to complete the connection again.

Luke was struggling to stand in the doorway, the wind seemingly focused on knocking him down. Kate was struggling and kicking, fighting him all the way. Her feet kept catching the bookshelves and the building seemed to shudder each time. Whether in pain or fury, Esme couldn't tell.

'I'm getting her out,' Luke shouted, his voice still clear amongst the howl of the wind and the shaking of the building. 'Let us leave.'

'Let him out,' Esme spoke to the shop. She sank back onto her knees and put her hand onto the floor. 'Please.'

The shop seemed to calm a little, although the wind was still whipping Esme's hair and she could feel a vortex of air pulling around her body as if trying to topple her. Through watering eyes, she saw Luke back through the front door, Kate Foster's legs kicking at him now, and her whole body bucking like a wild animal.

Getting up from the floor was a little easier this time. Her hand throbbed, and she used the counter to keep herself upright. She took a shaky step toward the door, and then another. The shop was still shuddering, and there were books falling, but they were no longer flying from the shelves and in danger of slamming into her head. She felt very tired, though, and the force of the wind around her body was too strong. It would be so much easier to just lie down. The smell of petrol was catching in the back of her throat and her head was dizzy with it. Her hand was still bleeding. Perhaps she had cut too deeply after all. Lost the knack. That was what she got for being mentally healthy, she decided.

She was moving. Crawling on her hands and knees

now, although she didn't remember falling back to the floor. The wrecked floorboards made the ground into an obstacle course. Splinters of wood were tiny spikes of pain, and they helped her to keep thinking. Little bright sparks of clarity. Stars in a darkening sky.

Esme felt tired. She was still inching forward because part of her had told her she ought to move. Ought to be fleeing. Or freezing. One of the two. She moved her uninjured hand forward and planted it on the floor. Followed with a single knee. Every movement a triumph. Hand. Knee. Pain. Pulsing pain.

A calm voice in her mind informed her that she wasn't making sense. That her thoughts were rambling and that she wasn't paying sufficient attention to her surroundings, her situation. The fumes were toxic. She had expended energy communicating with the shop. But she needed to do something. She couldn't go to sleep yet. There was something important.

'Take my hand.'

Her vision was blurry. Tears, wind, fumes, exhaustion. She blinked and it cleared enough to reveal a rectangle of light. The light was abruptly cut by a large shape. The shape spoke again, sounding sort of cross. 'Esme! Come to me. Take my hand.'

She was in the bookshop. The entrance was tightly packed with bookshelves, and the rectangle of light was the doorway to the street. She had crawled toward the exit, at least. The shape was Luke and he had his arm outstretched, crossing the threshold. His body was on the outside, and she wasn't sure if he was able to step inside. His arm was shaking, but his hand was reaching for her.

Time had slowed and everything felt impossibly difficult. She told herself to get to her feet. And that seemed impossible, but somehow she did it. Then she told her arm to lift, her fingers to find his, but it took its sweet time. Moving as if in a dream. A bad dream. The one where you were stuck to the floor, and the monster was coming.

Then her skin brushed his and time snapped back to normal. The muted sounds of the shop and the wind and somebody screaming obscenities all rushed in.

Luke's fingers wrapped firmly around Esme's, gripping tightly and pulling her forward. And then she was through the doorway and out. The fresh air out here was sweet and clean and she felt her chest expand, her lungs inflating with the first proper breath in what felt like hours.

She stumbled against Luke's chest and felt his arms wrap around her. She put her arms around him and held on.

CHAPTER THIRTY

Luke's head was still spinning from whatever Kate had thrown at him. He had been in the stockroom, looking for his mobile. Having not been able to get Esme on the landline, he had decided to send a text message to everyone on the island, figuring that would give him the biggest and quickest chance of success. The next thing he remembered was something hitting the back of his head. He had gone down hard, which must have been when he smashed his face and split his lip. He had definitely lost consciousness for a few moments and he hoped he had escaped without a concussion.

He drew in lungfuls of cold, clean air and felt his blood rushing in his veins. However muzzy his head felt, they were all alive. And the shop wasn't on fire. After he had manhandled Kate Foster out of the building, he had been joined by Hammer. Luke didn't know how he had known to come to the shop, he hadn't had time to finish his text messages before he had been knocked out by Kate, but he was extremely glad to see the man-mountain. Even more grateful when Hammer had simply taken charge of his hissing, spitting captive. He hadn't even had a chance to be irritated by how easy Hammer made it look. His attention had been taken by the more pressing need to find out why Esme wasn't directly behind him. He had gone back to the shop entrance and thought his heart was going to explode from fear when he saw her on the floor, struggling to move. It was as if a physical force was preventing her from leaving, the same force that didn't seem to want him back inside. He tightened his arms around her, as if reassuring himself that she was really there. Whole. Unhurt. Apart from the wicked cut on her palm where she had sliced into her hand.

Hammer was standing a little way up the street, Kate Foster against the wall of one of the houses, his arms boxing her in. He wasn't touching her, but he had formed a human cage and she was leaning against the wall, staring at him with hatred. She was no longer kicking or screaming into his face, so that was something.

Esme was in his arms. Something he had dreamed about for months. Her body was pressed against his and her hands pressed against his back, anchoring herself as if he was a lifeboat and she was drowning.

That snapped him out of his romantic reverie. She was traumatised. She was only holding onto him because he was her friend and she needed comfort. He told himself, and his body, to get a fucking grip.

And then she went up on tiptoe and kissed him. It was on the cheek, her lips brushing his skin so quickly he could almost have imagined it.

'Thank you,' she said, and he forced himself to meet her gaze.

'I think I should be thanking you. Did you know you could do that?' He knew he should release her now. She felt steady on her feet and was no longer in imminent danger.

She wasn't letting go of him, though, and he decided he would stop holding her the moment she stopped holding him.

'What's the play here?' Hammer called over his shoulder.

'Call the police,' Esme said, glancing over. She saw Kate's hand dip into her pocket and then up to her face. 'Stop her!'

Kate Foster had something at her mouth and then it was gone.

'Shit,' Luke said, dropping his arms and moving toward them.

Kate was already crumpling to the ground, her eyes rolling back in her head.

'Call nine nine nine!' Esme was on her knees, getting Kate onto her back and tilting her head back to open her airway. She swept fingers inside her mouth, even though she knew Kate had already swallowed the pill or poison or hexed object, whatever it had been.

'Causeway is out,' Luke said.

'They'll send the air ambulance,' Esme replied, starting chest compressions.

He hesitated for another second. He wasn't as good a person as Esme. She had snapped into action immediately and was trying to save the life of the woman who had, moments earlier, tried to kill them all.

HAMMER WATCHED the air ambulance touch down on the scrubby ground of the car park. He and Luke had carried Kate Foster on the stretcher down the track to the car park and there was a relief to pass the burden to the paramedics.

Two calm and highly efficient people moved in

synchronicity, speaking to Kate Foster and to each other in the shorthand of their business.

'Has she taken anything, do you know?' One of the paramedics asked.

Hammer shook his head. 'Maybe. Don't know.' He wasn't lying. Esme had said she had seen her put something in her mouth in the moments before she collapsed, but Hammer didn't know anything for sure.

The woman on the stretcher looked very small, now. Her perfect skin had a waxy appearance and the colour had drained away. Hammer knew that people could bounce back from worse. He just wasn't sure that would be a good thing. It had occurred to him when Luke had dialled the emergency services that it might be better not to bother. To let Kate Foster's unconscious body slip quietly into the sea. It wasn't a kind thought. Not a moral impulse. But Hammer had never pretended to be otherwise.

He watched the paramedics work. They clamped an oxygen mask over Kate Foster's face and one of them, a woman with short brown hair and a tiredness around her eyes, told Hammer which hospital they were going to and that he and Luke needed to clear the area. And then they were loading her into the helicopter and the rotors were moving.

THE NEWS about the events at the bookshop, and Luke and Esme's narrow escape, flew around the island. Esme didn't feel up to a meal at the pub, with everybody asking questions all at once, but Seren brought around a foil dish of casserole with instructions to stick it in the oven for half an hour. 'I was going to take one to Luke, too, but he's made it to the pub.'

Esme accepted the food gratefully and ate in her warm

kitchen. Most unusually, Jet curled up on her lap, as if he wanted to be close to her. She stroked him and felt the residual tingling in her fingers and arms from the spell in the bookshop. The palm she had sliced open was covered with an adhesive dressing and the wound throbbed a little, but otherwise she felt perfectly fine.

BEE SAT in the centre of her mirrors and steeled herself. Diana was in the garden behind the house and Lucy was elsewhere. Bee didn't like to think about her youngest sister and the ways she whiled away her time so, as a general rule, she didn't. The three mirrors, silvered and misty with age, rose to her left, her right, and straight ahead. She closed her eyes for a moment and brought the bookshop to her mind: the tall shelves, packed with books, and the old wooden counter with The Book Keeper standing behind it. Then she opened her eyes and looked into the future for the bookshop. She was content with what she saw.

CLEANING the aftermath turned out to be a bigger job than Luke had anticipated. Seren had popped in while he was standing in the front room wearing a pair of rubber gloves, taken one look around the place, swore, and then left.

Esme had called to see if he needed her help, but he told her that she should rest. Truth was, he didn't want her to see the place until it was all cleared up. She'd been through enough. On the phone, she had still sounded slightly dazed.

'We were looking on the mainland for the murderer, and she was right under our noses. I can't believe it. I mean, my instincts were right, there was something off about her, but I didn't listen to them.'

'Well, you're clearly smarter than me,' Luke said. 'I didn't pick up on anything.'

'You were probably blinded by her extremely smooth skin.'

'What?'

'Nothing,' Esme said quickly, 'ignore me.'

Luke pushed a hand through his hair. 'Did you think I was interested in her?'

'No. Maybe.' Esme's voice was strained. 'She was very-'

'I wasn't.'

'Good. Okay. Good.' He heard her take a deep breath. 'Not that it's any of my business...'

'It is your business,' Luke said quietly.

Tobias offered to help clear the sodden books from the shop, but Luke had called in a specialist cleaning service. 'I promised I would do my best and I think my best is probably engaging competent professionals.' They had dowsed the place with a powdery substance which had soaked up the petrol, before clearing it away. And Hammer had turned up with his woodworking tools and helped Luke to remove, repair, and re-lay the broken floorboards. He had understood, without Luke needing to explain, that they needed to re-use as much of the original boards as possible, and Hammer spent hours trimming down the splintered edges, filling and sanding cracks, and adding in small sections of hardwood from his own stash to fill the unsalvageable places.

Tobias looked at the repairs with approval, shifting the corner of the rug to examine the boards, before moving to inspect the rest of the shop. 'The new window looks good.'

Luke had gone onto the mainland to a builder's merchants and a glazier and had the window built. Instead of the one large pane of glass set in peeling woodwork, he had ordered a smart wooden frame, freshly painted in satin black and with three little panes along the top, all of which opened so that he would be able to let a little fresh air into the shop whenever he felt the need.

The smell in the shop was almost back to normal. There was still the faintest whiff of petrol, but Luke thought he might be imagining that. It might be the memory of the smell, the way it had clogged his throat and burned his eyes.

A lot of the books in the front of the shop hadn't been salvageable, but they had been easy enough to replace. Not all of them, of course, not the older editions, but he would track those down given time. Alvis had kept a meticulous stocklist, so he knew exactly what was missing.

Even luckier, having now found the hidden stockroom, he had been able to refill the gaps in the shelves from the books in storage. The shop didn't look empty or unloved. Luke had cleaned all the shelves a second time, after the specialist cleaner had dealt with the petrol, waxing them with the tin of polish and cleaning rags he had found in the kitchenette. Finally, after long days of labour, he could detect the faintest hum: the sound of a contented shop.

Esme was resting after her yoga and meditation session with Bee. It was strange to be back in the house and acting as if everything was normal. Luke had been busy tidying up the bookshop and refused all her offers of help, saying that she had 'done more than enough for the shop' and that she should 'chill'. She was trying to take him at his word and not interpret it as a sign that he needed space from her.

Bee brought two mugs of tea over to the cushioned seating area and handed one to Esme. 'You did better today,' she said.

Esme accepted the tea, but she couldn't accept the praise. 'My mind still wanders.'

'That's all right. The spaces in between the wandering are what matters.' Bee regarded her for a long moment. 'Out with it.'

'What?'

'Whatever it is you want to say.'

'Will Kate Foster wake up?'

'I don't know. I could look if you really want to know, but I don't think it will help. It's not the question you truly want to ask.'

Esme shook her head. There was no point trying to fool Bee. She ought to know that by now. 'What is she?'

'A woman. A very unhappy woman.'

'But she didn't look human. I saw her. At the castle. I thought it was my sight coming in and that I'd seen her true form. I guess I was hallucinating or something. Imagining things.' Even as she spoke, Esme knew that wasn't true. It was her old thought patterns kicking in. Self-loathing always waiting in the wings, desperate to take centre stage. She closed her eyes, just for a moment, and let the darkness fill her vision. When she meditated with Bee, that darkness had become her friend. It meant calm. It meant safety. Somewhere along the line, she had created – or found – something that was separate to her panicking, spiralling thought patterns and the fear and self-doubt that she had always assumed filled that place behind her eyes. Now she knew there was something else. A centre of calm that was immune to any of that noise. Bee had promised her that, with practice, she would be able to summon it at any time. Or, more accurately, go there whenever she wanted. In that moment, Esme knew that Bee had been telling the truth. And she knew, too, that she had been right.

She opened her eyes. 'She had just invited me to join her. It was a clear night and she was close to the fire, so there was enough light. She didn't transform, but it was like a filter had been lifted and I was suddenly seeing the truth. And she wasn't human.' Esme pictured the creature she had seen, its pale wrinkled skin and large eyes. She described it as best she could.

Bee nodded. 'I have seen that before. Maybe not as advanced a case, but something like it...'

'Advanced case?'

'Some people are born with particular abilities. Perhaps they belong to one of the old magical Families or perhaps some recessive genes have got together and randomly thrown in some affinity or potential. It probably happens with regularity in the human population. I mean,' she smiled, 'there are a lot of you.'

'You think she was human?'

'Definitely. Now ask me what happens if a human with a lot of motivation and a little latent affinity dabbles in magic.'

'But I'm human,' Esme said, suddenly feeling sick.

'You are our Ward Witch,' Bee said as if that was the definitive answer. And maybe it was, but Esme could feel the fear rising.

Bee patted her arm. 'You have to understand, you are not using magic in the way that Kate Foster had to have been using magic. Like anything, there's a safe way to do things and the other. You can't blame the hammer when you hit your thumb with it.'

'She really didn't look human. For a moment, at least.'

'She was wearing a glamour spell. I don't know how long she had been using it, but daily magical use, even something low level like that, takes power. And if you don't have any of your own, you have to get it from somewhere. You know how you got juice for that dehexing?'

Blood. Esme felt ill.

Bee looked serious. 'If a person takes power, uses blood magic they don't fully understand and are not powerful enough to control, it will exert a price. And that will twist them. It's like they are slowly hexing themselves until the only thing being fed is the desire for magic. All other desires, wanting food or sex or sleep, fall away. The creature you saw was Kate Foster. It was a person, but a starved and exhausted one. Seen in the flicking light of the fire she must have seemed like a monster.'

'She said she hardly ate,' Esme said. 'I thought she was being... I don't know...' An awful thought hit. 'Do you think she was asking for my help?'

'If she had asked you would have helped her,' Bee said.

'But what if she was asking and I missed it?'

Bee shook her head. 'It's not your responsibility to divine what people need. Just because you have the ability to do so, doesn't absolve people of their personal responsibility. You can't help those who don't want to be helped. You are missing something more important, though.'

Esme still felt sick to her stomach. She wrapped her arms around her torso and squeezed, trying to comfort herself. 'What?'

'You saw past her glamour. That's the sight.'

'I thought the sight was seeing the future.'

Bee was smiling. 'Don't knock it. Seeing the present clearly is just as useful. Maybe more so.'

CHAPTER THIRTY-ONE

I f she could see things how they really were, Esme could look at Tobias and see what he was. If she wanted. The thought was thrilling and frightening.

She knew the island had some unusual residents. Fiona and Euan could shift form. Esme had looked it up and knew the mythical term, selkie, but had no idea whether Fiona would identify as such or whether it would be an offensive term to her people. There was a possibility, she supposed, that Hamish might be the same. Esme didn't know how it worked, whether everyone in Fiona's family was the same, or whether it was a recessive characteristic that only came out once or twice per generation.

Jet was curled up in front of the wood burner and he stretched, rolling over and exposing his tummy. His eyes were blinking half-open as he regarded her. Unable to resist his implicit command, Esme dropped from the sofa to the floor and scratched his fur in the way he preferred. Purring, Jet twisted around and stood up, butting her hand until she stroked around his head.

Jet wasn't often in the mood for so much contact, so she pushed her whirling thoughts to one side and let herself enjoy the moment. She had always liked cats, in a theoretical sense, and could hardly believe that she now had one of her own. Not that she owned Jet, of course. He had simply come with the house. A lodger.

Once Jet had had his fill of the love and attention that was his due, Esme took her latest book from the special collection at the shop, an encyclopaedia of healing rituals, and curled up for a long session of learning. Kate Foster might have thought that knowledge was the root of all evil, but Esme rather thought it was what you chose to do with the knowledge that counted.

TOBIAS CARRIED the tea tray into the living room and found DS Kerry Robinson on the floor with Winter, petting him. Winter had barely moved for over a day and he hadn't eaten, either. Tobias pushed the thought to one side and put the tray onto the side table. Whenever he felt a little weary of humanity, he just had to think of a good-hearted soul fussing over a dog and he felt instant hope for the world.

Getting up in a self-conscious manner, Robinson moved to help him with the tea. He waved her away. 'It's in hand, officer.'

'Call me Kerry,' Kerry said and then looked surprised, as if she hadn't intended to say that at all.

Once they were both seated and with cups of tea, Tobias expected DS Robinson to get down to business. The body of the unfortunate young man had been removed from the cottage by the authorities and he assumed that this was a follow-up interview. Hammer had suggested they deal with it 'in house' but the boy had done nothing wrong. He deserved to be reunited with his kith and kin, and his family and friends deserved to know his fate.

Given enough time, the connection with the island would hopefully be lost in the labyrinthine system of the police service but, for now, DS Robinson was doing her job. She had had enough contact with Tobias and the island over the years to cement more memories of the place than most mainlanders.

'Between us,' Kerry said, 'there's enough evidence for the case against Elin Jones. As soon as she wakes up, she'll be placed under arrest.'

'She must be a very disturbed young woman.'

'We have no solid connection with the island community at this time. Working hypothesis is that it was a crime of convenience. We believe she followed the victim here and must have seen the disused cottage as an opportunity.'

'It's a quiet place,' Tobias said. 'But not a good choice. We're a small community, we notice things that are out of place. You know that.'

'We don't work alone like this,' DS Robinson said, surprising him.

He raised his eyebrows in polite interest.

'Official guidelines are for two officers to attend.' She shook her head as if trying to clear it. 'I interviewed people here back when...' a small frown crossed her face, 'Alvis. When Alvis Knott died.'

'Was that because it was natural causes?'

'You know, for a moment there I couldn't remember her name.' The officer seemed to realise she was speaking out loud and shook herself. 'Sorry. Sorry, I'm not here to talk about operational procedures.'

'Wonderful,' Tobias said warmly. 'It's not in my top ten.'

'Top ten?'

'Favourite conversational topics to have with tea. Operational procedures isn't bad, as such, but it doesn't make top billing.'

She cracked a smile. Then went serious again, the smile falling away.

'How's your tea?' Tobias asked and took a sip of his own. He had known this woman for many years and he didn't remember her seeming so uncertain and scattered. He worried that her regular contact with the island and its protective wards was having a detrimental effect on her mind.

'It's a bit of an odd one,' she said. 'And this isn't official. I shouldn't really be here...' She stopped speaking with what looked like an effort, closing her eyes for a moment to gather herself.

When she didn't resume speaking, Tobias sipped his tea quietly. Winter stretched his front legs and rearranged his head on top of his paws, and the fire in the grate crackled.

After a little while, DS Robinson opened her eyes. She looked directly at Tobias and said, 'I think something happens to me here. I thought I was going mad or had early dementia, but my memory is fine with everything else. Why can't I remember this place? Why do I struggle to remember your name, your face, this house? Is there something in the water? Do you put something in my drinks?' She seemed to realise what she had just said, looking horrified at her empty teacup.

'You are quite safe,' Tobias said. 'Please do not be alarmed.'

'Forgive me,' she said, 'but I think I am.'

Tobias waited for a moment. He felt a small pinprick in his conscience. If he was a good man, he would tell DS Kerry Robinson everything. He would explain that she wasn't losing her mind, but that she was being affected by ancient magical wards. Instead he waited, until the officer's expression cleared and she made a comment about the wintery weather, and he knew the topic had been forgotten. He wasn't a good man at all. He wasn't even a man.

TOBIAS HAD CALLED Esme to let her know that the police officer had gone back to the mainland. He said that he expected that to be the last of it, unless Kate Foster regained consciousness and the case against her proceeded.

Her hand was in Winter's fur, stroking around his neck as she looked around the cosy room. The sounds of Tobias making tea drifted through the open door and the fire crackled in the grate. She knew the ice would still be riming the glass of the windows and that, if she looked carefully at Tobias, she would see something that wasn't human. But she had decided not to look. It would be rude. She would wait to be asked.

A tiny electrical crackle, like a static shock, ran across the tips of her fingers. Her hand jerked back in surprise. Winter was breathing more quickly than was normal in a resting animal. Not quite panting, but getting close to it. His eyes rolled up and looked beseechingly at Esme.

Esme didn't know dogs very well and didn't consider herself an expert in canine communication, but her instinct told her that the animal was in distress and that he was asking for her help.

Without thinking, she opened herself up and looked, scanning Winter for the cause of his discomfort. There was something dark around his head. A miasma of tiny black particles that moved individually in a cloud. Like tiny flies buzzing around a swollen corpse.

Esme blinked. That was an unpleasant image.

But she got the message. That fuzzy dark cloud was malevolent.

It was also outside the body. Whatever was wrong with Winter wasn't from the expected ravages of old age, but from something external.

'Where does he sleep? In here?' Esme usually saw Winter slumbering by the fire in the living room, but she had to check.

'Mostly,' Tobias said. 'I often doze in my chair and we keep each other company.'

'How have you been feeling?'

He blinked. 'Fine. Why do you ask?'

'May I look around the room?'

'Be my guest,' Tobias said, still looking concerned.

Esme dropped to the floor and began to crawl around, looking under furniture. If Kate Foster had planted something in Tobias's house, this room would be the most likely location. She had had access to it while taking tea. She thought back to that first meeting, Kate sitting in her chair, looking shiny and perfect and as if she had never even heard of dark magic or cursed books.

She couldn't waste energy berating herself for her past failings. She could only learn and do better. That was the key, Esme decided. She was next to the guest armchair by the fire, the one that sat angled toward Tobias's favourite, inviting a person to sit comfortably, warm themselves and enjoy a civilised conversation and a cup of tea from the bone china that Tobias used. Maybe enjoy one of the slim lemony biscuits that he always seemed to have on hand.

She couldn't see anything under the chair, even with her mobile phone as a torch, but she used her hand to feel the underside of the seat anyway. Now that she had thought about it, this was the obvious place. It had to be here.

At that moment, her fingers felt the lump in the underside of the chair. Between the webbing that held the seat cushion, an unpleasantly soft lump that most definitely did not belong.

Gripping it between finger and thumb, she wiggled the object until it came loose from its hiding place. Thanks to her reading, she knew instantly that this was a hex bag. It was crudely made from what looked like the fur of a small rodent or rabbit, and it was tied at the top with a thin leather cord. She used her knife on the cord rather than attempting to untie the knots, and tipped it upside down.

She was expecting bones, but one was too small to have come from the owner of the fur and another of them was hollow, so it had to have belonged to a bird. That meant at least three lives had been used up. Whoever had put this bag into Tobias's home hadn't been messing around. It had to be Kate Foster, of course. Nobody else would do such a thing, and she had already shown herself to be adept with a cursed object.

The bones were clean and she wondered if that was because it had been in situ for a while, or whether Kate Foster had scoured them to prevent Winter from being drawn to the meaty scent and alerting Tobias. There was a shell, too, worn smooth by the sea, and almost certainly picked from Shell Bay on the island.

Tobias was carrying a laden tray, and she waited for him to put it down onto the stuffed ottoman before speaking. 'I found a hex bag under your chair.' She indicated the surface of the table and its unpleasant contents. She felt calm, despite the awfulness.

He took the news in his stride and simply picked up the teapot. 'Shall I be mother?'

'Kate Foster must have left it here. I'm not sure what it's meant to do. There are curses that are harmful, but there are ones which are meant to make people more amenable, or calmer, things like that. Have you been feeling all right?'

Tobias smiled at her gently. 'I'm not concerned by a witch's trick. No offence to you, my dear.'

'I'm more worried about Winter,' Esme said and then felt awful at Tobias's stricken expression.

They both looked at the old dog, his sides shuddering with every laboured breath. 'This hex bag is serious business and we don't know how long it's been...here.' She had been going to say 'poisoning Winter' but stopped herself in time. Tobias looked devastated, and she didn't want to upset him any further.

'I'm going to break it,' she said, channelling her best 'nurse knows best' voice, 'just to be safe.' The book had explained that removing and emptying a hex bag ought to undo its power. However, salting and burning was best for strong or particularly evil curses. Esme was a belt and braces kind of woman, so asked Tobias for salt.

When he returned, holding a china shaker, she applied it liberally over the objects and the fur bag and then swept the lot into the fire. She didn't know if she had been expecting a flash of coloured flame or a thunderclap, but nothing unusual happened.

'Is that it?' Tobias asked. His expression was both disbelieving and hopeful, and he bent to stroke Winter's side.

'Yes,' Esme said with complete certainty.

The fire crackled and the flames leapt and the evil burned away while she and Tobias enjoyed a hot cup of a tea.

· · ·

THE SKY WAS BRIGHT BLUE, the winter sun shining across the sparkling sea as if it would never consider doing anything else. The puddles in the track were iced over, but there was hardly any wind. Esme decided to take a stroll down to the shore before heading home.

There were three people walking slowly down the path toward the bay. Euan, far taller than Fiona, now, and broader than Esme remembered from even a few days ago, and baby Hamish. He was dressed in a bright blue waterproof all-in-one and was taking wobbly steps with Fiona hunched over and holding both of his hands to help him balance.

Esme thought about running to catch up to them, but decided against disturbing the small family group. Instead, she took the fork in the path toward home.

Half an hour later, Fiona knocked on the door with Hamish in her arms. Their cheeks were pink from the cold, and they looked delightfully wholesome and healthy. Esme ushered them inside. 'Stove's on in the living room. Go on through.'

'I won't stop long,' Fiona said as she efficiently stripped off Hamish's outdoor layer.

Esme picked up the damp waterproof and hung it over a kitchen chair in front of the radiator to dry.

Esme assembled a tray with teapot, mugs, biscuits and a sippy cup of milk. She didn't have baby bottles, but kept a small stash of plastic tableware for the youngest guests.

When she walked into her living room, a punch of strange longing hit her gut. Hamish was holding onto the edge of the sofa to stand up and was babbling nonsense while Fiona gazed at him with a fierce expression of love.

He stopped babbling and whipped his head around to stare at Esme. Then, evidently deciding she was safe, began babbling again.

'Yes, you can have some milk. Thank you, Esme.' Fiona seemed to understand Hamish. He let go of the sofa and sat straight onto the floor with a bump, his nappy-cushioned bottom making a soft thump. Then he reverted to high-speed crawling toward the tray on the coffee table. Fiona was sitting on the floor and she intercepted him, pulling him onto her lap.

Esme passed across the sippy cup and Fiona helped Hamish with it.

'Good walk?'

'Euan's gone for a swim,' Fiona said, her eyes still on Hamish. 'I wanted to check on you.'

'On me?'

Fiona looked at her, then. 'You've been through a lot. When I think about that woman... what could have happened.'

'I'm fine,' Esme said, mildly surprised to find that it was true. Kate Foster's conviction that she was evil and deserved to die had made her realise something at her core: she didn't agree. As a woman who had spent most of her life feeling not good enough, defective and weak, Kate Foster's pure and uncomplicated hatred had helped her to see clearly that she was fine. She certainly didn't believe she deserved to be burned alive, like all those poor witches of old, and that was refreshingly positive. Instead of trying to put this into words, knowing that Fiona didn't need to be burdened by the depths of her own self-loathing, even if the point of the story was to illustrate that she had discovered a tiny sliver of self-love buried at the centre, she just added. 'Honestly. I really am.'

'And what about our Book Keeper? I can tell I've missed something significant there.'

'Nothing.' Esme felt the rush of blood to her face. 'We've got closer, I think.'

'You think.' Fiona laughed and shook her head. 'The two of you can't stop staring at each other.'

'Luke doesn't stare at me.'

'Aye right. He wants you. Question is, are you ready for him?'

'I don't know,' Esme said, feeling her old worries come rushing back. She didn't panic anymore and had mostly banished Ryan's hectoring voice, but she was still the woman who had run away when Luke had moved to kiss her. She wanted to be ready. Maybe that would be enough?

'I'm sorry, hen,' Fiona said, concerned. 'I was only teasing.'

Hamish pushed the cup away and launched himself from Fiona's lap.

'It's all right,' Esme said. 'I do like him.' It felt good to say it out loud. She was allowed to like Luke. The toxic torrent had gone. Her ex had absolutely nothing to say. Being almost burned to death by a deranged woman seemed to have cleared him out for good.

Hamish made it across the carpet to Esme and began pulling himself upright, using her knees, chest and arm as if she were a climbing frame. Esme held her breath, blown away by the simple trust.

'He likes you,' Fiona said.

Esme found she couldn't speak, she was captivated by the soft skin of Hamish's cheeks, the way his long dark eyelashes fringed his clear eyes, the newness of him.

'He's going to be staying for a while.'

Esme glanced sharply at Fiona.

Her eyes were worried, but she kept her voice upbeat. 'Isn't that right, wee man? You're going to stay with Auntie Fi.'

'For a few weeks?' Esme asked.

'Mebbe longer,' Fiona replied. She smiled. 'If I'm very lucky.'

Esme lowered her voice. 'Is everything all right? With your niece?'

Fiona shook her head gently and reached for the television remote. Once CBeebies was playing, Hamish turning open mouthed to it like a flower to the sun, she moved closer to Esme and spoke quietly into her ear. 'Eilidh came through the op fine enough, but she's not wanting her wee boy back anytime soon.'

Esme wanted to ask why, but Fiona was cutting her eyes to Hamish, warning her not to dwell on the subject. 'She thinks he'll be safer growing up here. With us.'

CHAPTER THIRTY-TWO

E sme had renewed the wards, drunk a cup from her flask of gunpowder tea, and was heading toward home when she saw another familiar figure out enjoying the dry bright weather.

Better yet, there was a joyful bark as she got closer. Tobias called the dog back but Winter ignored his master, running up to head butt Esme in her thighs until she dropped to her knees to make a proper fuss. She sunk her fingers into the fur around his ears and neck and scratched vigorously.

'I don't know what's got into him,' Tobias said, mock-cross. 'He's behaving like a puppy.'

'He feels better, don't you?' Esme said to Winter, who answered her by attempting to lick her face. She dodged in time, but was thrilled he was moving so quickly. His muzzle was still shot through with grey hairs, but his eyes were clear and his nose damp and shiny with good health. As if keen to demonstrate his miraculous recovery, he jumped up and ran in an excited circle.

'Heel!' Tobias said sharply and the dog came and sat by his side, head low and ears back. His demeanour was contrite, but Esme estimated Tobias had about three minutes of good behaviour before Winter would be off chasing rabbits.

'I just renewed the wards,' Esme said. 'Everything seems fine.'

'Thank you,' Tobias said. 'Beautiful day for it,' Tobias said. He took in a deep, appreciative breath.

Winter's tail was thumping the ground and he let out a soft 'woof'. 'All right, go on,' Tobias said to the dog, who jumped up and began investigating the rutted ground and clumps of plant life to the side of the path.

Esme hesitated. There was something she wanted to ask Tobias, but she felt as if the subject didn't belong beneath the bowl of blue sky with the fresh clean island air moving her hair.

'What is it?'

She smiled ruefully at Tobias's perceptive nature. 'There's still something I don't understand. Kate Foster, Elin-whatever-her-name-is, is human. How could she remember this place? Or stay more than two nights? I swear I've been keeping up with the wards.'

'We are a place of safety,' Tobias said. 'You know that. Kate was wearing a magical glamour, and her soul was saturated in past magical use. It must have been enough to convince the wards that she required sanctuary. The wards can't be expected to discern the difference between benign or evil intent. That's down to us.'

'I should have seen it,' Esme said in a rush. 'I let you down.'

Tobias patted her hand. 'You have never let me down. It's just not possible.'

Suddenly, she was trying to swallow around a lump in her throat. Esme blinked back tears, turning to watch

Winter in his ecstatic investigations of the clearly suspicious gorse.

LUKE's favourite reading chair had miraculously escaped Kate Foster's liberal application of petrol. He had a mug of tea and his John le Carré to finish. It had been a busy couple of weeks of cleaning and fixing and airing out the building, but now the familiar scent of warm wood and old paper was once again asserting itself. The new window gleamed and the window display with driftwood and little twinkling lights looked cheerful and welcoming.

He was halfway through his tea and one chapter down when the front door opened. He replaced his bookmark and stood up to greet the customer.

Bee had a bag full of books that she put onto the counter. 'If you still need stock,' she said. 'Things I've bought over the years and always meant to return for a swap.'

'That's very kind,' Luke said. 'I will pay you for them, of course.'

'No need,' Bee waved a hand. 'Consider it a house-warming gift.' She raised a single eyebrow. 'Too soon?'

Luke laughed.

Bee turned to admire the window, the gleaming shelves, the neatly arranged books. 'You've done a good job getting this place back in order.'

Her sincerity made him suddenly choke up. He managed a nod in thanks and then mumbled something about having had plenty of help.

'It shouldn't have happened,' Bee said, not looking at him. 'I should have seen the hex coming to you.'

Luke knew that Bee meant the words literally. 'Your sister saved my life,' he said. 'I'm not complaining.'

Bee nodded briskly. 'I can't fulfil that debt. It's between you and Lucy, and she won't share. I can, however, do you a favour. I wish to make amends.'

'There's really no need...'

'You still want to find your brother?'

Luke closed his mouth.

Bee pursed her lips, hesitating for a second before she spoke. 'The head of the Crow Family owes me a favour. I'm going to call it in.'

ONE DOWNSIDE of living in a very close community was that it was difficult to go on a date without everybody else being on it, too. Luke knew that if he and Esme tried to have a romantic dinner at The Rising Moon, they would end up with half the village joining in. And if he spoke to Seren about wanting to stay private on a table just for two, they would simply have a curious audience for the whole awkward event.

Heading to the mainland in his car, the tyres crunching on the frost-rimed road and the low winter sun shining on the expanse of sand and sea on either side of the narrow causeway, and Esme in the passenger seat next to him, he felt as if he was flying.

They had been chatting easily enough, but he still had a ball of nerves in his stomach and he hoped she liked the restaurant he had chosen. A family-run Italian place with excellent reviews, mid-list prices, and an unpretentious menu. They were having a late lunch, rather than dinner, so that they could head back across the causeway before the tide closed it. If all had gone well, she might even invite him into Strand House and offer a glass of wine. His mind wouldn't let him think about what else might happen at that point. He knew that agreeing to a chaste daytime date was a huge deal for Esme, and he was willing to go as slowly as she needed. As long as she didn't hit the brakes completely, he could cope with anything.

'Can we stop?' Esme asked, in a horrible echo of his thoughts.

They had just joined the mainland, the road surface changing to the smooth tarmac of civilisation, and he wondered if it had triggered panic. He felt sick.

'Just for a minute?'

She was smiling at him, not seeming unhappy, and he told himself not to spiral.

'Sure.' There were wide turning points just off the road on either side. The Northumberland council's way of ensuring that nobody was forced to continue on the causeway if they didn't want to. Or had realised that they had drastically misread the tide table. The spaces were empty, a freezing January day not exactly drawing the crowds. He angled the car so that they were facing back across the causeway, wanting to show Esme that it was no problem if she had changed her mind. The thought brought a fresh wave of crushing disappointment, but he pushed it down. Whatever she needed. If this was too much, then he would take her straight home. He would leave her alone, even as it broke his heart. Whatever Esme needed to be safe and happy was exactly what he would do. There was something comforting about this clarity, and he felt calm when he turned in his seat to face her. He was ready to see the apology in her eyes and to meet it with equanimity.

'I wanted to see it from this point of view and I wasn't sure if it would be too dark on the way back. The island. I hardly ever see it from a distance like this and there's something... I don't know. Affirming, I suppose.' She was looking out of the windscreen, and he did the same.

The island was just visible, rising out of the silvered sand, against a pale opalescent sky. As he watched, it seemed to sink in and out of existence, as if it was resisting being seen. A trick of the light and cloud. 'It's beautiful,' he said, surprising himself.

'It really is.'

He dragged his gaze from Unholy Island to Esme and found her looking back at him. Her lips were parted slightly and her eyes bright. She was the most beautiful woman he had ever seen. Something seemed to shine from within, her skin and the whites of her eyes seeming to have a touch of the same unearthly opalescence as the sky.

'Do you want to go back?'

'And miss our date?' Her forehead creased a little. 'Do you?'

'No,' he said quickly. 'I just don't want you to worry if you've changed your mind. I don't want you to feel pressured.'

The smile that broke transformed her face from an unearthly beauty to something earthier and unmentionably sexy. He felt his body responding as his heart began hammering with an answering rhythm. If it was any other woman, he would be reaching for her right now. Instead, he held himself in check. Esme wasn't a woman you lunged at clumsily in a car.

The click as she undid her seat belt was loud in the quiet. And then she was leaning across to him, reaching her hands around his neck, and he met her halfway. He cradled her cheek and jaw with one hand and tipped her head back, the other hand finding the back of her neck. When their lips met this time, there was no hesitation, no restraint. It was as if this was exactly what they were meant to be doing, and both of their bodies knew it.

Happiness exploded behind Luke's closed eyes.

When they pulled apart, just a little, he rested his forehead very gently on hers, reluctant to pull fully away and back to the cool air of his side of the car. He didn't feel the need to ask if she was okay as Esme was leaning into him, smiling with her eyes so loudly that he couldn't mistake it. He knew his own expression mirrored hers and that he probably looked like a dazed idiot.

'I have food,' Esme whispered.

He caught his breath, wondering if she meant what he thought she might mean. 'You want to skip the restaurant?'

Her smile grew a little, but there was uncertainty in her eyes, too. 'Maybe. If you want? We could just go home. Right now. To my place. Eat there.' She took a little breath that almost broke all his gentlemanly restraint.

'I hate restaurants,' he said with complete solemnity.

She laughed, uncertainty banished, and he kissed her again, before releasing her. He waited for her to buckle her seat belt and revelled in the smile she shot at him as he put the car into reverse and then steered onto the causeway, toward the island. 'Let's go home.'

THE END

.

THANK YOU FOR READING!

I am busy working on my next book. If you would like to be notified when it's published (as well as take part in give-aways and receive exclusive free content), you can sign up for my FREE readers' club:

geni.us/Thanks

If you could spare the time, I would really appreciate a review on the retailer of your choice.

Reviews make a huge difference to the visibility of the book, which make it more likely that I will reach more readers and be able to keep on writing. Thank you!

ACKNOWLEDGMENTS

I loved being back on Unholy Island and getting to spend time with these characters. Thank you to all the readers who greeted The Ward Witch with such enthusiasm and made that possible.

To my writing coven, Hannah Ellis and Clodagh Murphy, heartfelt thanks for the inspiration, support and good times. Thanks also to Nadine, Sally, LK, and Julia. Writing and publishing would be a lonely profession without you.

Thank you to the excellent Stuart Bache for another fantastic cover, and to the team at Siskin Press. Also, thank you to my brilliant ARC readers for their early feedback: Jenni Gudgeon, Karen Heenan, Deborah Forrester, Paula Searle, Caroline Nicklin, David Wood and Beth Farrar.

As always, thank you to my wonderful children, Holly and James, and my lovely husband, Dave. You have been unwavering in your support and it means everything.

ABOUT THE AUTHOR

Sarah is a bestselling author of contemporary fantasy and magical realism. She writes the Crow Investigations series, a London-set urban fantasy featuring private investigator Lydia Crow.

Having always been a reader and a daydreamer, she now puts those skills to good use with a strict daily schedule of faffing, thinking, reading, napping and writing – as well as thanking her lucky stars for her good fortune.

Sarah lives in rural Scotland with her husband and extensive notebook collection.

Head to the website below to sign-up to the Sarah Painter readers' club. It's absolutely free and you'll get book release news, giveaways and exclusive FREE stuff!

www.sarah-painter.com

 facebook.com/SarahPainterBooks

 twitter.com/SarahRPainter

 instagram.com/SarahPainterBooks

Find out more about the magical families of London - the Crows, Silvers, Pearls and Foxes

The Night Raven is the first book in the Crow Investigations series

The Crows used to rule the roost and rumours claim they are still the strongest.

The Silvers have a facility for lying and they run the finest law firm in London.

The Pearl family were costermongers and everybody knows that a Pearlie can sell feathers to a bird.

The Fox family... Well. The less said about the Fox family the better.

For seventy-five years, a truce between the four families has held strong, but could the disappearance of Maddie Crow be the thing to break it?